DREAM TEAM: A NOVELLA

and

Other Stories of the Game

William J. McGill

Acknowledgements

Portions of "Dream Team" appeared in Peter Rutkoff, ed., *Going into Extra Innings. The Long Baseball Story.* Birch Brook Press, 2006, and in *Timber Creek Review* ((2000). "The Secret of Walter Johnson's Balls" appeared in *Spitball* ((1995), "Silent Sig Sprecher's Last Hit But One" in *Sou'wester* (1997), "Holding on and Letting Go" and "Homer Happy" in *Elysian Fields Quarterly* (2004 and 1999 respectively).

ISBN
978-0-61525998-7

An Abercuawg Book

Contents

DREAM TEAM:
A Novella

In the old movie It Happens Every Spring, *Ray Milland plays a chemistry professor at a small college "somewhere in the Middle West" who is an avid fan of the St. Louis Cardinals. Every spring he starts acting a bit peculiar. For example, students notice that in the middle of a class he moves about erratically behind the lecture-demonstration table, sometimes bending over, occasionally even disappearing from view, then reappearing with varying expressions of pleasure or pain. The reason for this erratic behavior is that under the counter he has a radio tuned into the Cardinals' broadcast. (These were the good old days, of course, when most games were still played in the light of day.) His odd movements allow him to pick up bits of the game in the midst of his lecture. Occasionally—well maybe a bit more often—events of the game prove too distracting and the continuity, if not the coherence, of his lecture suffers—though most students would not notice anything too unusual about that. Despite his peculiarity he is engaged to the president's daughter and all seems well.*

Then one day, quite by accident, solutions from two different experiments he's working on get mixed. He discovers that the resulting concoction has the effect of making a baseball avoid wood. He finagles a tryout with the Cardinals, signs on with them, and, abetted by his amazing dipsy-doodle pitch that jumps, drops, breaks away from any swung bat, leads them back into the thick of the race. But one day his catcher and roommate (played by Paul Douglas) mistakes the bottle of the secret solution for hair tonic and in using it breaks the bottle. The pitcher/professor is left with a very small residue to get him through the game that will clinch the pennant. In the last inning he has nothing left, except his own quite ordinary ability. Still he saves the game with a dazzling bare-handed catch of a line drive through the middle. He breaks his hand so that he can

6

never pitch again. He retires and goes home to marry his fiancée and, who knows, maybe ends up as a college president—small consolation for an all too brief career in baseball, but so be it.

It's a bit corny, but it's one of my favorite movies, and not only because I'm a Cardinals fan. As a boy in Alton, Illinois, I had the dream that once was the universal dream of American boyhood: to play major league baseball. For me, it faded out finally in college when I admitted to myself what others already knew—some had known for a long time—that I wasn't good enough. I turned to watching, thinking and writing about baseball as a substitute for playing it. And I've had a respectable career as a writer, first covering for a couple of newspapers the game I still love with the avidity of youth, more recently as a free-lancer, doing features for magazines and newspapers and even occasional gigs on NPR. I'm not exactly Roger Angell or Tom Boswell, but I write well enough and am known well enough that I can make regular and significant contributions to the family bank account. My wife, Eileen, a political science prof at Lebanon Valley College in Pennsylvania, is mildly skeptical of the social value of my efforts, but is otherwise supportive.

I've never had any particular interest in those fantasy baseball camps most major league teams run. Eileen offered to send me to the Cardinals' version for a birthday present one year, but I told her no thanks. I said I had outgrown that kind of thing. And I'm not much attracted to the fantasy league idea that so many guys are caught up in and which increasingly looks like a thinly disguised lottery. It's the game I love, the intricacies, the peculiarities. I replay in my mind the balletic grace of an eye-opening double play, the subtleties of infield shifts, the dazzle of a close call at home. I love the crack of the bat on ball (no metal bats, please), the slap of ball on leather, the smell of leather, the little rituals players go through to settle anxieties, to control anticipation. All these things and more engage the senses, stimulate our ways of knowing, even explain why a Renaissance scholar becomes Commissioner of Baseball. It explains, too, why a boyhood dream, the boyhood dream, doesn't just fade away, but transmutes into the pleasures I get from

7

watching and writing. And when Eileen chides me about it, I quote A. Bartlett Giamatti to her.

But, in the spring, every spring, wisps of the old dream niggle at my imagination. That's why I like the movie: because it nourishes the little boy fantasy in me that, even now, just maybe, I could have that one day in the sun-lit field of a major league game. And it is a day game, played on real grass, in a genuine baseball park. Now and again, it's a sweet and innocent pleasure to play that fantasy over and I will admit to indulging myself. Eileen can tell when it is happening by the wispy look in my eye, and she just smiles and lets the moment play out. She's gentle with me that way. I think she remembers what the wise old priest who married us said in our last counseling session before the wedding: "Don't ever forget you're marrying a child."

Most of the time I act more like the forty-year old man I am.

A couple of years ago—yes, in the spring—after completing my annual re-reading of W. P. Kinsella's Shoeless Joe, *I got to thinking about "Moonlight" Graham, the character in the book who had played in only one game in the majors and had never had an at-bat. Graham, of course, was not a figment of Kinsella's imagination: he's right there in* The Baseball Encyclopedia. *For the fun of it I started looking through my copy of the* Encyclopedia *to see whether there were other players who had only appeared in one game. As I did so the idea came to me of writing this book, of seeking out some of those players who had had the same dream, and who had been good enough, almost. They had pursued it all the way to the top, but had appeared in only a single game. Maybe they batted just once or pitched a single inning, then, for whatever reason—want of ability, the luck of the draw, injury—they had slipped back into the minors and finally unnoticed out of the game.*

I, who had hardly started up that long slope, wondered what it was like for those who had been to the Big Show, though only for a moment. Was it a memory they still cherished? Or was it laden with regret? Had the effort been worth it? Had it been it enough? How, if at all, had it affected the rest of their lives?

Paging through The Baseball Encyclopedia, *I found more than enough possibilities, so from early on I decided to limit the group to nine players, one for each position, a kind of one-day wonder all star team. And, I decided not to consider anybody who had hung around professional baseball as a coach or manager. Of course, they still had to be alive so I could talk to them, but they had to be out of baseball for at least ten years. That way I could assume they had gotten another life and had some time to reflect on their experiences.*

So here they are, my Dream Team.

A Dream Deferred

"Every spring I get this feeling that I'm in the wrong place. I don't think I'll ever lose that feeling."

When he said those words Danny Miller—he still called himself Danny though he was thirty-six years old—had a fierce sadness in his eyes. And he looked like he could have, should have, been some place else. Not just any place: the right place was center stage on a baseball field throwing, no-see-'um fastballs and wicked sliders past major league hitters. Though he had a tinge of gray at his temples and his good looks were not the fresh ones of youth, he retained the suppleness and grace of a competitive athlete. I could easily imagine him standing on the pitcher's mound at Busch Stadium, staring in to get his sign, then uncoiling with the rare force of a Gibson or a Clemens. After all, he had been there, but for one day, one day only.

Of all the ex-players who were on my list, he was the most famous, the one I was the most interested in and the one who had been the hardest to find. When I first got the idea for this project, I knew he would be my pitcher, so despite the difficulties in locating him I persevered. My usual method was first to check with the team for which an individual had played, then with the major league office. Next step was to try the hometown to see if he had just gone back there—or if there were still family there—easy enough to do in small towns, more difficult in cities. From there I might have to scrabble through the rosters of the minor league teams they had played for to see if there were any guys they had played with long enough they might be friends and had kept in touch. It was like searching my own memory. By the time I tracked Danny down, in a small town north of San

10

Francisco where he taught seventh grade and coached the junior high baseball team, I had already talked or corresponded with the other eight ex-players.

Of course, I knew something of his story, and I knew what he looked like. Two vivid images of Danny Miller had lingered in my mind for years, both images from pictures I had seen in *Baseball America*. In one his catcher is hoisting him in the air, surrounded by all his other team mates, at the end of the final game of the College World Series his senior year, his gloved hand thrust toward the sky in triumph, a smile of pure joy on his face. In the other he lies crumpled in the dirt at home plate after colliding with the Cubs catcher. It was a 1-1 tie in the bottom of the sixth. He had led off the inning with a double, then with one out he had come home on a single to left. The third base coach actually tried to hold him up, but Danny ran right through the sign and slid hard into the catcher just as the throw got there. He was safe—but out. It was an ugly picture, the kind ESPN would run over and over, piously advising viewers not to watch if they were squeamish.

When I first called him about getting together, he begged off until the junior high team he coached had finished its season, said he didn't have any time to think about anything except lesson plans and coaching kids. So I waited, then called again. With a vague reluctance, he agreed to meet me.

"Seven-thirty," he said, "at Henty's. It's right on the main drag which is only two blocks long so you can hardly miss it." In a city, Henty's might have been a sports bar, but in a small town it couldn't specialize. Still, it had the feel about it that the main topic of conversation was sports and it was quickly apparent that Miller was a regular. We sat in a back booth, dark wood with faux-leather seats. Probably "his" booth: I could see him sitting there, telling stories, drawing other one-time dreamers into the glow of what might have been. He spent the first twenty minutes of our conversation talking about how proud he was of his kids: they had gone 17-1 and won their league.

"...But you didn't come here to hear me chatter about a bunch of twelve- and thirteen-year olds, did you?"

"No, I didn't. Though it's interesting, I mean to hear you talking about teaching them. Any Danny Millers in the bunch?"

"God forbid." He said it almost with a laugh. To this point his voice had a false heartiness that sounded odd, even evasive, but as we moved into talking about his career, about the game and its aftermath, this tone vanished to be replaced by a voice muted and reflective. "You say you're writing a book about one day wonders. So what can I tell you?"

"Well, mostly I'm interested in what you've been do-ing— and thinking—since you quit playing, but I like to get a little background, too. Of course, I probably already know more about your career than I did about the other guys I've talked to."

"Me being a phenom and all?"

"Well, yes. And I'm a life-long Cardinals fan, so I was watching your progress in the minors with more than an idle interest. I mean they hadn't had a grade-A number one starter since Gibson. They would have had one in Carlton if they hadn't made that stupid trade with Philadelphia." I was on the verge of taking off on one of my pungent analyses of the shortcomings of Cardinal management that Eileen finds so funny, but I caught myself. "Of course I didn't come all this way to talk about that either. I guess I'd like to know a little about when you started playing, when you first started thinking you wanted to pitch in the big leagues."

"The first time I ever picked up a real baseball," he responded without hesitation. "From that moment baseball was the passion of my life, pitching in particular. Somebody like Brosnan or Bouton wrote that you spend your whole life holding onto a baseball, then one day you realize it's the ball that's holding you."

When he said this he wasn't looking at me, but at something that was far off in the distance, out beyond the walls of the bar, a sun-drenched field where everything was beginning anew. As he spoke I remembered a corner vacant lot in Alton, the grass permanently worn away from the areas where the bases and the pitcher's mound were located, the base paths distinct though not so completely worn. Probably even now an aerial view would

12

reveal the pattern, like the furrows of a long-abandoned field. I can still see that scrubby lot where the joy of playing the game seemed so innocent, and I knew what he meant.

"Yeah, it was Bouton," I said. "So why did you wait? You were chosen in the first round out of high school, the Orioles wasn't it? Why did you go to college?"

"Parents, mostly my mother. As a minor, I needed their approval and she insisted that I go to college. And I had my pick of places, all the universities with top programs were after me: Southern Cal, Arizona State, Miami."

"And Stanford."

"Yeah. And Stanford. My mother wanted me to go there. Said I would get a better education, even made me promise to get my degree. Not a bad idea as it turned out. What would I be doing now if I didn't have a degree?" He took a sip of his beer, slowly, thoughtfully as if savoring its mellowness—or something else. "And, in a way, it was no big deal to me. Sure I put off my dream, but I was young and cocky and never doubted it would all come. So I went to Stanford, I studied, I did the other things college students do, but most of all I played baseball and went on dreaming. Probably better than being a seventeen year old in Bluefield, West Virginia, two thousand miles from home. I don't regret going to college first. There wasn't any argument about that. Those were good years, senior year especially."

"Forty and five career record. Winning pitcher in the clincher of the College World Series, MVP in the tournament, NCAA player of the year."

"Yeah, good years. I don't regret them. Maybe the best years. I still have those trophies right out where I can see them. You hold on to the good things."

While he was doing all that, I was third pitcher on a small college team in the upper Midwest where weather meant two starters were usually enough and those two good enough that relief opportunities were rare. That's the way dreams end for most of us, the way it ended for me, slouching into the shadow past with nobody but me noticing.

"Then you were a number one choice again, this time with the Redbirds."

"Your beloved Redbirds."

"Yeah. But because of the College World Series and the usual push and pull of negotiations, most of the season was gone before you threw your first pitch as a pro. You went 3-0 with St. Petersburg, the Cardinals' top A-level team at the time, and it was pretty clear you had too much for the competition. The next season they started you at Arkansas and you dominated there as well, going 10-1 before moving up to Louisville. You went 7-2 and got the call up in September."

"Say, you've done your homework. I'm impressed. You know me almost better than I know myself." He raised his glass in a mock toast.

But all that hope, theirs and his, flamed out on a steamy September night in St. Louis when in his major league debut, he broke his leg sliding into home. It didn't heal quite right, he changed his pitching motion, he hurt his arm, and after several years of trying to get back, he disappeared.

I hesitated, took a sip of my beer. He seemed to be watching me anxiously. So I took a deep breath and asked, "Can you talk about that, the game, the injury, everything that came after?"

Wordlessly, he slid out of the booth and stood up. For a moment I thought he was walking out on me, a telling response to my question. Instead he picked up his glass, gestured at mine, and, when I nodded, took it too and sauntered up to the bar. The bartender drew two more drafts and Danny returned. He took a slow sip, played with the coaster, turning it, tapping it, balancing it on the edge of the table, then flipping and catching it deftly between thumb and forefinger of his right hand. He spoke softly, "The game, the day. I don't know what the other guys have said to you about their experience, but for me it was…it was, up to a point, everything I had ever dreamed it would be. Magical. 'The Day that I was crowned / Was like the other Days-- / Until the Coronation came-- / And then—'twas Otherwise'"

"Emily Dickinson."

14

"Correct. A gift of my Stanford education. My mother was right."

"And it did turn out otherwise."

"Waaay otherwise." He turned his glass, watching a world deep in the amber liquid. "You obviously know the details of the day, the stats. I don't know whether you can comprehend the sheer joy, the exhilaration. Or the pain. A day to remember. If one must." He took a long drink, half the glass, washing a bad taste away.

I wondered how far I should push him, how much graphic reliving of the one moment I should require of him. The image of that photograph was clear in my mind. "Forever--is composed of Nows" and I knew the sequence of nows from that moment to his departure from the game.

Too eager the following spring he started throwing before he should have. His leg was still bothering him and he changed his pitching motion. He hurt his arm and the Cardinals shut him down for the whole season. They had him pitch in the instructional league that fall, but he still wasn't right, the pain was still there, so they pulled him. The doctors told him complete rest was necessary and not even to think of picking up a ball till spring.

The following winter was an anxious one. He needed rest, but he was impatient to try again, to reach for the dream. The spring finally came. He tried. He threw the ball. The pain was gone, but so too was the extra zip on his fastball, the snap on his slider. They talked about needing to build up his arm strength again. I had read all the articles and columns in the *Post Dispatch*, remembered all the comments by Whitey Herzog, the trainers, the pundits, evasively hopeful or hopefully evasive. But the only thing he knew how to do was throw, so he just tried harder, threw harder. The pain returned. He gritted it out, throwing with his head and his heart, but without the bewitching trait of speed he was no longer a young phenom. There was surgery, the Tommy John thing, but not everybody who has it comes back with a newly young arm. Danny was one of the ones who didn't. Over the next few years, the Cardinals shuffled him here and there—Arkansas, St. Pete, Savannah—hoping, as he was hoping, that things would get better. Finally, however, they released him. He tried to hook on with another team, but no one wanted him.

I told myself I could comprehend the pain, though maybe I just didn't want to see again its residue in his eyes, in the set of his jaw. So I didn't ask him about those years when the memory of that shining day tempted him, drove him on, a thin gruel to feed the dream. Anyway, I moved on. "So when you left baseball where did you go? What did you do? How did you wind up here? You know I had a hell of a time finding you."

"I didn't leave baseball. Baseball left me. Every spring I get this feeling that I'm in the wrong place. I don't think I'll ever lose that feeling."

What was I hearing there?. Anger? Bitterness? Toward whom? About what? "Ashes denote that Fire was....," I started to ask him, "What's happening here? Something about the way you're telling the story has changed."

But I hesitated and he went on. "I drifted for a while, the kindness of my parents, and a few friends who didn't mind drop-in visits, and income from my signing bonus that I had banked rather than spent gave me that luxury. My parents were well off so I hadn't bought them a new house and fancy cars had never appealed to me. I thought about graduate school, maybe English, or an MBA, or even law. Worked for a while in the Bay area as a stock and mutual funds broker, but didn't particularly care for that uniform. I wasn't married so I was free to pick up and move on whenever I wanted. Oh," he said with a shrug, "I had some...what do they call them now? Relationships? But nothing that amounted to much."

"No significant others?"

He laughed. "Now there's a term that's never made sense to me. Maybe I was too preoccupied to get tangled up in a sticky web like that. A 'relationship' was about as far as I wanted to go."

"Preoccupied? With what?"

16

He looked at me, weighing something, almost spoke, then finished his beer instead. "Another one?"

"Sure."

When he returned with two fresh glasses he resumed talking almost immediately. "Three years ago, just about this time, I wandered into this little town, looking for a break from the urban scene. I found I liked it and decided to stay. Did some subbing in the local school. Though I didn't have all the credentials required, my Stanford degree impressed the principal. Turned out I liked that too and they liked me enough to arrange a temporary certificate. Now, I'm taking some courses over at Stanislaus State to get the credits I need for full certification."

He spoke with the nearest thing to enthusiasm I had heard from him. I ventured, "So is this it? Is this where you settle down, teach and coach kids. Or is it the first step toward maybe becoming a school superintendent, or getting a job in college, or...whatever?"

He looked around the room and again there were no walls. He was looking to see where the horizon might be. He sipped his beer. "No, no this is it. At least until..."

"Until what?"

He was silent for almost a minute then said in a voice so low I could hardly hear him, "Until." He drained his glass and then slid out of the booth and stood up, stretching his arms as if beginning a pre-game limbering up routine. "Look, I've got some papers to grade, that time of year you know. End of term, the rhythm of life. I better get moving. I'll give you one more question."

What was on my mind was my last question which he had not answered. What future now was he waiting for? Yet I retreated to his past, blurting out, "Would you do it again? Would you run through the coach's sign at third and slide into home?"

Softly, slowly, with no emotion in his voice, nodding his head almost imperceptibly, he replied, "Yes, yes I would. It was the winning run." He held his right shoulder, and with his elbow bent, moved his right arm, his pitching arm, in a circular motion.

The faintest of smiles and now I think one of the saddest smiles I have ever seen, flickered. "You got what you want?"

"I think so, mostly. I appreciate your taking the time. Maybe if I have more questions I can contact you again. Maybe show you a draft of what I've done."

"Sure, sure. If I'm around."

"And I'll pay for the beer. I can write it off as a professional expense."

He laughed, but it was a sound with precious little joy in it. Turning he walked away, waving to the bartender as he left.

I nursed my beer a while longer, jotted a few things in my notebook. Then I got up and went to the bar. As I was paying the tab I asked, "Does he ever talk much about when he used to be a ballplayer?"

"Used to be?" the bartender replied, looking toward the door. "No, he mostly talks about how things are going to be when his arm comes around."

Later, when I looked over my notes, one sentence struck me, a question I had written down even before I spoke to the bartender: do we always know when to let go of a dream, do we know how?

At the core of the story that Augustine recounts in his Confessions, *a story of pilgrimage, is the process of remembering what he had forgotten, of rediscovering what he had lost, ultimately of regaining his memory. The stories which I heard as I went about my interviews were hardly Augustinian. I was talking to ex-ballplayers, not spiritual pilgrims. But I was asking them to explore the past and, in so doing, I often thought of Augustine's observations about memory.*

I first read the Confessions *as part of a Western Civilization course my freshman year in college. I won't say I was particularly reflective in my reading. At that time thinking about memory and memories wasn't exactly high on my list: I was too busy living the now and dreaming the yet-to-be—making me not much different from most seventeen year olds, maybe from most people of any age. But something about the book resonated with me and I've reread it several times since, admittedly a peculiar habit for a sportswriter—just a gift of my liberal education, I guess.*

As Augustine knew, in entering those "fields and roomy chambers of memory, where are the treasures of countless images," we can call forth some things readily and they will parade before us in orderly array. Still others, however, seem hidden in dim recesses and we can bring them forth only with great effort, and then they appear in ragged disorder. We barely control and hardly understand our memory. Things lost from our sight may yet flow forth, often unbidden by any effort of our own, serendipitous eruptions like flares on the sun, yet which we recognize when they appear. And there are things utterly forgotten, things that we cannot even remember having forgotten if, by chance, they should present themselves to us again.

However they come memories or shadows of memories are not the past itself, but words and images of that past, traces

19

on our mind, never complete, never fully realized, only shards. The past could return really and fully only if we could transform the nature of time itself and we have no power to do that. We remember the past: we do not recall it, we do not bring it back living and breathing into the present. And if it is not the past itself which comes forth, but images of the past only, what can we say of them? Who knows how they are formed? From what we remember we construct an image, but it cannot be whole for we do not remember everything. Because we have not the real past to compare with our remembered past, we do not know how much is missing or how distorted the image is by the absence of particular memories. And we cannot even know with certainty whether what we do remember is accurate, no matter how bright the memory be. We can check our memory against those of others, but they too have the same limitations.

"There also do I meet with myself, and recall myself-- what, when, and where I did a thing, and how I was affected when I did it." But are we really who we remember ourselves to be? And even if we are not, is not our memory, however imperfect, the shaper of what we do now and therefore of who we are and who we might become? Can we forget ourselves, so forget ourselves, that who we are has no connection at all with what we were, become then entirely new? Or does our past, even without the memory of it, control who we are and can become? Can we ever remember what we have forgotten?

When we say we have forgotten something, how do we know unless there is some shadow memory that tells us we have forgotten? For Augustine, his conversion was finally an act of memory, a return to a knowledge which he had believed he had forgotten, but he had not, for how else could he remember it unless it had remained somewhere in the labyrinth of his mind. But that only leads us back to the issue of what it is that we remember: the thing itself or only an imperfect image of it. And if only the imperfect image, is that memory? or only a dream? Indeed, perhaps a fantasy?

Augustine wrote his Confessions, *not to tell God what He already knew, but to know himself as fully as possible. He strove then to be as honest as he could, which is one reason why he chose to write rather than conduct a silent monologue. In that way others could correct him, insofar as their own imperfect memories might do so. Finally he had to declare, "These writings are no true confession of mine unless I confess to you, 'I do not know.'"*

Are we all so honest with ourselves in the remembering? Or do we only remember what we want, what agrees with an idea of ourselves we treasure? And if the idea, the self-image, we have does not arise from memory, from whence does it come? Do we create it afresh from unnamable needs and desires? And, wherever it comes, from do we allow that idea to create the "memories" we require? Those were the questions in my mind as I talked with the various ex-players on my list. Of course, they were not the questions I asked. Instead I asked them to remember their past as if that were an easy thing to do.

And even as I was doing it, I wondered what business was it of mine to invade the lives of others with such questions? How would my questions affect the way they remembered, what they remembered? Even assuming--what was unlikely to begin with and what I must admit did not happen--that my questions were objective, unencumbered by my own baggage, my very presence, my very asking, "tainted" their memory. And, having led them to shape anew a memory of the past, what would be the consequences?

Dwelling in Possibility

"With a name like yours, you must have been born and raised to be a catcher."

"You'd think so, wouldn't you? But names can be a burden."

We were sitting on a bench in Forest Park on a pleasant mid-June evening, the typical humidity of a St. Louis summer not yet evident. Ivy Wingo Campanella was a short stocky African-American in his mid-fifties who, apart from tinges of gray in his hair, looked like he was still in playing shape. At first that surprised me. It was early in my project so I hadn't spoken to any of the others. There was no particular meaning to the order of my interviews, just whoever was the easiest to locate. And he was the easiest. A St. Louis native he had gone back there and one look at the phone book had found him: there can't be many Ivy Wingo Campanellas around. Till then I hadn't given any thought to what kind of physical shape these ex-players would be in. But after a couple of interviews I started to take notice. I began to wonder if there were any connection between that and how they had dealt with their "one shining moment."

"You any relation to Roy?"

He chuckled, a comfortable, rolling sound, "Hell no. Campanella's not really my name. Well, that isn't right. It's my name, but my daddy had changed his from Camp to Campanella when he was playing semi-pro baseball hereabouts back in the thirties. He was a helluva catcher."

"The thirties? Then it couldn't have been in honor of Roy. Why'd he do it? Was he trying to pass himself off as an Italian?

"You got it, man." He laughed again. "Only it wasn't his idea. He just went along for the ride, but he got to likin' the name so he kept it."

"So whose idea was it?"

"Fellah by the name of Ivy Wingo Ryan—that's who I'm named after, not the old-time catcher though I guess Ryan was. He ran a semi-pro team across the river, a good one. Like I said Daddy was a helluva player. Ryan was scouting around for a catcher and happened to see him play. Acourse, in those days there wasn't any mixin', but Ryan wasn't caught up in that. What he wanted to do was win and he figured Daddy was about the best catcher in the area, or was goin' be. He was just a kid at the time. So Ryan sidles up to him and says, 'How'd you like to play for the Granite City Rockers?'

"Well, Daddy's eyes got a little big since he knew Ryan was talkin' about a white team playin' in a white league. But if all Ryan wanted was to win, all Daddy wanted was to play, anywhere he could, as often as he could, as long as he could, so he says back, 'I'd like to, though isn't there a bit of a problem?'

"Ryan looks at him with a little smile and says, 'What's your name?'

"'Bobby Camp,' Daddy replies.

"'Funny,' Ryan comes back, still with that little smile, 'you look to me just like Roberto Campanella from the Hill. If you understand what I mean.'

"Well, Daddy was pretty light and his hair was straight and who knows there might have been some Italian in him somewhere. Certainly was some overseer or plantation owner in the family line. And like I said he loved playing ball, so he smiles back and says, 'I could be Roberto Campanella.'

"'Then, you're my new catcher.' Played for the Rockers for ten years till he went into the navy in '43."

"I like that story," I remarked. "Might want to use it. Do you mind, Mr. Campanella?"

"Hell no, I like it too. It's worth sharin'. And just call me Ivy. If we goin' to talk for a while I don't want to be mistered every other sentence. Makes me feel old."

"And I'm Will. Did your father ever think of continuing to pass?"

"Don't know about that. Might of, if he hadn't met my mother. She was dark and this wasn't a place for interracial marriages, still isn't, so he just kept the name and crossed back over."

We sat quietly for a time simply breathing in the uncommon freshness of the summer's air. Yes, I liked that story. Being raised in a different age, when racial questions, though hardly resolved, nonetheless had a different cast to them, I got some pleasure from hearing of someone subverting the old barriers, and making his own decision about which side of the barrier he would live on. Yet, the story had a troubling side to it as well. I recalled Emily Dickinson's poem that begins, "You cannot make Remembrance grow / When it has lost its Root—." Ivy's father seemed oblivious to roots and maybe that had served him well, but I wondered what the effect was upon the son. He had an invented last name, though serendipitously it had received some legitimacy by the emergence of Roy Campanella, and he had been named for an Irishman, who, in turn, had been named for an old catcher for the Cardinals and Reds. Ivy Wingo had a long (seventeen years), but mostly mediocre, career. A native of Georgia, he undoubtedly shared his contemporaries' views on matters of race (Ty Cobb, for example). My man knew the origin of the name, but appeared not to care. Or is that what he meant when he had said, "Names can be a burden?"

"Nor can you cut Remembrance down / When it shall once have grown—." Get on task, I told myself. I wasn't seeking here some primal tribal memory; I was trying to answer some straight-forward questions about Ivy Wingo Campanella within the framework I had set myself. The memory of his I wanted was about one particular day in his life and what he had made of it since. I knew the basics: he had a ten day stint with the Chicago White Sox in the middle of the 1973 season, called up when the starting catcher had gone on the disabled list. During that stint, he had appeared in the requisite one game to make my list. He caught the second game of a double-header in Cleveland, went one for three with a walk, and did his job behind the plate with no untoward incidents. But when the regular back-up catcher came off the DL, Campanella returned to the minors and a couple of years later retired.

"So tell me about THE game."

"It was a game."

"Just that? Nothing special?"

"Well, it was in the biggest place I ever played in, Cleveland Municipal Stadium, and, yeah, it was the big leagues and all. But baseball is baseball: that's the beauty of it. I mean, sure, the quality was different, better, than Triple-A or Double-A and so on right down to what those kids are doing over there." He gestured to a distant field where a pick-up game was going on. "But even from this far away I can tell you what's happenin'. And it was the same as that day. Nothing happened I hadn't seen before. It was the game."

"No different from any other game you ever played? So you can't distinguish it from any other one you ever played? You don't remember anything about it except it was in Cleveland?"

"Say there, Will, is this about what I remember or about what you want me to remember?" Ivy spoke, not harshly, but lightly, teasingly. Yet he knew as well as I did that he had me there. He laughed softly. "Let's make a deal. I'll tell you what I remember and you can make of it what you want, but don't put thoughts in my head or words in my mouth."

"Fair enough."

"First off, Steve Stone was pitchin' for us. He wasn't havin' a great year, but the whole team wasn't. He was only in about his third year up, so he didn't awe me—I wasn't a fresh young kid. And he was pretty easy to catch, normal stuff, ya know. I mean it could have been Wilbur Wood and his knuckleball; then it might have been a very memorable game indeed. So I caught him just like I caught lots of guys, some a lot better'n he was though they didn't make it to the majors. We used a couple of relievers, but I don't remember who. Just mop up action, because by that time we were out of it. Dick Tidrow pitched for them and I got a hit off him, single to left, but so what? We're talkin' Dick Tidrow, not Nolan Ryan or Jim Palmer. After that game I sat on the bench a few more days and back to Des Moines. So that's it, that's my memory. Come to think of it, there was one more thing. A coupla days later I was out in the on-deck circle waitin' to pinch hit for our pitcher when the guy ahead of me hit into a double play. Shows you how lucky I am. If he hadn't done that I would have been in two games and I wouldn't be on your all-star team."

Hesitantly, trying to stick to our deal, though still wanting something more, I asked, "How did you feel?"

"Feel? Same way I felt the week before when I was catching in Iowa and a week later when I was catching back in Iowa. I was doing my job, best I could. I always did my job."

"Didn't you enjoy it?"

"Acourse I did. Just like I did everywhere I played. I called it a job, but it was never just that. I love the game, the doing it, like my Daddy did, so it didn't make a whole lot of difference where I was."

"So why did you stop? You retired, what, a year, two years, later?"

Thinking back on the conversation, I have to admit that when I posed the question I felt a kind of vindication, a sense that I had sprung a trap on him, though I hadn't necessarily planned it that way. Hadn't planned it, but I was probably looking for it. There flashed through my mind the excitement that I had felt when I came up with my project, how I had framed the questions for myself. In retrospect, I have to admit the questions, some of them anyway, were the residue of my own dream. The answers I wanted were the ones I would have given, if only, if only I could have had that one day in the sunshine of my dream fulfilled. I have often invoked the cliché that baseball is about grown men playing a boy's game. As Eileen once pointed out to me, however—I thought, unkindly, at the time—men who spend their time writing about baseball are the boys who have been kept inside by their mothers because they have a sore throat or they have to practice piano or Aunt Elsie's coming to visit. So they're standing with their noses pressed against the window, watching the other boys play. But, that reflection came later. At the particular moment in my conversation with Ivy I was finally getting what I wanted.

Ivy Wingo Campanella looked at me, smiled, and replied, "Stop? I didn't stop, I just gave up traveling so far to play. Kept on going in semi-pro stuff till I was, oh forty-some. Still play in an over-fifty league though I gave up catching. All that squatting gets to you after a time. Play first base where you don't hustle around a lot. Long as I can see the ball and run the bases without puffin' too much, I'll keep on. Like I said I love the game, the doin' it, so it doesn't make a whole lot of difference where I am."

In his voice, his tone, there was all that "juice and joy" I like to rhapsodize about in some of my writing. I felt a little envious of him. Why had I stopped playing? I had not risen so high as he had, so wouldn't it have been easier for me to play on? Maybe I hadn't loved the game as much as I thought, as much as he has, despite all my words. Maybe what I had loved was the dream.

"That's great," I hoped he didn't detect my false heartiness, "but let me rephrase the question. Why did you give up professional baseball, going so far to play as you put it, and come back to St. Louis?"

"I got married and it made sense to me to think a little more long term, at least about some things. Evelyn, that's my wife, is a school teacher. She had summers free to join me wherever I was playing, but it just seemed like the right thing to do."

"Was it a tough decision for you?"

"No, not especially. Don't get me wrong. Maybe if I'd stayed up the rest of that year with the Sox, I mighta been tempted to hang on hopin' for another ride on the big carousel. And maybe I played that year or so longer thinkin' I would get another shot at it. But it finally made more sense just to come home, to settle down."

"So how did you meet your wife?"

"Like I said, she's a school teacher, mostly third grade. During the off-season when I was playing pro I had a part time job as a janitor in her building. We got to talkin' one day and one thing led to another. Her parents weren't all that happy with her takin' up with me. Her father was a minister and I'm not sure whether it was worse my bein' a part-time janitor or a professional baseball player. But I wasn't a mouth-breather, had a year of college, went to church, been brought up right by my own parents, and they softened up. So we got married. I played another year and we decided enough was enough. Got a full-time janitorial position in a high school, raised a family, and, like I said, I'm still playin' ball."

"You still working?"

"Sure. Only now I'm a facilities services supervisor."

"Moving up?"

He laughed. "When I started playin' baseball I was a Negro. For a while there in the seventies and eighties I was a Black. Now they tell me I'm African-American. Started as a janitor, then I was a maintenance man, now I'm a facilities services supervisor. Get the picture?"

"Yeah, I get it. No regrets?"

"No, not really. I've had a good life."

I'll admit I was still fishing. I liked Ivy, but his story— aside from the bit about his father changing his name—was too placid to suit me, or rather my project. Dickinson wrote, "The Past is such a curious Creature / To look her in the Face...." I wondered whether he was looking his past in the face. Or maybe he was, but to get at the real truth of it, you would have to examine it obliquely. Then again maybe I was just wrong, projecting shadows of my own discontent on somebody else's life. Could I as easily say I had a good life? What is a good life?

"Any family?"

He paused for a moment, then said "Have a daughter, Laurel, who's really made something of herself."

"How so?"

"She's like my wife, bright, interested in books and stuff. Graduated from high school top of her class. Got a full scholarship to Washington U. Did well there too. Went on to grad school, got a PhD in psychology, and teaches at Missouri."

"You must be proud of her."

"Yeah, proud, real proud. Wish I could understand better what she's talkin' about sometimes when she gets goin', but it sure is impressive. Evelyn understands it and she keeps tellin' me how good Laurel is in her field. She's made the big leagues and it looks like she'll stick."

He had a rich, resonant voice. It reminded me a lot of listening to Buck O'Neill on that Ken Burns special about baseball. And there was a subtlety of tone to it as well. While it rolled like the big river we were so near, there were depths and eddies to it that kept catching my ear. Like now: he was talking about his daughter and the pleasure was obvious, yet something else was there, swirling under the surface, what one of my old profs would have called a subtext. I watched him as he spoke and he was smiling, but his eyes, his eyes were like that river.

"Do you…"

"Don't ask."

"What?"

"I know what you were goin, to ask. Don't." He spoke with a sharpness unlike any tone I had heard in his voice before. Gone was the flow, gone even the sense of deeper currents. Here was the suddenness of an uncharted rock, a whirlpool of emotion. I started to speak again, but he rose and walked away from me briskly. He halted, perhaps twenty yards away, his body taut as if he awaited a collision with a base runner trying to score. He did not look back. I don't know what he was looking at or whether he even had his eyes open, but the picture I saw was of a man seeking something outside or inside of himself. Calm? Assurance? Finally, he seemed to fix his gaze on the kids playing baseball, watched them intently, and gradually, ever so gradually, he began to relax absorbing the easy rhythms of the game. His posture, which had been so tense, eased, as if, after

29

the collision he knew he had taken the shot and could shrug it off. Or needed to make it appear that he had.

What? What was this all about? Then it came to me. Campanella, Camp. Of course, I should have known. Jackie Camp. I walked slowly to him. He must have heard me coming, though he did not turn. I put my hand on his shoulder. "I'm sorry. I think I know the answer. I'm sorry."

Stillness for moment, then he spoke slowly, softly. "He was like me when he was little: couldn't get enough of playin' ball. And when he wasn't playin', he was watchin' me. Loved his name, too. Jackie Robinson Campanella. And he could play. Like both of them put together, way better then I ever have, or my dad. All-American his junior year in high school. Would have been a first round draft choice. Cardinal scout told me if he had a senior year like his junior year he'd be number one. But that never happened.

"Got hurt right at the start of the season. Nothin' that would keep him down permanently, but he was out for the year. Depressed him a lot, started hanging out with the wrong guys. Probably got into drugs. No. No probably about it, he got into drugs. Pro scouts got wind of it, and college recruiters, so nobody'd touch him. We knew, too. Tried to stop him, tried to help him. Things got pretty bad. That's when he started callin' himself Camp, instead of Campanella. I had no problem with that. But he had to make something big out of it, sayin' he was reclaimin' the heritage we'd....I'd denied him. Lots of screamin', lots of things said that shouldn't have been said. Maybe he was right, I don't know."

Names can be a burden, but we either let it weigh us down or we carry on. Memories, too, can be a burden. And what do we do with them: stumble and fall under the weight? absorb them into ourselves, assuming the weight of them as part of our being? or give them wings with our imagination?

"Thought we'd gotten through the worst of it though. Thought he'd gotten off drugs when he started attendin' community college. He was done with ball-playin' though. Said he wasn't goin' to be any man's monkey. That's the way he put it.

That bothered me. I had dreams for him and maybe those dreams were just me tryin' to make up for what I hadn't managed. Still I could live with it. Like I said, baseball's just a game. It's been my life, but it's just a game. He was a bright kid. Could've done what Laurel's done if he'd put his mind to it. Lots of other fields he could have played on. But then… then…"

I squeezed his shoulder. "I know. You don't have to tell me."

Yes, I knew the story. It was in all the papers, and on national TV. A young man barricades himself in a house with four hostages—a husband and wife, their twenty year old daughter, and her three year old son. Some say that the young man was the boy's father, that the older couple had sought a court order to keep him away from their daughter, that he had threatened to kill them. The siege lasted twelve hours, then ended in a blaze of gunfire as the young man came out the front shooting wildly. Inside the house the police found the bodies of the husband and wife and their daughter, their throats slit with a kitchen knife. The child was found locked in a closet. That is how a young man named Jackie Camp had ended his life.

For a time we stood there silently in the uncommon cool of a summer's day. I was watching Ivy out of the corner of my eye; he, in turn, was watching the kids playing baseball. One of them, seemingly the smallest of the motley group, came up to bat and on the first pitch hit the ball hard into left center between the outfielders. They hurried after it while the batter, running with his head thrown back, his arms pumping, raced around the bases, a joyous sprint for home.

"That's my grandson," Ivy said. "Runs like a deer. He's only ten, but he's already better'n kids three, four years older. He's goin' to be good one."

The first ex-major league ballplayer I ever met was Sparky Adams, who played infield (second, short, third) for the Cubs, Pirates, Cardinals and Reds in the 1920's and 1930's. The Baseball Encyclopedia *says he was 5'5 1/2" tall and weighed 151 pounds. When I met him he was a wizened little man with white hair who would have had to stretch to reach either figure. At the time I was 6'3" tall, weighed 160 pounds and had not yet decided whether I was Tom Seaver or Robin Yount, though I was leaning toward Seaver. As it turned out I was neither, but—wizened, white-haired or not—Adams had spent thirteen years in the land I only ever dreamed of.*

My memory is that it was Christmas time my junior year in high school. We were living in the Chicago area by then, my father having been promoted to the headquarters of his company. So I had moved on from that makeshift field in Alton and the only slightly more presentable little league fields, to real baseball diamonds, and to being pitcher and shortstop for my high school and the local American Legion team. A work colleague of my father had invited my parents to a party. At first they had begged off because my brother Jeff was just home from college, but the host, a hearty man who may have been in sales, jovially insisted that they come and "bring the boys along." Whether he really wanted a couple of teenage males there, thinking we would enjoy it, that he could get us to enjoy it, or just was willing to put up with us to have my parents there, I'm not sure. As I try to remember him, I think it was the former, so he must have been in sales.

Neither of us was what you might call socially adept, but Jeff had the advantage of being fresh off his first semester at MIT which was a fact of some interest to the suburban and corporate minds that were present, especially since he was in chemical engineering. I mostly stood by sipping on a coke, half-

32

listening to his efforts to provide varied answers to the same questions. Whenever Jeff mentioned his major, he always got appreciative and approving nods. Probably some of the men had no better idea what chemical engineering was than I did, but it had a solid practical ring to it. To the extent I really listened to the conversation, I recollect feeling a vague pride in the way Jeff handled himself, but no particular envy. I wasn't old enough to think well of social graces. Occasionally the interest turned my way and I would mumble some response to inquiries about whether I had decided where I was going to college and what I was going to major in, but the lack of clarity in my replies generally deflected the focus back to Jeff.

If somebody had mentioned baseball I might have been okay, because I could talk about that a blue streak. I did once say that I was hoping for a baseball scholarship to Northwestern, but that didn't raise much of a ripple. Most of the men were probably just golfers. And Jeff wasn't any particular help there because the only thing other than studying he did was sculling and what's to say about a sport where you don't even look where you're going. Mostly I just stood there trying to look attentive and comfortable, but wishing I was over at my girl friend's house.

It wasn't long before I started thinking I might just be able to slip out and make tracks across town to Shelley's. Before the idea got fully developed, however, the host came over and said "Will, there's somebody I want you to meet." He led me through the traffic to the next room that was occupied by clusters of men in earnest conversations. In the corner was this short little old man who was standing off by himself, not looking lonely or bored, just...sufficient. The host steered me right to him.

"Will, this is Sparky Adams, he's a neighbor and friend of my brother, but the thing that would interest you is that he played major league baseball for...how long was it Sparky?"

"Thirteen years, give or take a month." His voice was soft and still rooted in rural southern Indiana from whence he had come.

"Sparky, this is Will Collins, Art's younger boy. He's our local baseball hero, pitches for the high school and the Legion teams. Quite a star."

I blushed a bit and muttered something like what my mother had told me to say when I was introduced to people, but I did remember to shake his hand firmly. It was dry and leathery, cool to the touch. He looked at me with rheumy eyes.

"Pitcher, eh?"

"Yes sir, but I play some shortstop too."

He was still holding my hand. He turned it over and examined it as if he were trying to read my future in the length of the fingers. Then he fixed his eyes on mine.

This was more than twenty years ago. It had been almost fifty years since he left the big leagues. Can I remember accurately a conversation from that long ago? Could he remember what it was like to be a seventeen-year old boy dreaming about playing in the majors? Was he striving to see the world again as he once had seen it? to see in my eyes the length and depth of my dream? Or am I trying to instill significance into an incidental encounter between a starry-eyed boy and an old man?

I wasn't talking to Babe Ruth. Until that moment I had never heard of Sparky Adams. I had a friend who, if he had been there, not only would have known him, but could have rattled off all his career statistics from his .266 career average to the number of games he had played at each of three positions. He was the kind of guy who these days would be a whiz at fantasy baseball, but he was an indifferent first baseman even for a sand lot player. Of course, he had no illusions while I was preoccupied with what I hoped would be and therefore paid little mind to what had been. And the dreams that young men dream are not about being a journeyman player—or memorizing someone else's statistics.

Reality transmutes the dreams-- or kills them. To most of the "one-day wonders" I talked to, Adams would have been a giant, and an object of envy. And now, given all that I have learned from them, I wish I had learned more from him. That was my fault, not his, for I was young and too preoccupied with myself to know what to ask.

So, though I believe I remember how the conversation began, I have no idea of how long it lasted or even how it ended—and little enough of what was said. All I know about Adams and his career I learned from my trusty Baseball Encyclopedia— *and that only years after this encounter. The numbers tell me little of what I learned from him. In my subsequent life as a baseball writer I've talked to lots of players and ex-players about all manner of things, and probably Adams wouldn't have, couldn't have, said anything I haven't heard at least dozens of times since. But how do we ever know? Maybe that wizened, little old man was a Merlin with some special knowledge that, if only I had known, all else would have been different.*

Common sense tells me that at some point my father rescued me—more to the point probably, rescued Adams—from a morass of adolescent remarks and awkward pauses. Mercifully also, my parents decided to leave shortly thereafter. On the way home my father tried to get me to talk about the conversation with Adams, probably just to get me thinking I had had a passably good time at the party, but I assume my responses were pretty desultory. Finally, I asked if I could borrow the car and go over to see my girlfriend. My parents must have figured I needed some jollying up because they said yes a little more readily than usual.

Sitting on the couch in her living room, snuggling up as much as was proper with her parents in the next room and a ten year old brother who was likely to appear at any moment somewhere about, I said "I missed you Shelley." We hadn't seen each other since four o'clock.

"I missed you too, Will," she answered to my satisfaction. "Did you meet anybody interesting at the party?"

"Nobody half so interesting as you."

Funny thing is that I can see Adams clearly in my mind and I even have an image of what might have looked like when he played, but I have trouble remembering Shelley.

35

"Swish" Cartwright's Strange Bell

A drouthy day at the end of summer. Dust devils danced on the unpaved road, stirred to life by the ceaseless wind that swept the Dakota plain. I was seven miles from the nearest town, to use the word loosely, and fifty from one that would show up on anything less detailed than a county map. Why, I wondered to myself, am I here? The simplest answer was that I was looking for Clarence "Swish" Cartwright and, according to the owner of the combination gas station/ general store/ post office I had just left, he lived where this dirt road ran up against Cartwright Creek and stopped.

He had appeared in one game for the Chicago Cubs in 1966, their last awful season (59-103) before a period of revival under Leo Durocher that led to the monumental frustration of 1969. A first baseman in the mold of Steve Bilko or Dick Stuart, aka "Dr. Strangeglove" (that is, built for power and utterly graceless afield), Cartwright, of course, played the position oc- cupied by the Cubs' living and then still active legend Ernie Banks. Banks was in the waning years of his career, but there was no way he could wane far enough to be displaced by the likes of Cartwright. For one game, however, on a hot September afternoon Cartwright had taken his spot in the line-up. He batted four times, struck out three of them and managed a fly ball to center. He also made one error and may have been responsible for two others by Cub infielders. Not the stuff of legends. Proba- bly no one expected much else from him. While he had spent eight years in the minors and had shown considerable power, he also had displayed all the flaws that typed him as a journeyman minor leaguer. The only question was why the Cubs had bothered to bring him up in the first place.

"That I can't answer," Cartwright said to me after we met, "and there's a way in which I've always regretted they did."

Despite the remoteness of his location, I had not had much trouble finding him. For all the players on my list, if the major league offices didn't have any information on their whereabouts, I always started by checking out the area from which they had come and Cartwright was from rural South Dakota. He didn't have a phone so I had written him a long elaborate letter outlining my project and my credentials, and asking if I might meet with him. A month later I got a one word response on an old picture postcard of the Edgewater Beach Hotel in Chicago, which in the halcyon days of the fifties and sixties was where teams visiting Wrigley Field used to stay. In that regard it is most famous as being where Ruth Ann Steinhagen shot Eddie Waitkus, another former Cub first baseman. The one word was "Sure." I hoped he was more verbose in the flesh.

What I found at the end of the dirt road on the banks of Cartwright Creek was an old trailer home, vintage the late 1970's, set up on blocks. It looked to have weathered some hard winters with minimal attention to repair, a cracked window held in place by duct tape, which was also used to restrain some loose siding. When I arrived, Cartwright was standing barefooted in the water with his back to me. Only when he turned in response to my call, zipping up his pants with a big grin on his florid face, did I realize he had been pissing in the creek.

"Returning to nature what nature give me in the first place."

He had been a big man when he played: that was the source of his power at bat and of his awkwardness on defense. He was bigger now, having added weight as well as letting muscles sag. What remained of his hair had gone gray and while it made him look even older than his almost sixty years it lent him a peculiar distinction that made him look like something other than a fat old man. He had the leathery look of someone who has spent a good bit of time in the open air and sun. A lingering hint of rugged good looks marked his features despite the fleshiness. He gave the appearance of someone who laughed a lot, even when alone.

I introduced myself.

"Figured that out. Don't have many visitors atall out here—and no strangers. We can just sit over there if you don't mind." He waved toward a couple of aluminum folding chairs in the shade of one of the few trees in the immediate vicinity. A large styrofoam cooler sat between the chairs pretending to be a table in addition to serving its usual function.

"Beer?"

"Don't mind if I do. It is a warm day."

He opened the cooler and took out two cans of beer, some brand I had never heard of, and handed one to me. Settling into his chair, he opened his beer, took a long draught, smacked his lips, and invited me to start the interview.

"Well, as I said in my letter, I have two principal questions: what was it like to make it to the major leagues and appear in only a single game, and what did you make of the experience afterwards."

"You talked to manya the others on your list?"

"You're the fourth."

"Suppose you heard lots of pap about it was the greatest day of my life, the fulfillment of a boyhood dream and the like."

"Some of that."

"Well, it wasn't that way for me atall. Not that it wasn't interesting or that I don't think about it now and then. But you can only spend a certain amount of time thinking about roughly three hours outa yer whole life. That'll drive you buggy."

"Wasn't it a boyhood dream for you then?"

"Oh sure, what the hell. Any kid who ever played baseball and enjoyed it had some kind of dream like that. You probably did yourself though you don't look too a-the-letic. But it wasn't an obsession with me. And when I was called up to Chicago it was more puzzling than anything else.

Which is when I asked him why they had done so and he made his surprising response that he was a bit sorry they had.

38

"Oh, don't get me wrong," he said with a laugh and reached into the cooler for another beer. He looked my way inquiringly, but I waved him off. "I'll do two, for yer one. Do it with everybody else, might as well do it with you." He opened the can, took a swig, then continued.

"Everybody who plays the game professionally wants to make it to the bigs and I wasn't any different that way. And mostly they play until something inside tells them it's not going to happen—or more often when someone else tells' em. Some just keep on playing anyway because it's the only thing they ever wanted to do and there's nothing else they think they can do. You got the guys who'll play ten years or more in the minors without even the cuppa coffee I had in the majors. Career minor leaguers like that are interesting, some of 'em become local folk heroes in places like Little Rock or Salt Lake City or wherever."

"Was that what you wanted to be?"

He laughed again, took another swig of beer. "Well that's not bad. I mean don't 'Swish' Cartwright sound more like a folk hero in Wichita than a big leaguer. Razor Shines, he's *my* hero. So that call-up smirched my record." He laughed once more, but it seemed to fade and when he spoke again there was an edge of seriousness in his voice that had not been there before. "I knew several years earlier that I wasn't good enough. Up here I knew it." He tapped his forehead.

"Somewhere on a backburner though a notion was still cookin' that I could do it. I mean I had seen guys go up who weren't no better'n me. So there was this little something that said you can do that if they give you a chance. If I had walked away without that one game in Chicago I'd still have that...that... well call it an illusion. But being up there, playing that one game, seein' what was really needed to be there, fallin' flat on my ass like I did...." He shrugged, then added softly. "One dead illusion."

"But wasn't it better that way? Better than going through life thinking if only you had had the chance? Sort of on the order of 'Tis better to have loved and lost than never to have loved at all.'"

"Screw that, buddy."

There was a fierceness in his response that surprised me—and made me wonder if I had perhaps blundered into some field of his memory with a no trespassing sign. I glanced at him—a big, gone-to-seed ex-ballplayer pushing sixty, living alone in the middle of godforsaken nowhere, by all appearances a drifter on the surface of life—took a sip of my beer, and tried to figure out if there was a graceful way to discover what it was about or whether I ought to stay clear. He looked away across the creek, across the sun-baked rise that straggled away from its banks. After a pause he said, "Funny how ya think ya got somethin' in place and under control and suddenly it ups and bites ya. Sorry if I snapped a bit."

"No problem. Say what you want. This is an interview, not a federal investigation."

He took another swig of his beer, considered the logo on the can for a moment then with a shrug said, "When I graduated from high school I went pro instead of goin' to college. But I guess you can tell that. I was pretty ignorant about life. Oh, I had screwed myself a few cheerleaders like any big-shot high school jock woulda done, but I hadn't been serious about anything except hittin' a baseball. About the third year when I was playing in Des Moines and doing pretty well, about as well as I ever did in terms of homeruns and rbi's, so the local press was makin' out what a great prospect I was, I met this girl, Meredith McCoy. She was just out of college and workin' for some insurance agent in town. She was real good lookin' and we got it on pretty well. I was in love with her and one thing led to another as they say and we got married. I was on top of the world: half-convinced I was a star on the rise and with a loving wife, I thought. Another beer?" He was half-out of his chair already on the way to the cooler, so I said, "Sure while, you're up."

He tossed me a can, opened his while still standing by the cooler and took a long drink. "Well, two years later when I was back in Des Moines after a bad year in triple-A, she walked out on me. Seems she had thought I was her ticket to the big leagues: she wasn't any better at judging baseball talent than them sportswriters—or than I was at judgin' whether somebody really loved me." He paused. "She took up with the right fielder who everybody was ravin' about that year. The only thing that prevented what might have been a serious clubhouse problem was I got hurt and he got moved up to Wichita. She left with him thinkin' she was really on her way this time."

"Did she make it to the majors?"

He chuckled. "Hey, I like that. Good way to put it. But naw, she didn't. The following spring he tore up his leg sliding into second. Took him almost two years to recover and then he was never the same. Had lost a coupla steps and played a bit shy. He lasted one more year and retired. But by then she was long gone. She left him right after the accident."

"Looking for another rising star."

"Nope. She retired from baseball too." He gave a low sad, laugh. "She maybe was a little shallow when it came to matters of the heart, but she was smart. After two swings she decided to try some field she understood a little better. She went back and married one of her college profs who I guess had diddled her a few times when she was his student. Apparently, she guessed right that time: he ended up as a dean of the business school at some state university and then a college president."

"So you have loved and lost?"

"Yeah."

"Sounds like it wasn't that much of a loss."

"You'd think so, wouldn't ya. You married?"

"Yes."

"Kids?"

"Two."

"You happy?"

"Yeah." Did I sound convincing enough? I thought of what Eileen and I had been through together, the good times and the bad. Emily Dickinson wrote, "Memory is a strange Bell— Jubilee and Knell." I kept finding that out. When I had first set out on this project I had expected to encounter some ex-players who had come to terms with their past and some who had not, some who were happy and some who were unhappy. And I assumed there was going to be a real connection between how a guy had dealt with the ending of the common boyhood dream and how he had lived the rest of his life. But I was discovering that my thinking was too linear and it allowed for neither the double weight of memory, as both Jubilee and Knell, nor for the effect which probing other people's memories would have on my own. "No life is perfect, but yes I'm happy."

"Then you're lucky. I didn't expect perfection. I mean baseball is pretty humblin' that way. It lowers your expectations. Even if you're real good you make an out twice as often as you get a hit. I woulda been happy hittin' 300 in the game of life— God doesn't that sound puffed up! But I didn't. Like I said before I wasn't very experienced when it came to… to affections. Meredith burned me pretty bad, and despite all the evidence that it was just a bad choice, that I ought to get up and go on, I never did."

"What did you do?"

"Kept on playin' baseball as long as I could. Had the one fling in the bigs after eight years and played another three or four after that, just bouncin' around. Hell, if they'd had these here independent leagues like have been sprouting up now God knows how long I'd of kept goin'."

"And then?" We were coming back to the safer ground that I had defined for my project. I'm not sure which of us was more relieved.

"Then I came back to this area which is where I grew up. My parents had retired and moved to Florida, so they just deeded this land over to me. I mean, nobody was going to buy it. Pop had given up farming years ago and worked for the state highway department. The house had pretty well fallen down. I finished the job, then got this trailer cheap. Didn't live here year round, still don't though more'n I did."

He struggled out of his chair, ambled down to the creek, and again pissed into the passing waters, as he did singing an old beer commercial, "Live-a-ly golden, crystal-ly clear." Coming

42

back to shade of the tree he said, "Anytime you want to use the facilities, feel free."

"Thanks, I'm all right for the moment."

"I suppose it's one of the secrets of the universe that the older you get the more exercise your bladder needs."

"Gets you up and about. Keeps you from being too sedentary."

"Yeah, yeah. I like that. I'll remember that when I get up at three a.m. to join my stream with Mother Nature's. Nighttime exercise." He raised his beer as if toasting the idea.

"So how did you earn a living? Presumably playing minor league baseball hadn't exactly made you independently wealthy."

"That's fer sure. Did various things, mostly in the line of bar-tending and being a bouncer in clubs in places like Pierre or Sioux City. In the fall I'd go over to the Twin Cities and hook onto one of those rental car agency deals where they're tryin' to move cars to Florida for the winter season. I'd drive down there and get me a job. Made good money, sometimes enough just to relax up here in the summers. Didn't need much to keep me goin', bein' alone." A shadow crossed his face: a summer cloud momentarily obscuring the sun or memory's knell once more?

"You never thought of getting into coaching?"

He laughed. The shadow passed. "Me? Chrisakes, what would I coach? Hitting? Fielding? Most coaches are runty little utility infielders who sit on the bench and watch everybody so they learn something about everything. How many big coaches you ever see? Frank Howard's the only one I can think of and, hell, he could hit. Naw, the thought never crossed my mind. Beer?"

"Still working on this one."

He helped himself to another. "Be my guest. You don't need to wait to be asked." He leaned back with an audible sigh.

I looked over at the trailer. No sign of a TV antenna, so he didn't sit up nights watching sitcoms or the World Wrestling Federation—or baseball. So what did he do with himself besides the occasional hunting and fishing and pissing in the creek. Just sit and drink beer till it didn't matter that he was just sitting and drinking beer? Or ponder the mysteries of the universe? Or think about the eternal pinkness of memory?

"You miss baseball?"

"I miss playin', some. Funny, it's been better than twenty-five years since I stopped and I still miss playin'. I mean it was who I was since age seven or eight."

So, who was he now? Could I ask him that question? Would he have any answer? What he had described to me of his post-baseball life seemed essentially an aimless existence and not even one with the saving grace of a circle of friends, even just drinking or fishing buddies. I thought of a Dickinson poem: "Remorse—is Memory—awake / Her parties all astir— / A presence of Departed Acts— / At window—and at Door—...." Yet 'Remorse' seemed too strong a word to describe what I sensed lingering in this place. The thought made me wonder whether what I was feeling was simply disappointment at finding such a commonplace ennui: no rage against a failed dream, nor even against the failed marriage. Sadness, to be sure, but not a keening sadness which I could dramatize—and not a stoic heroism. I found myself oddly angry with the man and it was my irritation that led me to the question, hoping perhaps to provoke him to some memorable response.

"So who are you now?"

"Who the hell cares and what the hell difference does it make?" He spoke not in anger, but in mild amusement. He paused, took a long draught of his beer, then smiled. "I don't make a very good story, do I, writer man? Yer welcome to demote me and find yerself another first baseman.'"

"No, no you don't."

"Sorry you came all this way to find that out. But then I didn't ask ya in the first place. You came for yer own reasons."

I got up. I walked down to the bank. I pissed in the creek. Coming back, I stood there for a moment, silent. "I take that back. You do make a good story, or maybe you do. It's just not the one I had half written in my head before I got here. And I don't know if it's one I want to write, mostly because I can't figure it out, can't figure you out."

"You and me both, writer man."

"One last question. Just for the record, in case I make something of it. How do you make a living now? You couldn't have saved much from bartending and bouncing drunks. Did you inherit something from your parents?"

"Not yet. They're still livin', happy as clams. In their eighties, but us Cartwrights are long lived. I'm livin' on my pension."

"Pension? You don't have one from baseball and it doesn't sound like you worked anywhere long enough to be in any kind of pension plan. I suppose you'll get some social security, but you're not eligible yet."

Cartwright smiled, not a big hearty grin, but a Mona Lisa smile, slight, distinctive, suggestive, enigmatic. He reached for the cooler and fetched himself another beer. He seemed to be considering something and the deliberateness of his motions—opening the cooler, selecting a can, closing the cooler again, pulling the tab, taking a tentative taste of the beer—was obviously intended to give him time to think. Finally, he wiped his mouth with the back of his hand and spoke: "It's what you might call a private pension, provided by Meredith and her university president."

The look on my face must have revealed my bewilderment. Nothing that he had said about his former wife would have led me to believe that she might adopt him as a charity after so many years. "I don't get it. Why would your ex-wife...."

"I guess you wasn't listening as well as I thought. I said she left me. I never said we wuz divorced."

If bewilderment had characterized my look before, flat out utter astonishment touched with a line or two of absolute confusion must have been there now. I couldn't speak. He seemed to enjoy the moment.

"It's this way, writer man: when she left me for the right fielder she didn't take time to start anything so complex as divorce proceedings and that wasn't a particular matter of concern

45

to me. Whether it just slipped her mind subsequently or what, I can't say. All's I know is that when she got involved with her professor type she went ahead and married him. Well, you can understand that creates a kind of legal quandry, not to mention a potential public embarrassment for somebody like a business school dean or university president, let alone somebody who might have political ambitions."

Something like understanding began to shape itself in my mind, but I jumped ahead to misunderstanding. "My God, you're blackmailing them."

He gave me a look of amused indignation. "Now that's a bit hard. I'm helpin' some fellow human beings in a time of trouble, including my wife for whom I still have some abiding affection despite all, and they're helpin' me."

"Still sounds like blackmail."

"Well, you got to understand, I never brought the subject up. I was perfectly happy the way I wuz. Hadn't given any particular thought to what things might be like for them. I mean I knew she hadn't divorced me and I sure hadn't divorced her, but she had taken care of herself all right. Anyway, 'bout three, four years ago when I wuz sittin' right here thinkin' about just when I should head south, a fellah comes wheeling up the road in some fancy foreign car, plops himself down and tells me he's workin' for some people who have a serious problem and I'm the only person who can help them. Now I'm not what you would call a practicin' Christian, but my parents did try to teach me to help my fellow creatures in time of distress, so I naturally asked what I might do. Nice fellah, he wuz, though a bit slick. Anyway, he described the whole situation in some detail and kept referring to it as a catch-22 problem. I didn't quite know what that meant, but it was finally clear to me that things were sorta sticky."

"I think I see." And I did. If one or the other of them filed for divorce now, at the very least there would be a public record that an enterprising reporter— or political enemy— looking for a bit of dirt could easily uncover. And it was just as likely that the matter would come out in the open right then. Meredith's 'husband' could send her packing and announce he had been deceived, but not without having some muck on his shoes and raising a few questions about his judgment. They could have left well enough alone, but who was to know whether Cartwright, accidentally or malevolently, might not tell the story. The fair Meredith had certainly not spent any amount of time analyzing "Swish's" character—only his earning potential. "So this nice fellow asked what it would take to keep you quiet?"

"Yeah, and I said 'Not much.' My wants are simple. So now I get a nice little pension check every month."

No, this was a far cry from the story I had in mind when I had come down the road to this place and I hardly knew what to make of it. I still hadn't him out. "But you told me. That jeopardizes your pension, doesn't it?"

"Remember how I told ya that I'm a little sorry that I played that one game in the big leagues, that it sorta made it impossible to keep the illusion that if only I coulda got to the bigs I'd be good enough to stick."

"Yeah, I remember that."

"Well, I just gave you a real interesting story: one that could give some real pizzazz to your book, maybe attract some attention to you, get ya on the TV talk shows and all that. Make it to the writing big leagues. You thought of that?"

"It crossed my mind."

"Then maybe it also crossed your mind to ask: is old Swish's story true? How can I find out whether it is or not? Dare I use it true or not? What are the consequences of putting myself in a position to know?"

"I'm thinking those questions now."

"Then maybe ya know how I feel."

He pushed himself up from his chair, walked down to the creek, waded into it and once more started pissing.

"Well thanks, I guess I'd better be going."

"Nice talkin' to ya, writer man." He didn't turn, but continued at his work. "Don't drive too fast going out, raises a lot of dust, not good for the planet."

I drove away, slowly. "…My Hazel Eye / Has periods of shutting-- / But, No lid has Memory—."

We all aspire to a meaningful life. When we are young we compose epic poems in our minds of which we are the heroes, but most remain unwritten and therefore unrealized histories. When we are older we blunder about grappling with such beasts of the jungle as self-image, self-improvement,, and self-actualization. And finally when we reach a certain time of life, we venture into the fields of memory hoping that we might meet ourselves—or find solace by re-imagining our past

But who are we? Who is this self? What is its substance, its reality? Each of us has a particular image or understanding of our self, an image or understanding perhaps composed in part of considered reflection and assessment, but never entirely free from hopes and fears, anticipations and regrets, dreams and delusions. But we have other selves as well: the images or understandings that other people have of us. They too are composed in part of critical assessment, but, also, they are never free from expectations, preconceptions and prejudgments.

Usually when we talk about knowing ourselves we are referring to our self-image because we believe that our true self is the one we perceive and we presume that other people do or will or should perceive that self as well. Contrarily other people believe that our true self is the one they see and assume that we do or will or should discern the same image. But the true self is neither the one nor the other: it is at least both and if we would truly know ourselves we need more than self-knowledge.

Augustine remarks that out of the supply of images stored "in that vast chamber of memory...do I myself with the past construct now this, now that likeness of things, which either I have experienced or, from having experienced, have believed; and thus again future actions, events, and hopes...." But how do we account for the images that are not in our memory, but in the memory of others?. How do we see ourselves as others see us?

48

Worse yet, how do we remember ourselves as we are seen by others? The first is hard enough, the second perhaps impossible. And maybe that is the attraction of dwelling on the past: our memory becomes a means of creating a sense of self that is secure from the perception of others. The rootlessness of our society is more than physical. When we move away from home, and move and move again, we lose our connections from the people who knew us when, we lose a part of our past. Autobiography becomes a way of creating the self we would like to be, of composing our own songs of ourselves.

Augustine also wrote: "...The matter of the sound is before the form of the tune; not before, through any power it hath to make a tune; for a sound is in no way the workmaster of the tune....Nor is it first in time; for it is given forth together with the tune; nor first in choice, for a sound is not better than a tune, a tune being not only a sound, but a beautiful sound. But it is first in original, because a tune receives not form to become a sound, but a sound receives a form to become a tune."

The songs we compose from our own memory are not songs at all, not melodies, not tunes, for they are not in harmony with our true selves, only with our imagined selves. They are then mere sounds which, however loud, however pleasing to our own ear, denote nothing. We cannot give meaning to our lives without reference to others. The imagination of our own hearts produces only gossamer hopes for the future and mythic memories of the past. We are but "pleasing ourselves to ourselves."

There are people who would argue that the real past, "the past as it actually was," is unknowable whether one is talking about the lives of individuals or of nations. Then why look to the past at all? Henry Ford's "History is bunk" suggests that there is no reason for doing so. More imaginatively, but no less perversely, some would say that we should recreate the past to fit the kind of future we wish to have. Yet, finally, few of us are able to ignore utterly or manufacture totally our own pasts. Memory, unbridled and unrefined, will force its way into our consciousness. The sudden stab of a failure or a heartbreak, of things done or left undone, that arise serpent-like in our minds to tarnish our assumed innocence.

I used to tell myself—and others if they would listen— that I gave up playing baseball when I threw out my arm in a summer league game after college. The fact of the matter is that I gave it up when the last shreds of my dream shriveled. I can admit that now because for all my words, all my efforts, to make it otherwise, the memory of it kept coming back. When I am being honest, I know that there are other imagined realities that clutter the life story that I like to tell—some that I know and some that remain unknown to me.

What of the songs I was hearing? Few of the ex-players were what I would call reflective men—Sam Patch for sure, Felipe Ortiz maybe, Stoney Schmitt in an oddly negative way— and those few certainly weren't philosophical in their reflections. In a sense the likes of Campanella and Cartwright were at peace with their pasts, at least as it involved baseball, but more because they didn't look back certainly not with any regret. Bill Branch neatly packaged and shelved his. But each of them had moments when reptilian reality made itself felt.

Then there was Danny Miller. I kept going back to my notes and looking at what the bartender had said: "He mostly talks about how things are going to be when his arm comes around."

He, it seems to me, had made the hardest bargain with his memory, declaring that the past was not past, but the future—and the future was what he always dreamed it would be. I ached for him.

Had I Presumed to Hope

"Bitter? Damn right, I'm bitter. Wouldn't you be?"

I've always thought the army recruiting slogan, "Be all that you can be," was insidiously clever. It plays right to that juvenile notion the other kind of poster encourages, those misty ones of endless horizons and open skies with inscriptions like "You can be anything you want to be." Then some sergeant or lieutenant or whoever tells you just what it is you can be. Civilian life can be like that, too. The truth of the matter is that growing up means recognizing that some things are just not going to happen. When you're a kid you dream of stardom. In your make-believe games you get the game winning hit or strike out the big slugger in the clutch. Then, when it turns out you don't have the ability to play professionally, you fold those dreams up and put them away. Of course, the best thing is to do it on your own, read the signs and understand them, readjust your expectations without being kicked in the teeth.

But, even if you do, every now and again, watching a big league game, you feel the itch and wonder to yourself what you would give for one swing, one throw, one moment in that sun. Listening to somebody like Stoney Schmitt, however, you realize that it probably wouldn't have been enough, that maybe it's better to grow out of the dream early. So, yes, I had to admit to him, I would have been bitter, too.

"Ten years in the minors. Stats as good as dozens of guys who made it long-term in the majors. And what do I get? One lousy game. And you wanta know why? Because some scout

51

with blow-dry hair tags me as 'Not a prospect.' This is the same guy who tells his organization to draft another kid who was in the same league with me and who I played rings around every game we was in together. And why? Because the kid is five inches taller than me, hits a few homers, and runs two-tenths of a second faster. So I have to beg for a chance as a non-drafted free agent, but no matter what I do after that, it isn't enough."

"You're what? Five-eight?"

"Five-nine, hundred sixty-five pounds. Still."

But balding now which you can tell even though he's got a Reading Phillies cap perched on the back of his head. Chiseled features, sturdy build. Solid Pennsylvania Dutch stock.

We're sitting at the counter of Stoney's Diner on Route 422 near Reading. It's mid-afternoon and business is slow, just a couple of coffee customers and an old duffer who has been nursing some bean soup for an hour. Maybe he expects Stoney to offer to warm it up for him. Stoney is the second baseman for my "Dream Team," but I could have put him almost anywhere. As he bluntly put it, "An effing utility player, that's what they said I was. In Peoria!"

"But you did make it all the way up the ladder, however briefly. You had that chance."

"Some chance.Busted my butt for ten years for a crumb."

"Let them eat cake."

"What the crap is that suppose to mean?"

"Nothing, it just popped into my head. Tell me about the crumb."

Stoney got up, walked around the counter and poured himself another cup of coffee. He gestured toward my cup. I nodded. He refilled it, too. He made the kind of coffee that you can sip slowly and talk long with, neither bad enough nor good enough to divert your attention from your conversation or your private thoughts. He started to fix another pot, talking over his shoulder as he did. It was a process he had mastered by repetition, mechanical yet smooth like making the pivot on a double play.

"I'm in the Cubs organization for six years, scrapping my way up, but really goin' nowhere. I figure this six- year minor league free agent thing will get me a chance. So I sign on with the Phillies. I mean the Phillies! They've got diddley in their system in those days. Late August of that year they get themselves in a roster bind but don't want to waste an option on some kid they think is a hot shot—ask me about him some time—so they bring me up. I'm up for ten days. Day number nine, August 31, we're playing a double-header in St. Louis. Crazy-ass idea in the first place. You ever been in St. Louis in August? But they had to make-up a rain out and this was their last chance though it didn't matter squat if either game was ever played. Between games our second baseman gets sick—heat prostration, dehydration that kind of thing—so Elia, he's the manager, puts me in the line-up. I'm one out of three with a walk, handle six chances with no problem, including a nifty pivot on a double play…"

He had finished preparing the next pot of coffee by then, and had started wiping the counter. As he reached the part about the double play he deftly flipped the rag from one hand to the other, then without looking tossed it back-handed into the sink halfway down the counter, one for the highlight reel. For a moment, he smiled, the only time he did in our whole conversation—even the few times he laughed he did so with a frown.

"So I'm thinking Wally Pipp all over again, right. I'm flying. The next day is September 1, of course. They can expand the roster, bring up other guys from the minors, but I figure at least I'm there for the duration of the season, get in a few more licks and then who knows. So what happens? They waive me! They effing waive me!"

He slapped the counter, jiggling the cups and splashing some coffee on the counter, which he ignored.

"Stuck it out three more years. Bounced around from the Brewers organization to the Braves and the last year back to the Cubs. They wanted, get this, a veteran utility player to help young players at the Triple-A level! Cripes."

He paused. The soup dawdler finally decided to leave and Stoney took his money at the cash register, then poured some more coffee for the other two who, I guess, had lingered to listen in on our conversation. "Hey, Stoney," one of them said, "every time you tell that story it's different."

"Eff you, Mac." He came back and sat down beside me, then muttered soft enough to make it seem he did not want to be heard, but loud enough that he could be sure he was, "That's my effing brother-in-law."

"You didn't have any interest in coaching?"

"Hell, no. Not after the crap I put up with. I wanted out."

"Listening to you talk, I wonder why you stuck it out as long as you did. I mean after your 'cup of coffee,' as it were, with the Phillies and their waiving you I would have thought you would want out then."

"You'd think so, wouldn't ya. Got no idea why I stuck it out."

"Nothing else to do?"

"Naw, that's not it. I mean this place was waitin' for me whenever I wanted it. Place belonged to my Dad. I worked here all the time I was growing up—when I wasn't playing ball. And most off-seasons except when I was doin' winter ball some place. My wife worked here some, too. He'd already made me part owner before I quit and told me whenever I wanted to take it on full-time he'd just sit back and smell the roses. Didn't happen that way, dammit. I played ball three more years and right after I finally packed it in and came home for good, he died. Effing cancer."

He sat down next to me and took a sip of coffee. I wondered how much he regretted not quitting earlier, regretted that his father hadn't had a little time "to smell the roses." What had kept him playing? The residue of the boyish dream, of the young man's dogged hope? "Had I presumed to hope-- / The loss had been to Me / A Value...." We both seemed to have entered some silent place. Finally he spoke in a low monotone. "That's not true. I know why I stuck it out. It's just that there are things you don't like to admit."

"So?"

54

"I was a terrier. Had to be to stick so long. Had that dream in my teeth and I wouldn't let go. Just kept gnawing away at it. Bein' waived was only one more reason to keep goin'. To show the bastards. Oh, every winter I'd talk with Dad about it, and with my wife. But the conversations always ended up the same way with'em saying 'Stoney, it's your decision to make.'"

"And you'd say "One more year'?"

"Yeah. One more time around the carousel."

"But finally you decided to get off"

"Yeah."

"Why?"

"Cuz after that last summer I played, I came home, and started to have the same conversation with Dad, and he was still saying it was my choice. But I noticed something different about him and I stared real hard at him and though he hadn't said anything to anybody I knew he was dying. And I knew I had to let go, let that dream die."

"So you came home and became a restauranteur?"

He laughed ruefully."Yeah. Chef, waiter, busboy, dishwasher. The whole works."

"You change the name?"

"Naw. Dad had already done that, right after I signed my first contract. He was a believer too."

"What's it like flipping burgers instead of a baseball?"

"I open at six a.m. and close at six p.m.. Used to stay open till eight, but the only dinner trade I get is people from the retirement home up the road and they all eat early anyway, so I reduced my hours and didn't lose any business. Wife helps out while the kids are in school, kids help out on the weekend and I got a couple of part-timers who cover busy times." He abruptly raised his voice. "Everybody pitches in and helps except my effing brother-in-law who just comes in to complain about the coffee when he isn't watering the booze in his bar."

"Hey, Stoney, I ain't complained about this sludge in two days, maybe three."

"Then that's a personal record for you, asshole." He tossed the words out blandly without turning, like brushing away a fly. "Okay, there you have it: my life in the big leagues. Anything else you want to know."

"Yeah. So far you're the only guy I've talked to who was a non-drafted player. They've mostly been late-rounders, though one of them was a number one. Tell me more about what it's like to start out with that label on you."

"Scouting ballplayers isn't a science though some of those guys with their stopwatches and jugs guns try to make sound like one. Scouts are human and make mistakes, both ways. But the organizations don't like to admit that. Basically a guy who's drafted, especially an early-rounder has to prove he can't do it, and he doesn't have to show much to keep the organization believing. Because they want to, because they have to or admit they made a mistake. A free agent has to prove he can, over and over again, and one little stumble, one slump or bad spell, and he's back to ground zero. I mean it's in the organization's interest for him not to make it. Otherwise they have to admit they were wrong in the first place. Oh, they always cover their mistakes by talking about 'the intangibles.' You've heard some of that crap about you can't measure heart and desire."

"I've heard that," I said, "and I'll admit there's something to it. Doesn't that explain why some guys who don't get drafted, make it, and some players with a lot of natural ability, even some number one picks, never do?"

Stoney sat silently for a bit, turning his cup slowly, as if he were considering whether to acknowledge my point. Finally he shrugged, "Yeah, yeah, there's some of that, but it ain't that hard to tell who's puttin' out and who's doggin' it. The point is you take a first rounder who starts in rookie league or low A, and has a lousy first year. Everybody starts talking about adjustment problems, blah, blah, blah. They make excuses, give 'im more rope, send 'im to winter league to iron out the problems. I mean, I understand they probably blew a bundle on this guy, so they have an investment which, if they give up on too soon, the owner might start asking questions about how come they chose the guy in the first place. There was a guy in the Phillies organization, don't remember his name, first rounder who supposedly was one of these 'five tool' players. Well, maybe so, except for the little fact he didn't very often make contact. Oh he had a beautiful swing, picture-book ya know, but he diddled around just over .200 for four, maybe five years. I played with him two years and I can tell you he didn't have a clue. He tried hard enough. Wasn't on booze or drugs like some I could tell you about, whiz bang kids with too much bonus money. Ask me about some of them. This guy just didn't have a clue. But even when the organization got the hint, they didn't cut him. Tried to make a pitcher out of him and probably would have hung with him for another four years if he hadn't blown out his shoulder.

"But put a late-round draftee, certainly a free agent, in the same position and it's sayonara. Just like that. And if he has a good first year, but stumbles the second, that's all he gets. Every step of the way they're waiting for you to fall on your face, so they can tell themselves how smart they were in the first place. And if you call'em on it, they'll start sayin' you got an attitude problem."

"Did you get that label?"

He looked at me sharply. I had hesitated to ask the question. I didn't really need to because I already knew the answer, had known it from the beginning of our conversation. But I asked it anyway, maybe because I wanted to goad him.

"Sure, mister, I had an attitude. How the hell do you think I could stick at it so long without any support from the effin' experts."

"Hey, Stoney, put these on my tab. We gotta go get the manure off our shoes before I open." The brother-in-law and his companion slid out of their booth.

"Save some for your bar. You can put it on those moldy chips you serve." The men laughed and Stoney watched them out the door. "We're friends," Stoney said, almost in a whisper, "but don't ever quote me on that." He had hardly spoken the words when he slapped the counter as if to change the whole tone of the conversation. "You got time for one more question then I got to get ready for the cotton-top dining club. They'll start coming in at four-thirty."

"Some non-drafted players do make it. What about them?"

"They still live under the curse. Example: Cardinals had a guy in their system, Bernard Gilkey, signs as a free agent, a home-town player. He battles his way up through the system: nice hitter, wonderful fielder, good arm. But even when he makes it, back-to-back .300 years, the front office is still mumbling about having to improve themselves in left. So what do they do: they sign Ron Gant to a mega-bucks contract and get rid of Gilkey and for what. Sure Gant's got power, thirty home run power, but with that comes a .240 average, a hundred and fifty strikeouts and mediocre fielding. Dumb. Gilkey goes to New York, has a couple of real solid years, then one bad one and suddenly he's not good enough. Gets shipped to Arizona where they don't pay any attention to him. And I'll tell you why, that sign hanging around his neck, 'Non-drafted Free Agent.' No wonder he had a drinkin' problem."

"It's been what, eleven years since you quit?"

"Retired, mister, retired. I never quit. Yeah, eleven years. One for three, six chances error-free, and they effing waive me."

"Still a bitter taste?"

"Taste? An effing mouthful."

"You still pay attention to the box scores though?"

"What's that suppose to mean?"

"You still pay attention to the game."

He leaned forward, not looking at me, but attending vigorously, almost violently, to an imaginary spot on the counter. "Mister, you play the game since you were a kid—sand lot, little league, high school. You work at it, you dream about it. You fight to get a chance to keep dreamin'. You don't listen to scouts and coaches and organization creeps who tell you don't have what it takes. You struggle to make that dream come true for ten years, and you stop only because you have to, not because they make you. But there was nothin' wrong with that dream, nothin' wrong with the game. The problem is the effin' people that run it, but you can't let'em take it all away. Yeah, I still pay attention to it. It's a beautiful game." And in his voice was an edge of sorrow like what Roethke called "the loneliness of pencils."

He'd said one more question and I had asked several. But I was trying to find a way to end the conversation upbeat, so he wouldn't burn some retiree's dinner.

"So you married a hometown girl, not a stewardess."

"They never had stewardesses on minor league buses. Yeah, childhood sweetheart, all that good stuff. Actually it's the only thing I ever did that's lived up to expectations, mostly. Sometimes I wish I could have made the bigs, just for her."

To me one of the saddest sights is driving through the countryside on a beautiful spring day and passing empty fields. I don't mean pastures or cornfields. I mean ball fields. And I'm bothered driving in small towns and suburbs and passing vacant lots where there are no kids playing ball, and worse yet no tell-tale signs—worn base paths, makeshift home plates or pitchers' mounds—to suggest those lots are ever used for a pick-up game. I think I would even be happy if I saw some kids playing softball. For me that's a stretch, but, at least, it would be something.

Oh at the right time of day, late afternoon or early evening, when you go by a little league field you might see a game or a practice going on, but of course that's part of the problem. We adults have so organized games that the only times kids will play them is when we're there supervising them, managing them for our own purposes. To be sure, other sports compete for attention these days, but I don't even see those games being played in the fields and playgrounds. We've organized them, too, squeezing out the spontaneity and serendipity of play. One of my wife's colleagues who's into the sociology of sport gave me a long lecture one day about the whys and hows of this and even making it sound like some kind of civilizational imperative. To me all his words seemed to be simply another symptom, rather than an explanation.

A few years ago on an uncommonly warm April day when I needed a break from writing and Eileen was away at a conference and the boys were off at school, I went for a ride in the country to clear my head a bit. I don't remember the exact twistings and turnings I made on the back roads, but suddenly I came upon an Amish schoolhouse, one of those plain one room buildings that you find hereabouts in Central Pennsylvania. And in the schoolyard were a half-dozen or so kids in Amish dress, boys and girls alike, and they were playing baseball. To me it

60

was a joyous sight and I stopped and watched them for a while. But there was a bittersweet quality to my pleasure. Perhaps the only place where children can still be children and play baseball as it ought to be played by the young, unencumbered by the anxieties and expectations and agendas of their elders, is among the Plain People. They have no computer games to isolate them, no malls where they can gather and roam in packs, and above all no adults preoccupied with making this "a learning experience" or projecting their own needs on them.

But then, neither can they dream—as I did dream on the playing fields of my youth—that some day I would play this game before tens of thousands of people on major league grass.

When I was a kid, between the ages of eight and ten when we still lived in Alton, my friends and I would play baseball every day, all summer long. No matter how hot and steamy it got there we would be playing, usually in the lot across the street from our house. Charles and Charlie and Owen and Zeddie and Billy and I were the regulars and then whoever else was in the mood, including Jeff sometimes. I'd rush through breakfast, then grab my glove and bat and scamper over to the field. There didn't have to be any planning, any calling around to discuss what we were going to do, we just assumed that unless it was pouring buckets and hammer handles we would be playing ball. I was always the first one there with maybe Charles or Zeddie right behind. We'd play catch or field grounders until we had enough to start a game or it was obvious we had too many shirkers to get one up. Even then we would usually figure out some way to keep going, playing hot box, or inventing some new way to make playing catch into some vague semblance of the real thing.

Once we started we just played. All day with a break so we could run home for lunch. Our numbers would vary: Owen might leave, Jeff would drift over for awhile, Zeddie's sister might come, Billy would go to a piano lesson. The shape of the game would shift from teams to one o'cat and back, but it all happened like we planned it that way. We didn't keep score: that wasn't what it was about. We cheered big hits and good fielding plays and would remember them to tell our parents and to talk

61

about the next day while we were warming up. But the doing was the thing—running and hitting and throwing on and on through the day, even the steamiest summer day, until we were soaked with the pleasures of it.

When I was in St. Louis in 1998 working on a story about the McGwire-Sosa phenomenon, I rented a car and drove over to Alton, the first time I had been back since we moved. I drove around the old neighborhood. Miraculously, the vacant lot was still there, the base paths we had worn into it still evident. Of course, nobody was playing on it either. The next time I was there, spring of 2000, a brand new house was sitting there, smack in the middle of our home-made diamond.

The first major league game I saw was in the summer of 1968 when I was eight. My father took Jeff and me to a game at Busch Stadium, the Cardinals versus the Cincinnati Reds. The Cardinals won, 2-0, on a four-hitter by Bob Gibson. That was Gibby's fourth win in a row on his way to fifteen straight, and the Cardinals would win their second straight National League pennant, though they lost the series to the Tigers in a way I don't even try to remember. Gibby had a monster year, one that convinced the rule makers to lower the pitching mound to give the hitters a break. But to be honest we didn't spend a lot of time talking about Gibby or Lou Brock or Orlando Cepeda or Tim McCarver. We were not really baseball fans; we were baseball players. We might pretend to be those guys, but mainly we just played the game.

That was also the summer I had my appendix out. The doctor put me under strict orders about not over-extending myself and mother took him at his word. She made me stay around the house and kept a close eye on me until one day I had probably driven her close to buggy and she had to do some shopping. She told me I could go over to the field to watch, but only to watch. Well Zeddie had to leave and the guys said I should pinch hit for him, but just to trot real slow if I hit the ball. Even after the lay-off I lined the first pitch to center and I was just ambling to first. Then I saw the ball bounce away from Owen and knew I could make second so I took off, sliding in ahead of his throw.

My stomach hurt some and I had bruised my knee, but I was as happy as a lark. I was dusting myself off when Jeff came running in from right, his usual position--he was a good brother, but not much of a baseball player. I expected him to say something encouraging, maybe "Thataway kid", to recognize my grit, my enthusiasm for the game. Instead, he came running up to me and yelled right in my face "That's the stupidest thing you've ever done." And, of course, he told mother the minute she got home and I got grounded again. I told him afterwards that he didn't understand what it took to be a real baseball player.

I think it was about that time that I first began to dream about being a big leaguer. Maybe it was the trip to Busch Stadium that started it. Though I don't think I said anything about it, but then nobody asked me what I wanted to be when I grew up. After we moved to the Chicago area that question did come up.

When I was in seventh grade I got drafted along with a couple of other classmates to appear in the high school production of Our Town. *We were supposed to run out on stage with bats and gloves just before George and Emily get married. The director had them walking up the side aisles of the auditorium and we were supposed to come out on George's side and razz him a bit. Whoever was doing the program asked us what we wanted to be and I said "A professional baseball player." Unfortunately, the way it came out was "Will wants to be a professional baseball." So I got teased for weeks by the other guys who kept asking to see my stitches or was I a National League or American League ball. By then, however, I was too full of my dream to let something like that bother me. As it turned out, my dream was farther off the mark than the misquotation was.*

Moving didn't slow me. No more Charles or Zeddie or Owen, but now it was Roger and Dan and Andy and Ed and the pattern was the same. We played on the high school field or the community park or wherever, real ball fields now, and that made the dreams more real.

In my mind now when I think of those days, of those green fields, of the running and throwing and sliding, of the sheer innocence, I think too of some lines from Gerard Manley Hopkins: "What is all this juice and all this joy? / A strain of the earth's sweet being in the beginning / in Eden garden.—Have, get, before it cloy...." Then of course the only poetry was in the doing.

Shaking the Dust

Dear Mr. Collins,

    I enclose a document responding to the questions you posed in your letter of May 23rd. I regret the impression of being stand-offish by not speaking to you when you called. As my assistant indicated, I am a very busy man and this time of year, preparing for a busy summer starting new projects, is always particularly hectic.

    Quite literally, in the last decade I have not given much thought to professional baseball, either the game itself or the few years that I spent participating in it. As you are obviously aware, I have had a very successful career in the construction business and so, unlike some of those with whom I played, I have had little need to wax nostalgic about "The Game" or what might have been. Even so, I will admit that, in retrospect, the opportunity your project offered me has provided me some unexpected pleasure. Perhaps I might have enjoyed a conversation with you had my schedule permitted it.

    I hope the enclosure is helpful to you. I scanned it quickly after my assistant typed it, but have made no effort to edit it.

                Sincerely,

                William G. Branch

William G. Branch is the president of one of the largest construction firms in the Rocky Mountain region. It also happens to be one of the most successful African-American businesses anywhere in the United States. He is, I am sure, a very busy man, for he has built the business virtually from scratch. And, if one is to believe those business profiles that periodically appear in the newspapers, he is dead serious about keeping it prosperous, not so much for the obvious financial rewards as to sustain his fierce pride of achievement. It is an interesting irony.

Bill Branch was a first round draft choice out of high school, generally regarded as the most promising position player available. He ignored the Giants offer and accepted a scholarship to Wichita State University. There he played brilliantly on a team that regularly made it to the College World Series. Yet vague whispers about him began to circulate: not that he was into drugs or alcohol or was a behavior problem in the usual sense. The whispers were that he wasn't "serious enough," that he didn't have the dedication to realize fully his potential. The whispers probably began at Wichita State itself, because of his insistence on majoring in engineering and consistently taking overloads. They certainly became commonplace when, in his junior year he missed some games for "academic reasons," though again not the usual ones for athletes. A few scouts even tagged him as unsignable, saying that he had some uppity notion about going to business school.

The result was that he slipped into the second round of the draft his senior year. George Steinbrenner, who, for all his deficiencies, probably understood the situation better than most, insisted that his people draft him. So the Yankees took him. To the surprise, and probably the embarrassment of most other teams, he quickly signed. As it turned out ultimately, however, the whispers were true.

He had a different dream. Maybe that in itself should disqualify him from my Dream Team, but I had to admit a real fascination with someone who should have, could have, would have made the Big Show, but chose to walk away from it.

66

He's right: he was stand-offish when I called. In fact, I didn't even get to talk with him. I'll give his assistant credit: she's very good at protecting her boss. In a silky smooth voice she went through various evasive actions.

"Is Mr. Branch expecting your call?"

"No, he isn't?"

"Is this in regard to a current project or proposal under consideration?"

"No, it's not related to the construction firm."

"Mr. Branch does not accept personal calls at the office."

"This isn't a personal call, exactly. It's…a business matter, but not construction business."

"What is the nature of your business?"

"I'm a writer." A cool silence so I hurried on. "I'm writing a book about baseball and I would like to interview him."

"Baseball? Mr. Branch…"

"Could you do me a favor. Just ask him if he would talk with me. I'm writing a book about former baseball players who appeared in only one game in the major leagues. I'm talking to nine different guys, each of whom played a different position, and Mr. Branch is my third baseman."

A pause that, if I wanted to exaggerate a bit, I would call a stunned pause, then with an attempt at renewed assurance, she asked, "Are you sure you have the right person?"

"Yes. William Godfrey Branch, aka Bill Branch, born in Omaha, Nebraska, March 25, 1955. Graduated from Wichita State University in 1976, with honors in engineering and, incidentally, College All-American in baseball, two years. Signed with the Yankees. Played in one game for them in 1980. Retired to start a construction firm in Denver. The rest, as they say, is history."

Silence on the other end of the line. When the voice returned, the silk was frayed a bit. "Well, I've learned something new. If you'll hold, I'll speak with Mr. Branch."

I held and held and held. The wait was pleasant enough since their hold music was Duke Ellington instrumentals. Nice.

"Thank you for waiting. Mr. Branch regrets he does not have time to talk with you. But, if you would send him a list of your questions, he will respond to them in writing."

"But wouldn't it take less of his time if..."

"He will try to be as prompt as possible in his reply. Thank you. Have a good day." Click.

So I did as I was bidden and wrote Branch a letter describing my project, listing my questions, and identifying a few people he could contact if he wanted to check me out—including a sharp African-American lawyer from Philly with whom I knew Branch had done business. I still was hoping to soften him up to grant me a face-to-face interview. Wouldn't have minded having a look at that silky-smooth voice either. Sounds from his letter that I almost succeeded, but not quite. So what I have is the document he sent, which I reproduce verbatim with a few parenthetical notations.

Q: *What were the circumstances that led to your appearance in the majors?*

I gather from your letter that you have done your research pretty well, so I have to conclude that you don't want a lot of information readily available in the usual places. You are more interested in my perception of the events than the events themselves. The obvious fact then is that I was one of the usual post-September 1 call-ups. The Yankees, since they were in the midst of a pennant race, were very selective and only brought up a few of us from Columbus, all players whom they thought might give them some extra maneuvering room.

In that regard I was, perhaps, something of an exception. To be sure, I had had a good year at Columbus and,

in the only game I played in New York,
I acquitted myself well. I won't bore
you with the specifics that I'm sure
you already know.   [He's right. He hit .316 at
Columbus with 15 home runs, 73 RBI's, and 19 stolen
bases. He also led the International League third base-
men in fielding. In his one game with the Yankees he
was one for three with a walk and a stolen base and handled six chances in the field without an error.]

September call-ups are usually rewards for good performance in the minors, opportunities for the manager to
get a look at prospects for the next
season, or, as with the Yankees that
year, additions to bench strength that
might give them a critical edge in a
key game. I sense that, in my case,
they, or probably more specifically
Mr. Steinbrenner, thought exposure to
the atmosphere of the major leagues
and a pennant race would "improve my
attitude."

I was not a slacker, nor a trouble-
maker, nor a clubhouse lawyer. I simply didn't demonstrate the all-
consuming interest in fulfilling every
boy's dream that managers and coaches
thought appropriate. Now to some extent that was a false judgment. I
practiced hard; I played hard.   I
think I can say that I always gave my
best on the field. [Right again. In his previous
three years in the minors he averaged .323, made the
various league all-star teams, and popped up in numerous
listings of the ten best prospects in each organization.]

The problem was that instead of diverting myself off the field by end-

69

less gabble about the game or chasing women or going to movies or drinking beer, I spent my time in the closest university library or talking with financial managers and entrepreneurs. The typical minor league manager is not a person of large vision and therefore could not understand that those activities were my "release" from the grind of a long, hard season. [Those "best prospect" listings always mentioned anonymous concerns about his "commitment."]

The idea of promoting me, I think, was to wean me from my peculiar habits by seducing me with the thrill of the game. On reflection, I will confess that it might have worked. You have probably gathered I am a very focussed individual, but I did enjoy the game and at everything I've ever done I have had a passion to excel.

So I was not immune to the "dream." But, as I have also indicated, the 'baseball people" were not entirely wrong, because I did have another commitment, another dream if you will, which leads me to your next question.

Q: *What were the circumstances that limited your "career" to one game?*

The manager [Dick Howser] was trying to win a pennant. Probably, if it had been his choice, he would not have brought me up. He seemed to regard me with a certain disdain, the product of the easy assumptions about my attitude and his own narrow vision. Perhaps that is harsh: he was a good man and he, too, was focused. In his case the focus was on winning the pennant. So he chose not to play me, except for that one game, which I do not think was his idea. [Those of course were the years when Steinbrenner was much readier to interfere in things than he was in the later years of his reign—though it was a habit he never gave up. Branch obviously sees Steinbrenner's hand in the decisions to bring him up and to play him in the one game. He's probably right.]

I suspect Howser thought he would not get total effort from me, a misjudgment on his part, yet I understand it. Afterwards, though I had done well, he began dropping remarks to the press about having to get his play-off roster fine-tuned and of course I was not eligible for that. Perhaps, but I only say perhaps, had I played more that September I might have come back the following year, delayed a bit my other plans. Out on the field, playing the game, the essential beauty of it, the joy of it, might have enticed me. Being simply an observer, however, I frankly was bored by the "Bronx Zoo" mentality. So I decided to keep to my original schedule.

My overriding goal was to become what I have become: a successful independent entrepreneur. A successful African-American independent entrepreneur, providing an example for others to emulate instead of contributing further to the illusion that sports or entertainment (or worse yet, drug-dealing) offer the only avenues of success to young black males. To achieve that I needed capital.

Had I done what many people expected me to do after graduation, gone to work for some corporation interested in hiring a minority, I eventually would have worked my way up to a position where I had the income to pursue my objective. But it was not an environment that appealed to me, and I also wanted time to develop my plans. So I decided to use what I had ready at hand, my baseball ability, to get the capital I needed. The rhythm of the game—the free hours during the day and the off-season--offered me the time to do the research and planning I needed to do and the possibility of receiving a significant amount of money for signing was more certain than a bank loan. Of course, the assumption that I was unsignable hurt me a bit since otherwise I would have been a first round pick as I had been in high school and the bonus money would have been better. But it also meant that anyone who risked taking me, particularly if he had the mindset of a Steinbrenner, would pay a little extra to a second-rounder to prove how smart he was.

Every cent of that bonus money I invested and every penny above basic living expenses I earned in and out of season for four years I invested. [None of the usual buying a pricey car or a home for parents. In a story that appeared in the *NY Times* at the time he signed, he stated his intentions very clearly—though not referring to the particulars of his schedule. I think the reporter was too surprised by the response to his question to pursue it, but for the record let me note that Branch's parents had a comfortable home in Omaha where his father was a long-time postal employee and his mother a school teacher. Doubtless, they approved of his plan.] And I spent time assessing markets, developing a business plan, making contacts. I had told myself that wherever I was in four years whether still riding buses in the low minors or traveling by jet in the majors I would get on with my real life.

That winter I sat down and assessed the situation. I did look again at the issue of whether I wanted to play major league baseball and I admit that I felt some urge to give myself a good opportunity. After all, what would be wrong with lengthening my time-table a little? I knew that if I gave up baseball, it would be hard, perhaps impossible, to go back to it. But I concluded that the Yankees were unlikely to keep me in the majors the next year. In those days they didn't have a particularly good record of giving real opportunities to players from their own system. Of course, they could trade me. If they did so, however, I would have felt some obligation to give my new organization two or even three years. And I kept remembering a line from Langston Hughes about "a dream deferred." I knew what my real dream was. So all those scouts and coaches were right: I didn't have the commitment to baseball. I sent the Yankees a letter saying I was retiring.

Q: *What was your reaction to actually playing in a big league game?*

I was excited, of course. Despite what I have said to this point, I had been playing baseball all my life and as a boy I had certainly dreamed of being a major leaguer. [I was relieved to read that.] And to play a game at the major league level, indeed at Yankee Stadium, and before a big crowd, how could I not be excited. There is, it seems to me, a kind of magical quality to the game raised to that level. As I noted above, perhaps if I had played more that September the magical part of it might have captured me, blurred my judgment as it were. But I'm an engineer, not a poet. So I enjoyed the day and filed the experience away.

Q. *Do you have any reflections on the experience now?*

I imagine your real question here is "Do I have any regrets?" Quite simply, no. I have done what I wanted to do, and I believe what I have accomplished is a far better example for my people than anything which a successful major league career could have achieved. The fact that I used my athletic ability to get my start, as it were, only underscores my point. The enticing myth that young men, and, now increasingly, young women, can use athletic achievement to lift themselves in the world has reality only if one understands that it is a means to an end and not an end in itself. Nor is the end merely the accumulation of wealth.

The myth is that an athlete can use his or her ability to get an education not otherwise affordable. But how many really take advantage of that opportunity? How many opportunities are wasted because the false goal of being a professional athlete and earning enormous sums of money (indeed obscene amounts of money) blinds young men and women to the real possibilities they have? Most do not attain their inadequate dream and what happens to them then? If they have not actually used their opportunity to get an education, what have they left? And even those who do continue on to the professional level with significant success: what have they achieved for themselves? In what ways have they truly enriched their own lives in ways other than the purely material? More importantly, what have they really accomplished for their people? Given them pride? Pride alone is a paltry meal.

Certainly some of the superstars of sport who in the current climate have earned enormous wealth have contributed significantly to philanthropic causes in the communities from which they came. But to what extent have they really invested in those communities?

To what extent have they used their wealth to create real jobs? Who is helped when an athlete buys a half-dozen $200,000 automobiles or wears diamond studs in his ear? My firm not only employs many people of color in the Denver area, but I have recently acquired a major stake in an Omaha firm, which will, I promise you, become much more aggressive in offering similar opportunities in that community.

Excuse me, I seem to be shifting into my chamber of commerce speech mode. As I said, I have no regrets. I am doing now what I wanted to do. Another year or two or three playing professional baseball would probably not have prevented me from achieving my goal, but it would have added nothing to it.

Let me add that I do owe you some thanks for what I may first have regarded as an intrusion. You are perhaps aware that my assistant was taken aback to learn about my "former life." I do not endeavor to hide it, but neither do I make any effort to broadcast it either. She has two young sons and she couldn't help mentioning it to them, and I think in the right way, emphasizing the things that I hope my career illustrates. It made me realize that if I am really serious about providing an apt example, I should be, shall we say, more aggressive in recounting all the aspects of my success

story. That has produced the following story in the Denver paper as well
as some invitations to give talks in
the schools. I don't particularly
wish to be lionized, but, as I hope my
observations have made clear, I do
have a strong sense of social obliga-
tion. [He sent me a copy of the story. The headline
read "Denver Entrepreneur Chooses the Right Game." A
nice puff piece for his thesis. There was no indication in
the article that a personal interview was involved.]

Q: *Any other comments, observations, personal or otherwise?*

None. [Note no personal details. I know for a fact he
is married, have seen pictures of his wife in the papers, a
stunning woman with a high profile job in a Denver
bank. They have two children, a son and a daughter,
who attend private school. The girl is an All State basketball player.]

So there it is, crisp, direct (apparently), and impressive.
There remained a peculiarly impersonal quality about the picture, like the silky smoothness of his assistant's voice. Of all the
players I encountered I probably like him the least, but then I
don't really know him. I never met him: I only know the carefully delineated profile with which he provided me. I will admit
a great deal of respect for what he has accomplished. I wonder,
of course, if the line would have been so pat, so controlled, if I
had actually talked with Branch face to face, if there had been
some real give and take, if I simply could have observed him
operating within his environment.

The story doesn't really fit with the others I've heard, but
does it have to fit? Is there anything wrong with an American
success story that makes baseball a mere episode in a man's life?

If I was making all this up, I would tell the story pretty much the same. Except I would have Branch going home at night after he's made some big deal or had a tough negotiating session and settling down in a big, stuffed chair in his den. He would take out his old glove and a scuffed, darkened ball, maybe the one from his only major league hit. Then he'd just toss the ball into the mitt, time after time, listening to the slap of the ball in the pocket, smelling the leather, thinking about what might have been.

I wonder if he even has his old glove. I have mine.

In a musical appreciation course in college (which I took mostly because of Eileen), the prof told us that a piece of music consists of notes and movements and harmonies that are arranged in a temporal sequence. If you are listening rather than just hearing, you remember them, take notice when they recur, and gradually begin to build up a perception of the whole. You can't have this perception before you've listened, and you can't have it fully until the piece is over. Until the last movement, the last chord, the last note the music remains incomplete, because until then some new theme or direction can be introduced which can change the meaning of the piece. Like Yogi Berra is reputed to have said, "It isn't over till it's over."

Augustine viewed history on the large scale and the lives of individuals as moving in accordance with this musical conception of time. And, unless we regard all life as meaningless and all life stories as series of random and unrelated events, this conception at least provides us with a way of thinking about how we live and move and have our being in this world. There are successive seasons in our lives and while each may possess its particular qualities, its own sadness and joy, the whole of our life assumes its final sense and significance only at its end. Till the song is ended how do we know it. To compose an autobiography at age thirty is pretentious—or worse yet an act of despair.

Which is not to say we shouldn't reflect on our past at various moments along the way. Leroy "Satchel" Paige is supposed to have said, "Never look back, something might be gaining on you." I have been fond of quoting this line, usually to affirm my own efforts to move ahead, not to dwell with regret on things done and left undone. It's another way of saying, "Don't cry over spilt milk," and there's a certain practical appeal in that. Yet, in another way, that is probably bad advice. We are products of our past, both real and imagined. Through knowledge of the themes and variations in our lives, through understanding the pleasures and pains, we develop a sense of ourselves. From that knowledge and understanding we gather the resources to respond to what time brings and to continue the works in progress that are our lives.

At least that's what I think and if there was a particular idea I had in my mind as I began my project that was it. Specific to the context, I believed that the particular experience of reaching that boyish dream, reaching the major leagues, only to have it dissolve, disappear, in a twinkling, had to affect the subsequent lives of the men I was planning to interview. Not necessarily that it was itself the shaping event, rather that the way each responded either illustrated or contributed to who they had become, were still becoming. More to the point, probably, is the fact that while my own boyish dream had ended a long way short of the mark they had reached, it still had influenced me in many ways. And I was certain that if I had made it as far as the members of my Dream Team had, the influence would have been greater. Augustine says there are "four perturbations of the mind--desire, joy, fear, sorrow." Without trying to make the dream of being a major league ballplayer any more significant than it is in the great scheme of things, it seems to me that the particular experience I was trying to understand involves all four of those "perturbations of the mind," almost simultaneously. Other dreams, hopes, or aspirations that end with the same fleeting scent of success might serve the same purpose. But, of course, there was none other that I understood, or thought I understood, so well.

Yet that in itself presented a problem. Was I projecting my own desire on others? Certainly reading what Branch said I could conclude that. Here was a guy who saw what was "the end of my desiring" as simply a means to another end, an end that he apparently has achieved. Therefore, no real desire had been fulfilled in that moment, no particular joy derived from it, but

80

then no fear or sorrow came from the transitory quality of that moment. Yet in his words there were hints and suggestions. Even if the general framework of his "plan" was as he said it was, perhaps he has sanitized the story to fit what has happened. Perhaps he had forgotten, even intentionally forgotten, what it was really like. Augustine says that when we "forget" something a trace of it may still be there, a memory of a memory. "We have not as yet entirely forgotten what we remember that we have forgotten. A lost notion, then, which we have not entirely forgotten, we cannot even search for."

My appearance on the scene made Branch remember, but he wouldn't talk to me in person because he still wanted to control what and how he remembered. In that case my intrusion became an active agent in his life. He indicated that it had, yet he seemed still to be trying to control it, to use it in his own way. Even on the mundane level of how his assistant viewed him, she of the silky smooth voice, he wanted to bend it to his plan. Would she look at him differently now that she knew he had played professional baseball? I doubted that she would start talking about it all over the place, but what if she did? How does the picture we have of someone change when we learn something new about them, something that doesn't quite fit the pattern we have known? And what happens to the image we have created of ourselves, when we know that others have learned something new and different about us? Can we control the ideas other people have of us? What happens to the melody of our lives? So much for the notion that I was being an objective observer. Not only wasn't I objective, I was a participant in whatever came of his memories. That's an uncomfortable thought.

Or maybe I'm just projecting again.

This Dreaming Shore

I'm sitting on a bench near Pensacola, Florida, looking out at the waters of Perdido Bay, which, of course, is really only an inlet of the Gulf of Mexico, which is indistinguishable from the Caribbean Sea, which is only an extension of the Atlantic Ocean, which.... The ocean is really endless and we all live on islands. Some of the islands are just bigger than others and so to make ourselves feel more important we call them continents. Out there somewhere in all that is an island, really just part of an island, called the Dominican Republic and on that island is a town named San Pedro de Macoris which every baseball fan has heard about. It is the seedbed of shortstops.

But I am here rather than there because this is where my search for Felipe Ortiz has led me. And he's sitting beside me rather than being back in the Dominican because when it all ended, the pursuit of the dream, he never went home. "The wave of lost particulars" has a way of doing that, washing us up on alien shores.

He's the only one of the players on my dream team whom I actually saw play in his one game at the major league level. He was in the mold of the Latin shortstops, lithe, graceful, quick—still is. But he never saw a curve he could hit, and sliders were not much more to his liking. I thought when I saw him play—he made a couple of dazzling plays in the field—that he might very well stick around playing some as a defensive replacement and pinch-running for heavy-legged catchers. If circumstances had been right, it might well have happened. I mean, if Rafael Belliard can play more than ten years in the majors, why not Felipe Ortiz. But the choices that a manager makes when he gets down to the twenty-fifth slot on the roster can be pretty complicated. They depend as much, if not more, on all the other choices he has already made and the arcane rules affecting player options as on the abilities of a specific individual. So it just didn't work out for Ortiz. These days he might have had a better shot with all the roster juggling "to stay within budget."

Actually he had seemed to be in an ideal place. He came up to the Tigers in September, 1987, their last divisional title year before their 2006 run to the World Series. Alan Trammel was well into his long and productive career with the Tigers and neither he, nor his second base partner, Lou Whittaker, needed much in the way of rest. But, with the designated hitter rule in the American League somebody with Ortiz's particular skills seemed a decent fit: he could provide occasional relief for Trammel or Whittaker without weakening the defense and the team was strong enough offensively that his hitting deficiencies wouldn't matter much. Plus, he had the speed and the instincts to be a good pinch-runner. After the Tigers had clinched the division that year, Ortiz played his one game to give Trammel a day off. He was hitless in three at bats, played flawlessly in the field with, as I said, two wonderful plays, both grounders up the middle that required real athleticism for him to make the throws. He got a good round of applause when he came up to bat after the second one, including from me. At the time we were living in Ann Arbor while Eileen was finishing her dissertation and I was writing for a couple of suburban Detroit papers.

"I appreciate you remember that." He nodded his head as if agreeing with my description of the game, a slight smile on his face.

"So tell me how did it feel?"

"When it was happening just like picture I had in my head since I was little. And, of course, maybe better since Tigers so good that year. Very exciting to be with team that was so good. Just before first pitch I look around me, see Whittaker, Gibson, Evans, players like that, and I think, this one day I a champion too. Good, very good."

"Were those the best plays you ever made?"

He hesitated, then said softly, "No. I mean that was what I do best and there were many. But of course, those were big league plays, not minor league, so they felt best."

I detected no sadness in his voice, no hint of regret, only a quiet pleasure that he had done well, well enough for someone like me to remember more than a decade later.

"Did you think you might be able to stick with the Tigers, or maybe somebody else, as a utility player. Like Belliard?"

"Rafey, he hit better than me. I field better." He spoke matter-of-factly with the quiet pride of knowledge rather than the arrogance of imagination. He paused, looked away toward Perdido Bay, maybe to all the sparkling waters beyond, the frothy crests of imagination. "No," he finally said, "I have no illusions by then. I enjoy the moment, that's all."

"But you kept on playing in the minors?"

"Where else could I get so good a job?"

As they say, it's all relative. Had he made it to the majors, even as a utility player in the late eighties, he would have had an income that, wisely used, could have set him for life. The salary of a minor league player, though nothing much, was more than he could have earned as a poorly educated, unskilled worker in the Dominican, so why not stick at it? And there were always the pleasures of the game which, as became evident to me in so many ways, he savored. "How long did you play?"

"Twenty years. Dodgers sign me when I was fifteen."

"The rule is you have to be sixteen."

He laughed ."Rule is you have to show certificate that says you at least sixteen. Dodgers always know where to get certificate like that. They sign me and I play in their organization for six years. Then Reds for two, Tigers for five, Indians for two, Pirates for two, finally Cubs."

"You've got it down pat."

"I remember. I remember every place I play. You want to hear them all?"

"I believe you, but go ahead."

84

"Vero Beach, Fort Worth, Albuquerque...." They rolled like a litany, all names I had heard or read from poring over newspapers and media guides, small towns, big towns, wannabe big league cities, the song of America, of baseball...."and Orlando."

"You did move around a lot. Join professional baseball and see the world, or at least North America. Were you released, traded?"

"Traded, always traded." There was almost a hint of pride in his voice. "I was good enough fielder that teams like me as throw-in on deals."

"Any favorite place?"

"No, no favorite. They were all beautiful to me while I play. Could have played more I guess. But finally I was tired. Play baseball since I was seven. All year sometimes. So finally I stop when I thirty-six."

"Your time or Dodger time?"

"Dodger time, of course. Afterwards I get younger." He smiled.

"No interest in coaching? I would have thought you'd be a natural for a minor league fielding coach. That was your strength and you're a Latin player with a good command of English. With the increasing number of Latin players, your language skills alone would be an advantage."

"There was talk of that. But people talk. Baseball people talk most of all. In clubhouse, by the batting cage, in hotel lobbies. Hints, vague promises, but always somebody else get call. Would have been good, but no matter. I find job here at Naval Air Station."

"You didn't go back home?"

"Where's home?"

"The Dominican, San Pedro de Macoris."

"This is home now." Till then the lilt of laughter had always seemed to be just under the surface of his conversation. He had seemed as light-hearted as he was light-footed in the field. At worst his voice was matter-of-fact, no tones or gestures or facial expressions that betrayed sorrows about goals not achieved, dreams unattained. He exuded a sense of complete-ness, of contentment. And something about that enticed me, in-trigued me, made me wonder if maybe it was enough to have played a game one loved so long, to have extended one's boy-hood. When, I asked myself, is it best to have conceded the big-ger dream? Now, subtly, yet unmistakably, a grayer tinge had appeared, a wistfulness, a plaintiveness.

Carefully I ventured, "No family back there then?"

By that time we were no longer sitting, but walking back and forth along the shore. In the ease of our conversation we had made that choice unconsciously, but mutually. We had found a rhythm, a harmony in our gait. Now, abruptly, he stopped. The rhythm was broken. He still stood close beside me, but he had moved far away. We seemed separated, isolated. Then he stooped, picked up a stone and with remembered grace threw it in a swift, sweet side-arm motion that brought me back to a sunlit afternoon in Tiger Stadium.

Watching him, it struck me that the things we do in mo-ments of stress, the diversionary actions we take to relieve ten-sion, themselves reflect something of our nature. They are the outward and visible signs of our imagined places of retreat in moments of pain, like the tree houses of our youth. I thought of myself, sitting in a darkened study with my old glove, a Mac-Gregor G44, Gil McDougal model, and a scuffed, grass-stained ball. The only sound is the repetitive slap of the ball in the pocket as, time after time, I toss and catch it. This rhythmic beat was—still is at times, I must confess—the music that takes me out of myself, or deeper into myself, to find rest from anxiety or anger or hurt, and the means to work through them. Was it to those few hours in the sunshine of Tiger Stadium, or to his memory of those few hours, that Ortiz had gone from me?

Only when the stone had skipped and skipped and splashed and sank, did he turn and, walking slowly as if he had added again that one year and far more on his age, he returned to the bench. He sat down, his eyes on the water, and rubbed the palms of his hands together. A careful gesture, automatic, but not unconscious. Brushing off the sand? or some layer of the past?

"I have three sons."

Pride, anger, loneliness, grief conflicted in the simple words. I felt that I had struck home, the place of sorrow. Instantly I felt regret that, without intending it, I had somehow injured this graceful, good-tempered man. I could not think of what to say for I had no sense of the realities I had made him confront.

"I have three sons." The voice was gentler now, less conflicted, saddened. "And a wife."

Well researcher, I said to myself, there's a story here that will help my book, but how do I proceed without appearing to be hard-nosed. I like this guy. I want him to like me, which has only happened one other time in this project. I took a deep breath and asked, "When did you last see them?"

"February, 1988."

I am not dumb. I think: when he left for spring training the year after the game we had been talking about, that is the last time he saw his family. Is there a connection?

"I was eighteen when I marry her. She was sixteen. Young. Too young as it turn out. I saw only her beauty, only her pleasure with life. I saw none of the other things. So we marry and I go on playing baseball. Every year I send most of what I earn back home to her. I even skimp on meal money to have a little extra for her, and in time the boys. Most winters I also play. Mexico, Caribbean leagues mostly. And what I make I send home. When I am in Dominican I also work at whatever I can find. We are not rich, but I am good steady provider.

"For a few years all is good. I am doing what I love and still thinking somehow I will become big league player. She too is thinking same thing and I hear she talks much to people of how it is going to be. That pleases me. We dream together I think. But then I begin to see our dreams are different."

As he spoke the words came more slowly as if they were coming from farther away, deeper down. Their tone was unemotional, yet the very absence of emotion heightened the sense of sorrow. I was not sure he would continue, so I ventured, "Different? How different?"

"She was dreaming how rich we would be. Not like it might happen, but like it was sure to happen. Like it was not a dream, not even a hope, but a certainty. It wasn't just the money. That I could understand. We both come from poor families. And in my dreams I think how much I can do for them. But what I begin to hear is how we will be better than all them. I begin to hear how she says and does things when I am away that I do not like so much. And when I am home we argue and she begin to say things to me about how I fail her, how I not try hard enough, how.... "

His voice cracked and he could not continue. We sat there silently for a time and I struggled to find something to say, not to get him to go on so much as to ease his hurt. We all know the stories of players who reach the "Big Show," only to waste their careers with alcohol or drugs. There are more we never hear of whose careers die away in the minors for the same reasons. We read about career ending injuries. Sometimes a life is cut short. But there are other sorrows that invade the lives of the men—or man-boys—who work at baseball: all of the sorrows that can affect other men, other man-boys. And we never really know the price of those sorrows.

I thought of Eileen, of the troubles we had had, troubles rooted at least in part in my own difficulty in discovering what I really wanted to be when I grew up. We were saved, our marriage was saved, by two things. Eileen had her own thing, her own dream, and she is very good at it. She got a PhD in political science and teaches at a small college where she is a much respected teacher. She's done her share of publishing, too, more than usual for someone in a teaching institution. In other words, she never defined herself in terms of what I was doing or wanted to do. No less important than that, I grew up enough to take pride in what she has accomplished and continues to accomplish. So we could survive my failures and her successes. That doesn't always happen in the game of love, and sometimes there's no way it can happen. Was there ever any real chance for Felipe and his wife?

Finally, he broke the silence, quietly, firmly. "After long time I go to Detroit. I play my one game. It is good to have that day, to be for that little time in the eye of my dream."

"That day it was no dream," I said. "I saw the game, remember. And anyone who saw it would say you were a big leaguer."

Again that fleeting, slight smile. "I thank you for your words. Like I say it is good, very good. But I have no illusions then. I have no belief it will ever be more than that. By then I know my limits. I not even a banjo hitter. But I love what I do and what I do good I do very good and there is joy in that. So I go home happy. But is worse than ever. She make so much of that one game. She wave it in front of everybody. She say things that hurt others, so it hurts most myself. I try to tell her what I know in my heart, but she scream at me like I hit her. Tells me to go away, tells me she will find better man than me, one who is not so weak, so much a coward."

He stood up and walked away from me, toward the water. For a moment I thought he meant to keep on walking, into the bay, into the deep. Instead he repeated the action of picking up a stone and throwing it, watching it skip and splash and sink like instant replay. Once more I admired the gracefulness of his movements. There are shortstops who are acrobatic, like Ozzie Smith, and there are shortstops who are balletic. Lopez was like that. When he played it gave him a elegance, now it gave him dignity. He watched the rippling circle spread out and fade and disappear in the quiet waters. Then I understood: inextricably bound in the memory of those few hours were both the greatest joy and the greatest sorrow of his life, golden moments entwined with searing fire. Rising I walked slowly to his side and stood with him. Three jets from the air base burst through the silence.

"I have three sons. And a wife. But no home there. My home is here. I send them money. My mother writes and tells me they are good boys, are growing up, playing baseball. She does not mention Maria. Maybe someday...."

I think Sparky Adams probably asked me whether I liked pitching or playing shortstop better. At least, that's the kind of question he might have asked. I don't imagine I gave him a very articulate answer, but maybe I mumbled something like, "Pitching, I guess." The fact was at that time I had only been pitching a little more than a year and I hadn't hit my stride, while I had been playing shortstop from the first day I picked up a glove.

It was 1975, the summer after my freshman year in high school, in the county recreation league that I first pitched in a real game. We were playing Chicago Heights and were down 8-7 in the seventh. Bill Knecht had gone all the way, but obviously was pretty shaky. He was one of those bulldog types who are always pitching in trouble and more often than not get out of it. This was one of the other days. Fred Harris, our coach, had left him in there probably because we had a double-header coming up the next day. In the seventh Knecht loaded the bases with nobody out, then ran the count to three and nothing on their clean-up hitter, a burly catcher named George Graham. He already had three hits. Coach ambled out to the mound and called the infielders to gather around.

As usual, I was at short. At fifteen I was already tall, but still skinny. Coach always called me "Slats" after the old Cardinal shortstop, Marty Marion, a hero of his when he was growing up. Bill Knecht had obviously lost his interest in pitching that day so finally Coach looked around at us and said, "All right, who wants it?"

Harris was a funny guy. He had a lame left arm, the result of a shrapnel wound in the Korean War. He would pitch batting practice for us and even play in pick-up games sometimes. When he hit, he always bunted and everybody knew it, but eight out of ten times he'd beat it out, he was that good. He was pretty testy and nobody really liked him much, but he was a good *coach. He knew baseball and he could make himself clear to teenage boys who loved the game and were ready to lap up everything he said. After he asked the question, he looked around at us. When nobody answered right off, he took the ball from Knecht, tossed it to me and said, "Slats, you've got a good arm, it's your show."*

Later I wondered if he was trying to take me down a peg. I admit I put on a show of being pretty cocky. I was the youngest guy on the team and thought brashness might be taken for maturity. At that moment, however, I didn't have time to think of anything much, there being no room for error. So after warming up I just threw three straight fast balls past Graham. He took the first one and swung late on the next two. He stood there staring at me for moment, then walked back to the bench laughing as he tossed his bat away. We would have some great battles over the next few years and he hit me better than anyone else did, but we also became friends and I think the way we reacted to that first encounter was the reason.

I struck out the next two batters as well, then went the next two innings without allowing a base runner. We tied it in the eighth, then won in the ninth. I relieved again the next day, pitched another scoreless inning and started a game the next weekend, taking Bill Knecht's place. It was one of those "almost too good to be true" beginnings, but it was true. I remember. I remember those years as the glory days.

That summer, I wasn't great, but I was pretty good. I had nothing but a fastball at first. Harris, however, was quick to see the possibilities and taught me how to throw a sneaky fast curve by holding the ball differently. It didn't break much, just enough, andt it didn't put any strain on my arm. "Try the fancy stuff, later," he said, "after you've built up some arm strength. You haven't thrown enough yet to get fancy." By the time of the league championship game I was throwing the curve and had my best game. We lost to Harvey 2-1 in ten innings after I had gone nine, giving up one run and three hits. Harris took me out because he said I had thrown enough, so it was Knecht who ended up taking the loss.

That winter couldn't go too fast for me. I played jayvee football and was seventh man on the basketball team, but they didn't really interest me. Baseball had always been my game and now it had a new fascination for me. I liked shortstop, but pitching puts you at the very center of things. It's the only position from which you can control the game because when you're out there everything depends on how you throw the ball. When you wind up and let fly with that baseball all kinds of things can happen, but none of them can happen until you throw it. That's dazzling power for a sixteen year old boy.

I remember Coach Douglas on the first day of high school practice the following spring. He yelled out, "Outfielders to the outfield, infielders to the batting cage, pitchers and catchers over by the bleachers." I started walking toward the bleachers when he barked, "Collins, I said infielders to the cage." I turned and looked at him, and then at the guys, all of whom had stopped and were staring at him. Then suddenly it struck me: he didn't know! Dan Douglas must have been the only man in Flossmoor who didn't know. When I thought about it the reason was obvious. As soon as school was out in the spring he headed north to Wisconsin where he ran a summer camp. He didn't come back until football practice started. And football was his main interest, so all he thought about was how things were shaping up for the fall. Since I played only an indifferent game at end, he didn't pay much attention to me. Nor did he notice what was happening around him on that spring afternoon, so when I saw he was just going to yell at me again, I turned toward the cage, shrugging my shoulders.

A week later, just before a practice game, he came up to me. "Collins, I understand you did some pitching last summer."

I played it casual. "Yes sir, I did."

"Well I'll try you for an inning or two today."

The inning or two turned out to be five. We were already trailing 3-0 in the fifth when our starter, Jimmy Phillips fell on his shoulder trying to field a bunt. As he went out to check on him, Coach signaled to Knecht to warm up, but then he got to the mound he noticed the other infielders were all looking at me.

92

"All right Collins," he said. "It's yours. I want to see Jenkins at short for a bit."

By the seventh we were tied 3-3 and I had given up one bloop hit. It was only a practice game and Coach Douglas didn't really have his heart in baseball, but he liked to win. He left me in and I gave up one more hit, a clean one to center. We won with a run in the bottom of the ninth.

Turned out it was John Maier, sports editor of the local paper, who had clued Douglas in on what everybody else knew. Maier wrote a nice column about it after I had started (and won) my first game for Douglas: how he had dropped by to get a story on the season and Coach told him he was a little short on pitching, naming the guys he was looking at. Maier asked him, "What about Collins?"

"Collins? He's a shortstop. Good arm, but I don't know if he can pitch."

"Well, Dan, you are apparently the only coach in the county who doesn't know that."

I still have a copy of that column.

During the summer after my junior year in high school I was pitching for the local American Legion team and was having a pretty good time of it. Still mixed pitching with playing shortstop, but the magic of gripping the baseball had me. We played on a field right next to the commuter station. It was a decent field though there wasn't much seating for spectators, one small wooden stand, painted green, on the third base line. Of course, we didn't have much need for more than that since the only people who came were parents and girl friends. Whenever somebody showed up we didn't recognize, there would be buzzing about maybe he was a scout, but the only time we knew that for sure was when we played Blue Island.

They had a pitcher, Mitch Tracey, who had dominated the high school league he was in and was All-State in his junior year and would be again as a senior. The local papers always referred to him as a "pro prospect." He wasn't very big, shorter than me and about as skinny. And he wasn't any faster, in fact, probably not as fast. But he had great control and had a nasty

93

curve ball that made him very tough for most sixteen and seventeen year olds. Eventually he did sign with the Tigers, but never made it past Double-A. I think his lack of a "big league" fastball did him in. The jugs gun mentality among scouts and player development directors makes it pretty hard for a finesse pitcher to get very far unless he's lucky.

Anyway, that day we knew for sure that there were a couple of scouts present, both middle-age guys with the look of having spent a fair amount of time out in the sun watching ballgames. They both had little notebooks that they periodically scribbled in, but other than that nothing to differentiate them from anybody else—except that they were strangers, obviously knew one another, but didn't sit together. They might as well have had signs on their backs.

Tracey was pretty good that day: he gave up six hits, walked nobody and struck out nine. The hits, though, included two doubles each by our third Baseman, Jim Britton, and me, back to back both times so I scored twice. We topped a lot of curveballs into ground outs. Pretty good, but I was better. They got a run off me in the first when I was little wild. (My control was never quite as good as it was that first time I pitched and some guys called me "Wild Will). Our catcher had a passed ball and the run scored on it, but after that they didn't touch me. I gave up only two hits and the one run (which, of course, was unearned). I walked four and struck out twelve, including the last three in a row, after I had walked the lead-off man. We won, 2-1. It was a non-league game so it didn't count for much, but you would have thought we had won the state title.

We didn't have dressing rooms, so we came to the field in our uniforms; the only thing we had to change was our shoes. After that game we took an uncommon long time untying our spikes and putting on whatever shoes we had to walk home in. A couple of us, at least, were wishing, hoping, praying, that one or the other or both of those birddogs would come up to us, pat us on the back, and say, "Nice game, kid." Maybe they'd even ask our name and say something redemptive like, "I'll keep my eye on you." They did speak to the coaches and I saw one of them

94

talk to Tracey, but neither one said anything to me. Jim, who was a bit more forward than me, asked our coach what they had said. He just replied, "Not much."

Walking home I thought about that and made up my mind Coach didn't want to say anything that would give me a big head. I didn't quite believe it though and somehow the victory didn't seem as shining as it had at first. A year or so later when I heard the Tigers had signed Tracey, I said to about everybody who would listen, "I beat him straight up, head to head, and could do it again."

That's how I remember it all anyway and who's to say it didn't happen that way. I've lost touch with my high school buddies, so I don't have anybody to check with. Maybe I prefer it that way. I'm fond of quoting Augustine and his lofty remarks about "the fields and palaces of memory," but, looked at another way, memory is a puppet show and we're the puppeteers. Of course, puppet shows are never very realistic, except to children, so it's hard to convince even yourself that the story's true. On the other hand, it's the self who most wants to believe and the self is often childish.

Even the puppets of the past, however, have a way of getting out of our control. I can't avoid the fact that by the time I was nattering on about being able to beat Tracey, there was a certain shrillness to my tone. I hadn't seen another scout and Division I coaches weren't exactly pursuing me with scholarship offers. I did have some feelers from the likes of Southern Illinois and Central Michigan. That should have told me something, but all it did was stimulate a kind of "I'll show you" attitude that probably wasn't very pleasant and certainly was adolescent. It did prompt me to work pretty hard, trying to add velocity to my fastball. I didn't end up going to any of those places. Both my parents had gone to the University of Michigan and they were encouraging me to go there. I thought about it and half-convinced myself to go to Michigan and be a walk-on in baseball. My mental scenario had me dazzling the coaches and leaving them wondering why that hadn't recruited me. Maybe it was the worm of doubt, the fear of failure, or just contrariness, but I ended up insisting I wanted to go to a small college. I said I was in a big high school and wanted a place where I wouldn't be a number. That appealed to my parents and it wasn't a problem of finances so that's how I ended up at Beloit.

Looking back on it now, I wish I had gone over and talked to Tracey, not to find out what the scout had said to him, but to ask him what he was thinking himself, what he was really dreaming. But that's a forty year old looking back. Then, I was too busy thinking I was every bit as good as he was, maybe better. Dreams have a way of clouding your judgment, especially if you are a sixteen year old boy who lives and breathes baseball. Even more to the point, given how brief a future life my dream had, I should have talked more to Bill Knecht, whose place in the sun I had obscured with the scudding clouds of my own adolescent dreams.

Reading the Signs

Stories of hitters with Ruthian power litter the columns of sports pages, especially those published in the spring of the year. In most cases, however, the sequels also tell of the failures to make contact with a pitched ball or to catch a hit or thrown ball sufficiently often to make it worth the agony. For some of these March *wunderkind*, their power potential is entrancing enough to allow them to have adequate careers at the major league level: Dave Nicholson, Dick Stuart, Dave Kingman, Rob Deer, Pete Incaviglia, Russell Branyan to name a few.. Occasionally you even have a player like Gregg Jeffries who is a pure hitter, but for whom the search to find a position in the field where he is not an utter liability is fruitless. The creation of that peculiar institution, the designated hitter, has offered some refuge for such players. Oddly, however, few players are brought up to the major leagues with the specific purpose of being a DH. Rather that position seems to be a place of honor reserved for veteran players who have "lost a step" (or more) in the field or who, after an earnest effort at one or several positions, have somehow earned the safety of being a "one dimensional" player.

Then, there are all the untold stories of minor league players with great potential who never quite hit well enough to allow those who make personnel decisions to feel comfortable exposing them and their fielding deficiencies to the more critical eye of major league fans. If you read the annual summaries of the best prospects in various major league organizations that appear in such publications as *Baseball America*, you invariably see some players described as having major league power who will never ultimately grace the roster of a major league team. Indeed, if you examine the descriptions carefully, you can identify them by two tell-tale signs: at least a passing reference to the organization's attempt to "find a position for them," which usually means playing them for a while at first base and then in left field. (In sandlot baseball we always put the awkward kid in right field. That's a difference worth pondering.) The second indicator is that the statistics show that they strike out more than one-third of the time. Even in this new millenium, when the lust for power has eliminated the sense of embarrassment players use to feel striking out more than one hundred times per season and managers use to have at fielding a team with several whiffmasters, there are limits though the statistics of Ryan Howard make one wonder.

Which brings me to Sam Patch. Sam was six feet four (still is) and 235 pounds (wishes he still were) and played a pretty good tight end in Division Two football at Slippery Rock as well as leading Division Two baseball in homeruns three straight years in the late seventies. He was drafted by both the San Diego Chargers and the Padres, but opted to play professional baseball because his hero was Bob Robertson. He wandered through the Padre organization showing the classic signs: hitting with enough power to make managers and hitting instructors dream of what might be if only…. If only they could adjust his swing so he would make contact a bit more often and if only they could find a position for him to play where he would not endanger himself and others.

In 1985 he had what an inverately optimistic observer called a "break out year" in AAA: he hit .257 with thirty-three homeruns and was playing left field about as well as he ever would. The result was a September call-up and his one major league appearance. He played left against the Dodgers: he went one for four with a long home run and three strikeouts and had three putouts in the field and would have a couple more if he hadn't made a wrong first step. Since two of the three strikeouts were on foul tips, the team felt sufficiently encouraged to bring him to spring training the following year. However, he ended up back at AAA, was a throw-in when the Padres made a trade in early July with Texas. In August of that year he retired.

So how had he gotten from there to being a social studies teacher and head football coach at McGuffey High School near Pittsburgh?

"Simple enough," he told me when I asked that question. "From the Rock I had everything I needed to get a Pennsylvania teaching certificate, I had always lived in the area during off-season because my wife had a teaching position in Washpa [Washington, Pennsylvania, for those not in the know], and they had an opening. In fact I had already applied for the job before the trade so I was planning to quit anyway. Spent three years as assistant, then became the head coach."

"Football, not baseball?"

"Yeah. Fact is I was probably a better football player than I was a baseball player, though I doubt if I would have cut it in the NFL. Maybe I might have managed a stint on the taxi squad for somebody like New Orleans, but I wasn't fast enough. Not that my hopes were all that high for making the Big Show in baseball, though I could almost imagine it, and stranger things have happened. Baseball had two attractions: it's easier on the knees and there's the minor leagues. In pro football you get cut and where's to go? These days you've got that silly European league and arena football, but they're a long way from the minor league systems baseball teams have. Didn't somebody write a book called *Good Enough to Dream*? That's the minors and that was me. All around though, I was better at football, and I probably understand more facets of the game." He laughed: "I mean can you see me teaching some sixteen year old kid how to field or make contact with a pitch?"

I had an easy time locating him. Employing my usual principle of checking first the hometown—in his case Oil City, Pennsylvania—the first person I contacted, the editor of the local paper, turned out to be a cousin of Sam's by marriage. He laughed at the thought of Sam being on anybody's dream team. "Oh, he could hit a ball a mile, but there was this little thing about doing it more than once a fortnight. Sam lives down in

Washington County now. Teaches and coaches at McGuffey High School. Doing well."

"So are you doing well?"

"Can't complain. Have a good bunch of kids and we win more than we lose. This coming year we should win a lot more. And the teaching is good too. These are mostly rural kids, small town kids, like I was and I think I know where they're coming from. My wife teaches in the Trinity district, where we live. That's a different environment. She likes it well enough, but I prefer this. If I had my druthers I'd probably live in Claysville, too. Would like my kids to grow up in a place like that where there's less concern about the labels on your clothes."

It was spring, a late April evening, and we were sitting on the back deck of their house from which we could see the junction of I-70 and I-79. It was a bit nippy, but the air was fresh and the hills of Western Pennsylvania were turning green again. Pretty country, unless you're looking at the leavings of a worn-out coal mine or a shut-down steel mill.

"So tell me about that day."

"That day. *The* day. The day all my dreams came true." He smiled, took a sip of his Iron City beer. "Well, I figure I don't need to tell you the stats. You want to know how it felt. I'll tell you: it felt good and it felt bad. Good because, well hell, that's why you play professional baseball, at least in the beginning, because you do dream about making it to the majors. I knew I had limits. I mean if I was too slow in football, I was at least slow in baseball. But I was as fast as Bob Robertson, my big hero. And most players who make it have deficiencies. They're always talking about these five tool players, but there aren't that many of them and even the ones there are don't always use them all. Mostly because they lack tools six and seven, smarts and heart. They can make up for a lot.

"I like to watch the real super stars—though there are a lot fewer than the sportscasters seem to think. Like this guy Vladimir Guerrero of the Angels. There's a genuine five-tool player,. Or Albert Pujols of the Cards, not great speed, but he's got everything but that and he knows how to run the bases,.

100

Even more fun, though, are guys like David Eckstein.. I mean, there's a guy who made it on smarts and heart. Sure, he's not a super star, but he's made it in spite of all the scouting reports. Maybe it's ironic me saying this, but the sport needs more guys like that, and fewer would be Ruths and McGwires."

"Like you?"

"You got it right there." He hoisted his beer in a mock toast. "You know I think I could've stayed up in the majors longer in times like today." He paused, emitted a low chuckle that seemed to be laughter at himself, then shook his head. "Somewhere along the line you wake up, well most guys wake up, and realize you're not going to make it. For some that comes pretty fast, for others it takes longer. Heck, there are some who never quite admit it despite being told pretty clearly by the organization."

"How long did it take you?"

He looked thoughtfully at his Iron City. "Three years. Yeah, three years. By then I had seen enough other players to get a good read on how I stacked up and, being optimistic, I concluded I was a marginal prospect."

"But you played, what, three more years?"

"Yeah, three more. Why not? I had folded up the dream, but I hadn't put it away. And once I stopped there would be no going back."

"Plus, if you had stopped then you never would have had that one game."

"And I would have lost the chance to be one of your dreamboats or whatever you're calling them."

"So you're glad you stuck it out those extra years?"

"Sure. No doubt about it. Besides, that was my only shot at extending my adolescence. And Nancy, that's my wife—she'll be home in a bit, so you can meet her—had a good job here, no kids yet. First one was born in '86."

"The year you quit?"

"Say you're quick, aren't you?" He raised his glass as if in salute. "And, of course, the year after that magic moment, the day all my dreams came true."

So back to my stock question, my effort to get at the nub of what I might have missed by my own early exit from the yellow brick road. "So how did it feel?"

"Feel? Like I said, good and bad. I mean anybody who's ever played baseball as a kid has at least, even if only for a moment, fantasized about being in the big leagues. Look at yourself. It's running out your pores. I mean anybody who cooks up a project like the one you're working on is probably trying to satisfy some interior psychological need that comes out of that boyhood fantasy." He looked at me out of the corner of his eye, a sly grin on his face.

"You caught me there," I said, not entirely happily.

"Thought so. Chalk that up to my courses in developmental psych at the Rock. The advantage of going to a Division II school—you have to go to class. Anyway, if you actually do it, if you actually walk out on the field of a major league ballpark and play a game, hell an inning, a third of an inning, it's got to feel good. And for the rest of your life you can go around saying 'I played in the majors.' Probably good for a free beer in half the neighborhood taverns in Washington County."

"But bad too? Why?"

"Because you know you don't really belong there. You know this isn't going to last. I mean I told you already I had no illusions by that time. Well, not many, so it shouldn't have mattered. I should have taken it for what it was, enjoyed it, and gotten on with the rest of my life. I knew it was a fluke, the result of some complicated roster juggling the Padres had blundered into, but the next six-seven months were probably the dumbest months of my life."

"How...." My question, whatever it was going to be, was interrupted by the distant sound of squealing brakes and then of a crash.

"Godamn, there's another one." Sam lumbered to his feet and hurried over to the railing of the deck and looked down toward the intersection of the two interstates. I followed. "I don't know how much money the highway department has spent on that intersection. They've got rumble strips down the hill, signs, flashing lights, concrete barriers. They even reconstructed it to make the turns from 79 onto 70 more gradual. But there's always some dummy who thinks he knows better. They come racing down that hill on 79 and they either run up somebody's back, or bounce into a barrier, or roll over. Damn, I should be keeping score. Can't those lulus read the signs?"

We could just see one of those sports utility vehicles rolled on its side on the eastbound ramp. The traffic began to back up behind it. Westbound cars and trucks crept past, suddenly made cautious. Those going east were stuck. We watched silently. It didn't take long before we heard sirens and saw the flashing lights of police and emergency vehicles.

"Years ago, right after we bought this place, a truck went over down there, burst into flames. The driver was trapped inside and people just stood by helpless. They said they could hear him screaming, begging the state trooper on the scene to shoot him, kill him quick rather than let him burn slowly." Sam shook his head slowly. "Maybe that guy down there is lucky. There's no fire. Maybe he just got himself some bruises. And a hard-earned lesson. Damn, why don't people read the signs."

Reluctantly we wandered back to our chairs. It seemed somehow inhumane, unconcerned, to go back to our conversation. Yet it also seemed ghoulish to continue to watch, though from that distance we couldn't see much. Good and bad. For several minutes we were silent, then finally I figured I'd better get us back on track. "You were saying."

"Yeah, yeah, I was saying it wasn't a good time. That winter my wife was pregnant. We'd decided earlier that summer would be my last and I would go out and get a real job. Instead I started working out harder than ever, getting ready for spring training because they'd told me I was going to the major league camp. Well, Nance, was good about it, but she was having a hard time with her pregnancy, and I wasn't as helpful as I should have been. I mean the lost illusion had reappeared it seemed and I put more stock in it than was smart. So it was a rough winter, emotionally I mean. Looking back on it I figured I had come close to really blowing it, what we had right here. So I went off to spring training and blew that instead big-time. Batted .159, didn't hit a dinger and damn near ruined a couple of fences running into them. That was a good reality check. I started looking for a teaching or coaching job around here and promised Nance I'd only play until I landed one, then I'd quit. There you have it."

"No regrets?"

"Yeah, I guess a couple."

"Like what."

"I regret I put Nance, us, through the difficulty of that one winter. I mean deep down I knew I wasn't good enough, but the hook gets in your mouth and it's hard to thrash free, no matter what you say, and she didn't need that. Oh I think I've made it up to her in lots of ways. I mean we're happy. Things are good. But there was no call for that. I saw all the signs clear enough." He paused.

"That's one regret. You said a couple."

He took a deep breath and resumed. "And I regret that I don't regret it enough, that if I had it to do over again I know I'd make the try."

A door closed in the house. "Nance, that you?"

"Yes, it is."

"Boys home too?"

"In all their glory."

"Come on out and meet a genuine writer, soon to be world famous."

"Be there in a minute."

He smiled. "She took the boys to practice. Usually I do it, but you got me excused."

"Baseball practice?"

"Naw. And not football either. They all play soccer. Sign of the times."

Somewhere I read that our efforts to reconstruct our past involve "The inevitable tango of memory and imagination." The more I consider that the more I like it.

I began this project with the notion that I could sit down with these ex-ballplayers, ask some questions, and come up with the makings of their stories. Of course, I wanted their stories to answer some questions that they may never have thought of. They were my questions and I was trying to get answers out of their lives. To put it into the language my wife would use (her specialty in political scientist is studying polls), I was "tainting the sample" by my own assumptions which, of course, colored the questions I was asking—and how I understood the answers I was getting. She told me that more than once and I finally listened to her.

So I asked myself whether I needed to revise my approach. That got me to thinking about my own story and I began to wonder how much of what "I remember so clearly" is, in fact, my imagination working, rather than my memory. But that only made me wonder whether you can have the one without the other, memory without imagination, imagination without memory. Then I ran across that phrase, "The inevitable tango of memory and imagination," and it made sense.

Augustine talks about the memory as if it were a great warehouse--to be sure, one that doesn't have an up-to-date inventory and certainly not a readily accessible data bank despite the talk about the human mind being a kind of computer. We don't know what's there until we start looking and some things thieving time may have stolen from us. Augustine doesn't use the term imagination to describe what we do when we start pawing around in our store of memories, but he makes clear that what we find is not the past itself, but images of it—and seldom, if ever, whole images. The question is how we put them together to form a coherent picture. What I think is that we do it through imagination informed by reason. That is, we fill in the gaps between the memories by using our imaginations, but our imaginative leaps have to make sense in some way. However, imagination is a rambunctious sense and at times takes the lead. That's why the tango metaphor is so telling.

I'm no expert on the tango, but I have this image of it from watching old movies. I think of it as a lively dance, one that involves abrupt shifts and turnings and in which first one then the other partner seems to be in control. So it is, I think, when we enter the palaces of the mind, of memory and of imagination.

Sometimes the memories seem to be whole. They are full images of a past event and the easy temptation is to regard them as true, almost as if the event itself were recurring before our mind's eye. Yet, in truth, the details may be the work of our imaginations, filling in lacunae. In such cases the process is unconscious and memory itself leads the dance, moving the imagination as it requires.

More often our memories are fragmentary. We are conscious of the dark, unclear spaces, and we work, we hope rationally, to fill them. The very consciousness of the act, however, accentuates the reliance on the imagination, and that vivid partner may seize the lead. But we strive to work with it within the formal patterns of the dance.

And there are times when imagination takes wing, when sweet reason does not have the strength to control the imagination of our hearts and the patterns are lost and the tango becomes a danse fantastique. Looking back on my own life I have some vivid "memories" of things which, upon further review, I am fairly certain never happened at all. Were they dreams which were so vivid that they assumed the character of reality? Or *were they merely wishes that I made into horses so my beggarly experience could ride? And there are a few "memories" which I don't want to look at too closely for fear that they are purely imaginary: the no-hitter I pitched in Legion ball, for example. Did that really happen or was it merely something I wanted so badly I made it happen in the arena of my imagination?*

The wings of imagination can become, consciously or unconsciously, the means of escaping from the claims of memory into fantasy. Some fantasies are benign. If my "memory" of out-pitching Mitch Tracey is mere fantasy, it's a harmless one. But if I had built that into a belief that I was better than he was (and there were moments when I did so), that the failure of the scouts to recognize my ability was an injustice, that my dreams of being a big leaguer were somehow thwarted by unnatural forces, where would that have led me? If one constructs a view of real-ity from the purely imaginary, the consequences are far from benign. That is delusion and madness lies that way.

I read recently about an English professor who said that a good biographer will not allow "the tyranny of facts" to trap them in reconstructing the life of a subject. Instead they will find a "mythos" that will give shape and meaning to the events. I suppose that's what we all really do when we try to find meaning in our lives though we may not do it as consciously as a biogra-pher might. Yet there is something unsettling in that idea. I'm no intellectual, but I'm not dumb, and "mythos" sounds like one of those wiggle words that allow people to create the truths they desire—which to my mind are not truths at all, but fantasies, fi-nally even delusions.

The tango is a passionate dance, seemingly wild and freed from all restraints. That freedom, however, is illusory. In fact, the tango is stylized, moving within its own sphere of rules and conventions. It must be so. Each of the partners must know his or her role, what to expect from the other, how the steps fit into a greater pattern. Otherwise it would disintegrate into mere disorder. The dancers would not be partners at all, but dervishes whirling in their separate worlds without meaning and without hope.

If we have only shards of memory our lives are frag-mented; if we have only imagination, our lives are a danse ma-cabre.

Strange Honesty

Their names are legion: Jim Delsing, Chuck Diering, Hal Rice, Jim Busby, Ken Berry, Hal Jeffcoat, John Cangelosi. They are the joy of managers with heavy-footed, slugging left and right fielders—fast, smooth-fielding center fielders with at least decent arms who had long careers in the majors without ever frightening any pitcher when at bat. There are, after all, a limited supply of Joe DiMaggios, Mickey Mantles and Ken Griffeys. Center fielders are like shortstops: they have to be able to cover ground and catch and throw. If they should also happen to be able to hit, what a treasure and to hit with power, what a wonder. Yet, of course, they have to be able to hit just enough above the Mendoza line if they are to hang around as long as the above mentioned players. Jeffcoat, of course, is an oddity in that list. Partway through his career he switched to being a relief pitcher (he didn't hit enough) and managed a respectable few years in that role. And Delsing is the answer to one of the great trivia questions, but that's another story.

I mention them only because they are the role models for another veritable legion: center fielders who fielded a little less well, perhaps, and hit not so much, so they didn't quite make the grade. Which brings me to Willie Bush, "Fast Willie" as he was commonly known.

He ranks with the likes of Moonlight Graham and Dan Jesse for the brevity of his major league resume. He appeared in only one game, but had no official at bats. Unlike them, however, he had one statistic, a caught stealing. He appeared as a pinch-runner for Jesse Gonder of the Mets in the final game of the 1964 season. It was a memorable game because the Cardinals' victory over the Mets in that game clinched the pennant. And perhaps, "Fast Willie" contributed in a small way by his failure to succeed in the one offensive category he was good at, stealing a base. Bush had led every minor league in which he had played in stolen bases. Given the relative infrequency with which he reached base, that was no mean feat.

Among the candidates for my dream team, he was the easiest to find. And, once I located him, I had no fear that I would lose track of him since he was midway through a sentence at the Michigan State prison at Jackson, the alma mater of Ron LeFlore, who would have been on my list of role models except that he hit too well. Once more Willie had been not quite fast enough. I pondered the ethical question of whether it was right to put a convicted felon (armed robbery) on my Dream Team, but gave way before the weight of two practical considerations. First, with Sam Patch in left and Walt Armbruster in right I had an outfield roughly equal in terms of fielding ability to the legendary 1953-54 Cub outfield which included Ralph Kiner and Hank Sauer plus whatever poor soul had to play between them. And second, I needed a base-stealing threat.

"Man," he said when we first met, "I couldn't believe that letter of yours. I mean it's been a long while since anybody axt me about my ball-playing. Half my fellow residents here didn't even believe me when I tol'em. But man, you have made me a regular cee-lebrity."

I hadn't known what to expect. His reply to my letter had been terse and perfunctory. "Okay. I'll be here. Willie Bush" was all it said. So I wasn't expecting anyone quite so open and convivial. I thought he might be a tough interview—wary, taciturn—but he quickly dispelled that presumption. A lithe, wiry man, looking like he was put together with rubber bands, only

110

the lines in his face and the distinct grayness in his hair differentiated him from the young man I had seen in an old photograph. When I commented on his apparent fitness, he replied, "I exercise, man, I always have. Otherwise, I'd go stir-crazy," and he slapped his leg and laughed.

"I signed with the White Sox right outa high school. I mean those were the days, we're talkin' mid '50's, when the opportunities for a black man in collitch weren't quite so many as these days. These days I mighta gone to collitch. I wasn't too bad a student, never flunked a thing. Mighta ended up bein' a lawyer, instead of needin' one. But hey man I'm not complainin'. Got traded by the Sox to Cleveland in '59 as a throw in when they wuz tryin' to solidify the team. That wuz the 'Go-go Sox" team. I mighta fit right in, but that's how it goes. Didn't fit at all with the Indians, and they sold me off to the Cubs."

"How did you end up in the Mets organization?"

"Another trade. They'd taken somebody in the expansion draft the Cubs wanted back, so they worked out a twofer with the Mets with me as the icin' on the cake. I was good trade bait. Dazzled people with my speed so they sometimes forgot a few of my shortcomings. Man, I was fast."

"Fast Willie."

"You betcha," he retorted laughingly. "Course I shoulda known if I wasn't good enough to make the Mets in 1962 the future wuz none too bright. I mean, they wuz awful."

"Forty wins, a hundred and twenty losses."

"That's what I mean, awful. They had Ashburn in center. He could still hit, but the whiz had gone outa that kid. I coulda subbed for 'im some, probably won two or three more games for 'em." Another thigh slap, another laugh.

"But you kept on playing."

"Well, it was steady, if seasonal work. Good for a few free meals in the off-season. And even if I wuzn't goin' nowhere in baseball there wuzn't nowhere else to go. Then, of course, I

111

got that call up in at the end of '64. Forget why they bothered. Maybe an injury, maybe just an error in the front office, maybe they wuz showcasin' me for a blockbuster trade."

He had this way of drifting from a possibly logical explanation of events into some wild assertion. It was not a movement into fantasy, for he was not deceiving himself. Rather it was a conscious venture into comic absurdity. I wondered if he was always like this, or whether he was playing a part, like an old soft-shoe routine that he knew would keep a white man amused and at arm's length. Yet it also struck me that we often do that with our memories: is it a means of easing the pain?

"Well, tell me about it. What were you thinking? Did you think it might be the breakthrough?"

"You shittin' me, man. Like I said, I don't know why they bothered. Probably some fuck-up in the front office. I mean these were the Mets, wasn't much they could do right in those days. But I can't complain. I mean I was wearing a major league uniform for a coupla days. And I did get into a game. That was a ticket to more'n few free snacks in the winter. If T. V. talk shows had been big back then, who knows, I mighta made the rounds of them and gotten into show biz."

"As the result of pinch running for Gonder and being thrown out trying to steal second?"

"Man, you're brutal." But he laughed.

"Were you stealing on your own, or on a steal sign?"

"Man, you're smarter than that. What's a no account rookie goin' ta be doin' stealing on his own in a game like that? Fact is, I didn't ever steal on my own till after I left baseball." Another thigh slapper.

"How close was the play?"

"Oh, it was close, real close. I mean I was fast. But that Gibby was good. I just didn't get the jump I woulda gotten on somebody else, even so the catcher had to make a perfect throw to get me. But it was bang-bang."

"Were you out?"

He laughed again. "Man says I was out, I was out. Won't see me trying to rewrite no history book."

"Not even your own?" As I asked the question I was thinking, why not your own? Bush, of all my dream teamers, would have been the easiest to excuse for indulging in a bit of fantasy as an escape from reality—or maybe as an explanation for it, turning himself into the victim of a bad call.

For the first time he gave no rapid response; his risible manner seemed checked. He looked away from me at something only he could see. Finally, in a low voice, almost a whisper, he said, "Some things don't bear thinkin' on."

The laughter had gone out of the air and I feared I had put the quietus on our interview. Should have been smarter, more subtle, I thought to myself. Yet his unaccountably cheery manner had led me on to being a bit careless in my approach. Apparently, the result was that I had come too close to penetrating his protective shield. I retreated to safer ground.

"What were you thinking when you trotted off the field after that play."

He stared at me darkly for a moment and then abruptly the soft shoe dancer was back. "I was thinkin' I'd never catch Ty Cobb that way."

"Stengel say anything to you in the dugout."

"Nothin' I could understand."

"That was the last game of the season for the Mets. Did you have any notion it was going to be your one and only appearance in a major league game."

"Oh sure, I didn't have no doubt about that. I mean, I knew my limits and figured I was already a step or two beyond 'em. But I had fun the few days I was a major leaguer. If you can call bein' with the Mets in '64 bein' a major leaguer. Got no invite to spring training the next year, but that didn't surprise me. Woulda surprised me more if I had."

"So how long did you keep playing?"

"As long as anybody would have me, which was as long as they thought I had speed. Like I said before, it was steady work. Saw a lotta towns, rode a lotta buses, but there sure was nuthin' else better to do. Guess I proved that in spades."

We were back to the brink and he had brought us there. So I asked, "Do you care to say anything about what happened afterwards? How it was you ended up here?"

"What's to say. Kicked around here and there, workin' at what you'd expect a black man with no collitch degree and no particular skills outsida being able to run fast might do. I mean it was honest work at first, but it was driftin'. Had no fambly. No fambly to speak of, so there was nuthin' in particular givin' me direction."

"You never married?"

"Naw. When I was young and frisky and fulla myself, I was havin' too much fun. And I was too quick to get caught." He paused, shook his head, sadly smiling. "Have a son some- wheres. But ain't seen him since he was a toddler. Hell, he's a grown man now and who knows what he's become. It's a sure thing though he has no idea who his daddy is."

"You ever think of looking him up?"

The sad smile flickered again. "Naw. What'd be the point? I'd disappoint him for sure, and he might disappoint me. Oh, I think of him some.Think about his momma too.Good woman. Only one I coulda imagined myself settlin' down with. Wonder sometimes what it'd be like havin' a fambly. But don't go far with that one. How'd I support 'em? Hittin' up banks in- stead of 7-11's? Like I said, after I quit playin' I wasn't exactly a prime attraction."

"You never thought of staying in baseball as a coach?" I knew the answer to my question before I asked. It was, after all, the late sixties when he left the game, or it left him. And in those days there were precious few black coaches. Baseball hasn't exactly had an inspiring record on that front, but back then it was even more dismal. Why did I even ask? Probably because I wanted him to be angry about it. That's what I was missing in this story, anger. He had to be angry about something. But he just laughed at my question, the way one would laugh at a child who asks a question the answer to which the child could never understand.

"Anyway I got a little too attached to cheap red wine and that led to a few overnights in local jails, which acourse made it harder to get even the piddlin' jobs I had managed to get before. Finally I started hittin' up convenience stores for a livin'. Fur awhile I got a decent wage that way, and I was pretty good about not over-exposin' myself, movin' around. But, as you can tell, I finally lost a step—and here I am."

He made it sound simple and easy. He had told me everything and nothing. His narration of his "life in crime" was as unemotional as his "life in baseball." Neither story particularly satisfied me. Again I missed the anger that I thought should be there: anger because the dream had been so prosaic, so ephemeral, and because the rest of his life had been so pointless, so inevitably pointless because of the nature of American society. Or, I wonder now, was I angry because he was dancing around me, evading me. Fast Willie still had a step on me.

"Can I ask you something?"

"Seems to me you've been axsin' a lot."

"Granted, but I did tell you in my letter I wanted to interview you which by definition involves asking questions."

If he caught the edge in my voice, he gave no indication. He simply gestured with his hands as if to say "Okay, I'm not going anywhere."

"I've been listening to you talk. You seem…well, content about what happened in your baseball career. And probably you didn't get a raw deal in the game. You sound as if you got as far, maybe even a little further, than you expected. You could

115

run, but you couldn't hit. There were some center fielders in the majors in your day that matched that same description—though they were all white. But you're shut out of the game in the end. You kick around doing jobs that don't pay, you start robbing stores, and end up in prison. I mean, aren't you frustrated by what's happened? Aren't you angry that your chances were so few?"

"Like I said, man, some things don't bear thinkin' on."

I made a gesture encompassing the drab visitors' room and everything it represented. "All you've got is time to think."

"Man, you've got some kinda bug up yours, doncha. Did you come here to axt me questions or to tell me somethin'? Are you writin' a book about baseball or do you got some other axe to grind and your usin' baseball as a cover? Well, that may be all right, that's your business. But it's my past we're talkin' about. I don't own much, but I own that."

Oddly, he spoke calmly, without urgency, but there was a quiet firmness in his tone like an old homesteader declaring "Get off my land." Emily Dickinson says "Remembrance has a Rear and Front--/ 'Tis something like a House—." and, yes, maybe we can say we "own" our past. And it has various rooms, including a "Garret" and "a deepest cellar," which we may not want to enter (though we do not always control our own wanderings) and to which we may refuse others entrance (*that* we do control). I might not think much of Bush's dwelling, but a man's house, even his house of memory, is his castle.

"So you're satisfied with this, with being here?"

"Well," Willie said, "there are a lot worse places to be than in prison. I mean if I was outside, I'd probably still be trying to hit up convenience stores for bread money. And that's no kinda life for a man my age. I mean, I've lost more'n a step. This is kind of my retirement plan. Besides," and his eyes twinkled as he spoke, "you might never have found me then, and I woulda lost a chance to be an all star. You ever get your book published,

I'll be a real celebrity here. Maybe even the warden will have me over to dinner. ."

[Note: Jim Delsing was the pinch-runner for Eddie Gaedel, the midget who walked as a pinch hitter for Bill Veeck's St. Louis Browns in 1951.]

My first year in college I was the number three pitcher behind two guys, one of whom made it to the majors and had a twelve year career and other got as far as Triple A before he hit his ceiling. Which is to say the only time I pitched was in practice games, though I remember warming up to come in as a reliever once. It was the only time Chuck Poholsky, the soon-to-be major leaguer, had a bad day. We were down 6-0 going into the bottom of the seventh so the coach sent in a pinch-hitter for Poholsky and started me warming up. Well the pinch-hitter doubled, the opposing pitcher unraveled and before you knew it we had seven runs and the lead. About the time we got to 6-5 the coach told our other starter, Dave Moore, to warm up and when we got the lead he went in and I sat down.

But the handwriting was on the wall long before that. In the late fall of my first semester, I was in a gym class run by the head baseball coach, Howard Daniels. He sent us outside to play softball. It was a cold blustery day with no sun to take the edge off the winds of November in southern Wisconsin. Poholsky and I were shagging flies and tossing them back to the infield. We had been at it for a couple of minutes when Daniels sauntered over and told Chuck to roll the ball in so he wouldn't hurt his arm. The next time one came my way I rolled it toward the infield.

"What the hell you doing," Daniels barked from thirty yards away.

"Trying to protect my arm."

"No way you can hurt your arm."

That night was not the best one of my life. I alternated between depression and anger and occasionally managed to combine them.

I won't say that I was recruited aggressively by Coach Daniels, but he had spent some time with me when I visited the campus senior year in high school. He had encouraged me, I

118

*thought. I knew he was a bit crusty, but this wasn't crustiness,
this was downright meanness it seemed to me. To say it in the
first place hurt, but he had shouted it in front of twenty-some
other guys at least a few of whom knew my hopes and that
burned. And blindness! I mean he hadn't ever really seen me
pitch. How could he say something like that? But a still, small
voice kept whispering, "Sure he's an S.O.B.—but he's a correct
S.O.B."*

*I went out for the team anyway. I loved the game and
wanted to be with guys who shared at least some of that passion
and with whom I could talk. And this was a small liberal arts
college in Wisconsin, Division III where you played for the joy
of it. It was an absolute fluke that, without athletic scholarships,
we happened to have two pitchers with the skills (and futures) of
Poholsky and Moore. Poholsky was a local boy whose father
had worked in the maintenance department at the college, but
was now an invalid. Chuck simply didn't want to go away from
home. Knowing that, Northern Illinois had been after him hard,
but he had tuition remission at Beloit, and he liked the place.
Moore was a late bloomer. He had started at the Naval Academy and pitched a little there, but decided that environment
wasn't for him. Daniels knew the family—I think he had gone to
school with Moore's father—so he lucked into another pitcher
with real promise.*

*Because of the location of the college and the iffy-ness of
spring weather, it wasn't often that you needed a lot of pitchers.
A "Spahn, Sain and rain." rotation wasn't a hope, but a reality.
A couple of the position players could also pitchers and would
have provided relief if the two horses had ever needed any. But
the one year I played there was only that one near chance of
anyone else pitching.*

*I knew about Poholsky before I went there. I knew he was
good, though not how good. Moore was a surprise. He was just
transferring in when I arrived since it was mid-summer when he
made his decision to leave the Academy. Daniels may have led
me on a bit before I enrolled. Back then I would have said he
had. Now I'm not so sure. But then, he didn't know he was going*

119

to get Moore when I was visiting the campus. If I had known that I might have gone somewhere else. Probably if I had gone to one of the other colleges in our league, I wouldn't have faced that kind of competition for innings. In fact, on seeing some of the other teams I was pretty sure I would have been no worse than number two starter on most of them. But that's not the stuff of which dreams are made.

And if I had worked at it, built up my arm strength, refined my control, really started thinking about strategy and pitch location, by senior year I might have been something. Then maybe a tryout, a free agent contract, and.... Admittedly I played out that scenario in my head a few times that first year and even looked into transferring. I talked to my parents about it. While they weren't too keen on it, they would have gone along with it. My father did ask, "Is this about baseball or about the rest of your life?" Put that way I had to confess to myself that realistically transferring somewhere that I could pitch would only have delayed the inevitable by extending the life of my dream—might better call it a fantasy by that time. And I liked Beloit just fine, was doing well, planning to major in English and philosophy, had friends—including Eileen, though it was junior year before that got serious. So I stayed and the next spring went out for track, running the mile and two mile.

There is one last scene to the story of my baseball dream, one last indignity.

All the time I was in high school, in addition to playing at school and in legion ball, I also played in a recreation league. The team was pretty much the same bunch of guys who were on the other teams, really the same bunch who had been together ever since grade school playing one o'cat and then little league. It was a cross between a church league and a county league with about half the teams being sponsored by churches and the other half by businesses. Our sponsor was always Peace Lutheran Church that about a third of the guys belonged to, at least nominally. When we dispersed for college it looked like that team was history.

For college, most of the other guys had stayed closer to home than me, three of them even commuting. A couple of them hadn't gone to college, but were working in the area. I had seen one or two of them Christmas break, but had been pretty preoccupied breaking up with Shelley. It was mostly her choice rather than mine and there had been a long, painful afternoon or two of heart-to-heart talks that left me not feeling very social. So I lost contact with the guys.

The summer after my freshman year I got a job at the R. R. Donnelley plant in Chicago, basically loading mailbags into boxcars. It was hot and heavy work, bag after bag of Sears Roebuck catalogs or Fortune magazines, but I enjoyed it. It was good for me, helping me work off some of the frustrations I felt after the whimpering out of my dream. I didn't do anything dramatic like announce I would never play baseball again, but knew that when and if I did it would be for love of the game, not because it was tangled up in the now dissipated dream. Usually when I got home from work, I just took a long, hot shower then ate dinner and vegged out around the house.

The end of my first week on the job I arrived in town on an Illinois Central commuter train about six o'clock. As I got off the train I looked across the tracks to the field. There was a game going on. Momentarily I smiled, imagined a new generation of players, some of them maybe dreaming as I had, thought I would go over and watch for a bit. Then I realized that the third baseman was Jim Britton, the shortstop was Buddy Smith, the second baseman was Bruce Whitman.... All the old team except the pitcher. I recognized him right off, Brian Kennedy, who had been the pitcher for our arch-rival high school, and who I had beaten six times in three years.

Nobody had called me. Nobody had asked if I wanted to play. I exited the station on the opposite side and walked the long way home so I wouldn't have to pass the field.

On the Fly

As I said before, in sand lot ball right field is where you put the kid who can't run or catch, the assumption being that's where such limitations cause the least damage. That kid always bats last, too. Charles Schulz's Lucy Van Pelt is the prototype, except you also want a kid who keeps his mouth shut. But in the pros you look for at least passable speed and a strong throwing arm as well as more than average power at the plate. Often you hear the cliché that the right fielder needs a good throwing arm because he has the longest throw, which makes sense only if you're talking about the throw to third.

Walt Armbruster was one of those guys who, on scouting reports, was described as having "a cannon for an arm." However, it was a sixteenth century cannon with similar accuracy. Increasingly, as he worked his way up in the Cleveland organization, it became evident that the flaw was not correctable, much to the despair of various coaches who thought they could solve his problem. Coaches, being like the rest of us, always assume they can solve somebody else's problems. Still, Armbruster hit well enough in the minors, mostly in the .260's with "occasional" power to earn him the distinction of being a marginal prospect. If he could get the power up a bit and the strikeouts down, who knows? After all, there was always the designated hitter slot where his most glaring deficiency would not matter.

"So how come you never learned to throw accurately?" That was almost the first question out of my mouth after I finally tracked him down outside Austin, Texas, where he owned a gas station, served as part-time coach for a small college team, and substituted frequently playing bass in a blue grass trio of some local distinction. It was, perhaps, not the kindest of openers, but it was a question that intrigued me.

He responded with a laugh. "Mister, if I knew how come, I could've fixed it."

Armbruster was a lean, angular man with rugged good looks. He looked for all the world like a refugee out of a grade B western right up to the crooked smile, but straight teeth. Even twenty years away from his brief stint with the Indians he looked fit to play and, as it turned out, he still did with a local recreational team. He not only seemed fit, but happy.

We were sitting in the cramped office at his gas station, a space that looked more like a nesting place for memorabilia from his varied activities than a place of business: pictures, autographed baseballs, plaques, sheet music, the neck piece from an old bass. Most of the time we talked his hands were never still, but played idly, randomly, with this object, or that, often with the neck piece on which he fingered invisible strings, hearing music that eluded me.

He had come out of a small town in West Texas where he had set all kinds of local high school records in football, basketball and baseball. He spent two years playing baseball at the University of Texas, then turned pro and began the slow climb toward that one day in the sunshine of a major league stadium.

"You spent, what, six years in the minors, working your way up in the Cleveland organization."

"Yeah, six years. Was the spring of '79 when I finally went north with the Indians. Spent two weeks with'em, played one game. But you know all that stuff. I mean that's why you're here: because Walt Armbruster played one game in the majors. God, you've got strange interests."

"I admit it. But humor me. Tell me about it. Did you ever think you wouldn't make it at all? And what was it like to have it over so fast after all those years?"

Sure, I knew "all that stuff," all the details of his career at least on the surface. I had pored over the sports pages of the *Plain Dealer*, had read the Indians' annual media guide for the years he was in the organization, knew all the puffery around his career, and the bald, plain facts of the statistics. I knew also we were talking about the Indians of the darker years. They had come off a 69-90 season in '78 with an outfield of Jim Norris, Rick Manning and Johnny Grubb who had managed nineteen home runs among them. Things would be better in 1979. Grubb was gone and they had brought in Bobby Bonds (his fifth team in five years and on to a sixth after that season) who hit twenty-five dingers on his own. So even the illusion that an outfielder had power was appealing. And Armbruster made the team that spring mostly because of an injury to one of the regular outfield-ers—and an empty cupboard in the dreaded designated hitter de-partment.

To be sure he had had "a good spring" and the *Plain Dealer* even suggested early on that he gave evidence "of filling a real need in the Indians' arsenal." That evidence earned him two weeks of bench-sitting and, toward the end of that fortnight, a start as DH against the Yankees. He went 0 for 4 with two strikeouts. The most notable thing about the day, however, is that, for reasons which are unclear even after a careful reading of manager Jeff Torborg's post-game comments, Armbruster played right field in the top of the ninth. On a double down the line by Chris Chambliss, Willie Randolph came all the way around from first. He might have scored anyway, but it was made certain by the fact that Armbruster's throw, all the way on the fly from the right field corner in Municipal Stadium neatly bisected the third base line and surprised a customer in the twenty-third row. With a nod to the player's good looks, the beat writer for the *New York Times* called it "high, wide and hand-some."

Two days later Armbruster was back in the minors and two months later he was released, not so much for that one errant throw as for the fact it epitomized his inability to show any pro-gress toward "harnessing his talent," perhaps an apt comment for someone of his background.

So I knew all that and the knowing of it probably ex-plains, though it may not excuse, the particular edge to my questions. Despite his appearance and his general affability, I will admit to not particularly liking him. Was it the apparent ease with which he accepted his failure? Because that is how I regarded him: somehow I was less interested in knowing how he felt about that day, about sharing whatever particular sense of magic there might have been, than I was in knowing why and how he had failed. And in letting him know, subtly of course, that he was a failure.

"I probably knew by the end of my third year that my chances were iffy at best. I listened hard to all the instruction and practiced all the suggestions this or that coach made, but somehow I wasn't putting it together. Oh, I had spells where I showed improvement, at least in practice, but I always reverted to the error of my ways. I was kind of like one of those pitchers who shows great control in the bullpen and lose it all once they face a batter. I suppose, despite my apparent effort, my mind was elsewhere, thinking about other things."

"What other things?"

"Music, for one." He picked up the neck piece of the old bass and fingered it as if it had strings, as if the whole instrument were there. "I'll betcha one thing you didn't know. I wanted to be a music major in college."

"No, you're right. I didn't know that. But you weren't, you were some kind of general studies major."

"Yeah, that's what they called it. Or jock major as most of the other students called it. The coach advised me against music because of the practice time. So I never even tried the audition that was required. And there were other pressures too."

"Like?"

He shrugged. "Other pressures. But we were talking about the things that were on my mind when I was playing in the minors."

"What else beside the music?"

"More music. By then I was already playing a lot around here in the off-season, having a good time doing it. And there was this soprano with one of the groups I played with."

"*Cherchez la femme?*"

125

"No, actually her name was…is Brenda." He laughed at his own joke.

"But you stuck at the game, at least until you had the one shot."

"Yeah. I still liked playing ball, still do, and I wasn't quite ready to settle down. I mean I knew that I wasn't about to become a recording star either. Between playing bass and playing baseball, I figured I might as well stick with the game for a while. And there was Pop."

Your Dad?"

"Yeah. He had been a ballplayer too, a pretty good one, better than me. He could hit for average and the cut-off man. He played in the minors a coupla years. With the Cardinals. Then the war came, he got drafted, and that was that."

"He didn't try to come back after the war?"

He paused, reached for a small picture frame on his desk, looked at it wistfully and then without a word passed it to me. The frame contained a photograph of an old man standing by a battered snow fence. The face was weathered, the features sharp and distinctive, chiseled, the still abundant hair white. The man wasn't looking at the camera, but off somewhere like he didn't want to meet the camera's eye—or the photographer's. He had one arm. Finally, in a low voice, Armbruster said, "There was only one Pete Gray. It wasn't Pop."

"War injury?"

"Yeah. Omaha Beach."

"So you stuck at it because of him?"

"Why not? He had it tough after the war. One-armed farmers in West Texas aren't big either. But he stuck at it, had the good luck to meet Mom who was a school teacher who respected grit. Which he had a lot of. And things got better after that. I think the best was watching me play sports. Playing was also a habit with me. I mean I had been playing since I was knee-high. It was something I did when the season rolled around."

"It happened every spring, eh?"

"Yeah, something like that."

126

"So tell me about *the* day."

"What's to tell. An ofer at the plate and in the field I made somebody's day in the twenty-third row."

"But wasn't there a feeling, an excitement, about actually playing in a major league game?"

"Except for the last inning, I wasn't playing, I was only hitting. Isn't the same thing. You'd think a galoot like me would fit right in as a DH, but I never did like it. There's a rhythm to playing baseball, like in music: running on and off the field, tossing warm-ups between innings, making adjustments in the field, pounding the glove. Just walking up to the plate every two or three innings and sitting on your duff in the dugout in between doesn't do it. It's like a cymbal player in an orchestra hanging out in the dressing room and then coming on stage at the end of a movement, banging the things together then going back to the dressing room till the next movement was ending. I got a feeling Torborg thought that too, though maybe he wouldn't use a music metaphor. Probably he already knew he was going to cut me so he put me in the field that last inning so I could say I had actually *played* in a major league game."

"Did it make a difference?"

He swung back and forth in his swivel chair a couple of times, then with a half-smile, replied, "Made it more memorable. Hell, that ball went into the twenty-third row. On the fly. Probably a team record."

"Then it was over."

"Yeah, back to the minors. Should've quit right then, but hey, Willie Mays didn't quit when he should've." He laughed and looked away. Was there regret here, some sorrow, a sense of failure? What did I want him to say? "Even thought about trying to hook on with some other organization. Maybe these days I might've tried one of those independent league teams. Like I said playing was a habit. It was something I did. Still do, but it's simply a diversion, exercise, now. But hell, I had known for two-three years that this wasn't my future, that this wasn't really what I wanted."

"What did you want?"

127

Silence, broken only by the squeak of his chair as he swung back and forth again. He seemed to be groping, not for words, but an idea. "To get it over with?"

"What?"

He drummed his fingers on the desk, as if what he really meant was getting the conversation over with, getting rid of this guy who had barged in on him and disrupted something important. Now I wanted to laugh. What indeed? He wasn't any Bill Branch with big fish to fry: he was a glorified gas jockey who played as a pinch hit sideman for local bands.

Finally he spoke. "The dream. I wanted out of it and into real life, however commonplace that might be."

He has that right, I thought to myself. Dickinson writes, "To flee from memory / Had we the Wings / Many would fly…." And from youthful dreams as well once they have grown brittle. Perhaps also from the memory of those dreams, a proposition which raised some questions about my little enterprise. I asked myself again what I was doing, and why and how I was doing it. And why did I react the way I did to some of these guys? What was I blaming them for? Armbruster came awfully close to saying what had been niggling at me. Was this project simply a way of getting me finally and absolutely out of my dream and into real life?

"So did you make it?"

"Yes, I did. I married Brenda, bought this place, had a family. And things are all right. All right."

"So, no regrets."

"Back home, Bildaw, where I'm sure you've never visited, there's still a welcome sign at the edge of town that says 'Bildaw (unincorporated): the home of Walt Armbruster, greatest three sport athlete in Crane County history and future major leaguer.'" He smiled, "It's a bit faded, of course, but there it stands."

"Hasn't anybody thought of taking it down? or at least, editing it?"

128

"Well, nothing much has happened there since. I suppose they could add a p.s., 'He didn't make it.' But Pop likes it the way it is. I guess it reminds him of the days of hope."

"And there's no hope now?"

"Not for that dream. I gave it up a long time ago, and it didn't cost me all that much. I mean," he made a sweeping gesture which took in the office and all its accumulation, "when you got all this, what's to regret." He laughed, but it ended abruptly as his gaze fell again on the photograph of his father. "Pop took it harder than me. I think maybe he thought if I made it big it would set everything right again, like having his arm back." He paused, took a deep breath, and with a surprising sadness, added, "Funny, a gritty old farmer with one arm and a son with too much arm to control. Sorry, Pop."

Augustine wrote: "If an instant of time be conceived, which cannot be divided into the smallest particles of moments, that alone is it, which may be called present. Which yet flies with such speed from future to past, as not to be lengthened out with the least stay. For if it be, it is divided into past and future. The present hath no space." But as human beings we live in that fleeting moment. At times we may cling to the present, but such times are rare, for the present can seldom fulfill our desires— it is too fleeting, time present too swiftly becomes time past and we cannot hope toward the past.

Our fate is ever to seek some compensation and consolation either in memory or in dreams. If we turn to memory, however, we are quickly disappointed. Images of the past are too frail to bear the burden, for they are but images—the past itself is gone, beyond hope. In our youth, we have too little past to sustain even the frailest images and in later years our pursuit of happy memories too often costs us the recurrent pricks of remembered sorrows. Of course, we can invent a past and some of us do, but therein lies madness. The idea that we can rewrite the past, our own, our people's, our nation's, in terms of the kind of future we want to have—an idea which some people seriously advocate-- is exquisite insanity.

Nostalgia is not an effort to rediscover the past, but to populate memory with pleasant images, to remember only the good things, and so nostalgia too is delusion. Like all delusions it can produce only false joy. The passion for tracing our roots also offers only spare consolation for present uncertainties, for it possesses the same dangers as searching our own pasts, the dangers of unpleasant discoveries. I remember once when I was in high school getting all excited about looking into my ancestry, probably as a result of some social studies assignment. My father said to me, "Don't bother. You won't like what you find." But even if a search produces heroes and heroines, those images remain remote and can provide little sustenance, little real sub-stance.

Thus we try to borrow happiness from futurity. Images of the future, however, are only tentative: they are hopes, or fears, since the future is not yet. And the future too has its limits. If we are persons of courage and talent we can dream that, through some vigorous assertion of our abilities, we may fulfill our best hopes. If we lack courage or talent we still too readily dream that somehow all our happy expectations will come to be in spite of our fears. In either case our future as we conceive it has limits which our imagination dreads to approach, but which we must admit are not far distant. Our lives remain brief and fragile.

The felt awareness of our own temporality comes to each of us, though at different times and different seasons. Once it comes it can threaten our sense of reality and of our own significance. That awareness initiates many of our inner anxieties, as well as our public actions, creative and stupid, noble and pite-ous.

The awareness of temporality emerges in the frightening intuition that we are no longer a ""promising young man or woman". One day we suddenly realize that we can no longer measure our significance in terms of our potential, the golden realm of possibilities in which great achievements and memora-ble deeds await our enactment. Actuality must now dominate our self-assessment. Unwillingly, we are fixed in the fleeting present. Shocked we recognize that the significance of our life is limited to what we have already become, and to our past, or to what we imagine our past to have been. The passage of time closes off the future, restricts possibility to the present. It is the "pile of years" which tempts us to re-envision the past.

Perhaps that is why we sometimes cling to golden mo-ments and wish that those moments might never end. Perhaps that is why we cry into the darkness "I wish we were still play-ing. I don't want to quit. I don't want this to come to an end."

Most of us do not have just a single dream; most of us do not finally define our entire lives in terms of one potentiality. We have several. We live. We grow. We move from one dream to

131

another; we envision new horizons and new possibilities. But the passage of time relentlessly, inevitably, constricts. The new horizons disappear; the new possibilities diminish. The mediocrity and the frustrations of the present, constantly relieved by the magic of future hopes, as constantly reassert themselves.

"These days have no true being," Augustine said. "They are gone almost before they arrive; and when they come they cannot continue; they press upon one another, they follow the one the other, and cannot check themselves in their course. Of the past nothing is called back again; what is yet to be expected is something which will pass away again; it is not as yet possessed, while as yet it has not arrived; it cannot be kept when once it has arrived."

Yet how we will prance and preen, dreaming dreams. We imagine that our pride is exaltedness, that our curiosity is a desire for knowledge, that our ignorance is simplicity, that our sloth is rest, that our luxury is abundance, and that our prodigality is liberality. But none of our imagined futures, none of our potential careers, gives us the new life which we seek: the new life which will give our existence a permanence and significance. We are mortal and we cannot give ourselves immortality. We have finally to look to our present, fully and realistically, and to accept it as both ordinary and fleeting. From this abyss we cry, "Out of the depths have I cried unto thee, O Lord. Lord, hear my voice. ." (Psalm 130: 1-2)

A Dream Ends

As I consider again the ex-players with whom I spoke, I ask myself what I have learned—about them and about myself.

I had always told myself that I gave up playing baseball relatively painlessly. After a little thrashing about and a few moments of posturing, I shrugged my shoulders and went on. But, perhaps for that reason, I never gave up loving the game itself, and I have continued to find in it joys and sorrows, tranquility and excitement, and the makings of prose and poetry. If I haven't had a "life in baseball" I have had a life around it, using the skills of observation and writing I do have and my appreciation for the baseball skills which I did not have in sufficient abundance. That's what I've always told myself.

I recall going to a game in old Memorial Stadium in Baltimore a year or so before they moved to Camden Yards. I had hardly seated myself when I noticed a gaggle of people gathering down the right field line. There were fifty of them: tall and short, fat and thin, more fat than thin. The disembodied voice of the public address announcer, Rex Barney, the ex-Dodger pitcher who never quite learned control, proclaimed "Today we welcome the Orioles Fantasy Campers of 1991." Then he announced the names with the appropriate hometown. When his or her name was announced each one ran—no trotted, chugged, lumbered, presumed to run, from the right field corner, down past first base, around home plate, and joined a staggered line in front of the third base dugout. They each, male and female alike, wore an authentic imitation major league uniform with their name on the back. None were young; only one could even evoke the memory of athletic grace that hinted this could be more than a youthful fantasy grown middle-aged. For that one it might indeed have been a dream deferred.

When the last had struggled into place, the voice declared, "And there they are, the Orioles Fantasy Campers of 1991. Give them a hand." And politely the crowd responded with a rippling of applause. Perhaps they deserved it: for having wives or husbands or lovers willing to spend or willing to allow them to spend three thousand dollars to feed a fantasy. Not a bad price, if you come to think of it, especially since they got to keep the uniform.

As I said in the beginning, I have never been tempted to participate in one of those camps, nor have I any interest in the fantasy league business. Give me the real thing, I tell myself. As they made their laborious progress, however, it occurred to me that the scene might be symbolic of the differences between my memory and the reality of my past. I have a real past in baseball, but truth to tell, imagination may control my mental tango. And maybe I really played like those fifty fantasizers looked. No, that's overly harsh. I was almost "good enough to dream," close enough that no one could laugh at me. I tell myself.

I have wondered sometimes what it would have been like to play one game as a professional: not one game as a major leaguer, but as a professional in the lowest rung of the minor leagues. To know that somebody thought I had enough ability to take at least a semi-serious look at, to be able to test myself against other bright-eyed dreamers. Maybe it's better the way it was. Maybe it's better to see the dream for what it was, a childish fantasy, than to let it take on too much of the illusion of reality, to have too much flesh and bone, and so have it hurt too much when it ends.

I set forth innocently, or perhaps naively is a better word, thinking I had only the curiosity of the observer—an informed observer, of course—motivating me. In the end I was led back to Bouton's statement that you spend your whole life holding onto a baseball, then one day you realize it's the ball that's holding you. Baseball is about remembering, maybe that's why it has such a grip on the heart and mind. To borrow again from Dickinson: "No Passenger was known to flee— / That lodged a night in memory— / That wily—subterranean Inn / Contrives that none go out again."

For someone so fond of quoting Emily Dickinson, a habit I acquired from my American lit prof in college and which amuses my social scientist wife, I should have known better: "Through these old Grounds of memory, / The sauntering alone / Is a divine intemperance / A prudent man would shun."

I could piously or pompously say I know myself better now, but am I any more comfortable with that knowledge? Have "I achieved any meaningful integration of my past and present and potential future selves?" Not likely: life is not like that. For the most part we try to live one place or the other though the past always lurks there ready to rise up on us unbidden, unless it's the past in which we're trying to live. Then we're just treading water.

And what of my Dream Team? What can I say of them? In an odd way I find that three of them are mostly living for and in the future: Campanella in his hopes for his grandson, Ortiz in his hopes that one day he will again see his sons and know them, and Branch with that drive to excel and to store away the past. Three others are bound to the present infinitive: Cartwright wallowing in the present like a hippo, Patch in his comfortable sense of being in the right place, and Bush living off his state-sponsored "retirement" plan. Schmitt nurses still the frustrations of the past, gnaws at them like a dog at a bone. Armbruster, more quietly, yet no less sorrowfully tends the sense of having failed his father. But all of them have reached some kind of truce at least with their pasts.

And then there was Danny Miller. I had imagined various things I might say of him. I retain a vivid memory of my last sight of him ambling out of Henty's bar in that small California town and, most of all, the bartender's words to me after Danny had left. Not just the words, but the way the bartender said them, the tone of his voice: "Used to be? No, he mostly talks about how things are going to be when his arm comes around." I have gone over the notes from my conversation with Danny time and again and always I I come to and dwell on that one passage, something I wrote even before I had talked with the bartender: "Do we always know when to let go of a dream? Do we know how?"

Now I know that Danny Miller did not.

On an early April morning he stood on the home field of Stanford University. He looped his fingers through the wire mesh of the backstop and leaned into it, his forehead pressing against the early morning cool of the metal. The grass glistened in the beginnings of the first sunny day after a week of gray rain, the abundant green contrasting with the muddy brown of the base paths. A day of sun would mute the contrast, evaporating the glitter into the spring air and drying the infield to a dusty tan. At some magic moment boys would suddenly appear to unlimber their dreams in hopes of a game, in the promise of the game.

But Danny was not watching the coming of the new day. Rather he saw yesterday and yesterday and yesterday crowding past in slow, yet antic profusion, descending by fits and starts to this moment, this hour, this April morn. All the yesterdays save one tangled together in some dark and ominous pattern. Only the shining days, when his lifelong dream verged on reality, were bright and unsullied. I would have called it memory, but for Danny it was still the dream, the dream he had never let go of, could never let go of, because it was the very heart of him.

Slowly he walked to the middle of the diamond. He sat down on the mound, for him the hill of glory. In his right hand he held his NCAA plaque and his diploma. In his left hand, his pitching hand, he held a gun. Clutching these trophies to his chest, he put the barrel of the gun into his mouth, and blasted the last shreds of the dream into darkness.

I was not there, of course. I know only what I read in the newspaper. I only imagine how it must have been, yet there is something that tells me that is how it was. And I weep for him. Sure it's fine to keep a little boy fantasy around and indulge it every now and then, maybe even every spring, but dreams can kill if they are not folded up and tucked away.

136

April is the cruellest month, breeding
Lilacs out of the dead land, mixing
Memory and desire, stirring
Dull roots with spring rain.
      T. S. Eliot, "The Waste Land"

Can a broken dream really hurt so bad?

Other Stories

of

The Game

Holding On, Letting Go

"Whatsa matter, Geezer? Those old bones can't take a little ding?"

"Getcher self back to the retirement home."

"Yeah, this isn't an old timers game."

Ed Duncan hardly heard the taunts, the cackle of laughter coming from the Pirates' dugout. Kneeling in the dirt behind home plate he concentrated on wishing away the pain in his right hand, stinging from the wild back swing of yet another young phenom who hadn't learned to hit, probably never would. "Sweet Jesus," he muttered to himself, "how many times is this?"

No way of knowing, not after catching for twenty-five years in high school, the minors, the bigs. You don't count things like that, you endure them and go on. But his gnarled hands, his misshapen fingers, told innumerable stories of foul tips, of pitches in the dirt, of other wild swings. While the phenom sauntered off unconcerned with anything but the fact that the count was now 0-2, Mark Ashford, a good ump, slowly bent down to dust off the plate. Without looking up he said, "You all right, Ed?"

"Yeah, Mark, I'll be okay. Just give me a little time."

"You got it," and with ritual effort Ashford slowly whisked away dirt that wasn't there.

The Cardinals' trainer, Jack Ohan, chugged out of the dugout, followed more slowly by the manager, Jim Rawley. Duncan rose to his feet and automatically held out his hand. Ohan took it gently, cautiously probing. "That hurt?"

141

"Hell yes, it hurts. That sucker has one of those maple bats."

"Is it broken, Jack?" Rawley, an ex-catcher himself, studied Duncan's hand like it was a topographical map.

"Could be. We'd better do x-rays."

"You're coming out, Ed."

"The hell I am. It isn't broken."

Rawley shook his head slowly. "You haven't changed in twenty years."

Duncan forced a smile, "You wouldn't want me to."

"You're right about that."

They had a history, a long history, all the way back to Duncan's first season with the Cubs. Rawley was the starter, a veteran almost as battered then as Duncan was now, but knowing too much to give way to a raw rookie, no matter how brash. A year later, when yet another rebuilding effort began, their roles were reversed. Then Rawley became a coach and started off on the road that had led to two stints as a manager, with the Reds and the Rockies, before coming to the Cardinals two years ago. Their roads had crossed a couple of times. Rawley was a coach with Atlanta during Duncan's brief stay there, and Duncan was playing with the Reds when Rawley arrived in Cincinnati, was still there when he moved on. After Rawley got the Cardinals job he told the GM, "You've loaded me up with a lot of good, young arms. I don't want a kid catching them. Get me Ed Duncan."

"Can you throw?"

"Gimme a ball, Mark." Ashford carefully handed him one. Duncan gripped it, briefly averting his face so neither Rawley nor Ohan could see the wince, called out to his second baseman and fired a low bullet right on the bag. Nonchalantly he picked up his mask and started putting it back on. "Yeah, I can throw."

Rawley looked at Ohan, shrugged, and they returned to the dugout.

"Okay, hotshot," Duncan said to the batter, "get back in there and see if you can't do it right this time." He called for a curve and chuckled to himself when it nipped the outside corner for a called third strike. He rolled the ball back to the mound and said to the ump, "See you next inning, Mark."

"Hope so."

He sat at the end of the bench away from Rawley, away from Ohan. He folded his arms so his right hand was nestled under his left arm pit, but without any pressure on it. It hurt, hurt bad, but he didn't want them asking about it, looking at it. He knew he wouldn't say it didn't hurt, but he also knew he was going to finish the game. Rick Higgins, the rookie right hander, was in a groove and he wanted to keep him there. That was his job, a job he had grown into over the years. It was why he had stayed in the big leagues, why Rawley had traded for him. The game was too close, the race was too close, to risk giving way to Seth Miller, the back-up. Miller was okay, a strong arm, probably as good a hitter as Duncan, at least now, but better off catching the veteran pitchers who could call their own games.

And he didn't know how many more games he had left.

"Did I wake you, hon?"

"No, not really. I was just between here and there." The voice was low, languid. He could imagine her stretching her free arm toward the ceiling, palm upward, maybe moving it slightly to let the ring catch the light from the bedside lamp, watching the twinkling star. She still played with it that way after all these years. It pleased him though sometimes he wondered whether she was asking ""Should I or shouldn't I?"

"I'll be home soon."

"End of another road trip."

"Yeah. Almost another season, too."

"And another and another and another...."

The old song, the song that always brought silence between them. Sometimes pained, sometimes just embarrassed, but always silence till one or the other of them, usually Cindi, found a way out of it. Most of the time by denying it because behind it there was the abiding, accusing pain: where were you when I needed you most?

Working, playing ball, because where else could he make the kind of money they needed for Billy's medical expenses. Or was it where else could he run from the dailiness of watching his only child waste and die? Sure he was there all that dark, hard winter, but dammit playing baseball isn't like shop keeping or going to the office. You had to keep in shape. It was year round. It was road work. You had to be away to do it. Had to be? Silence and behind the silence....

And afterwards? Should he have quit then? Could he have quit? How? It was what he did, who he was, for as long as he could remember. Even before he had met Cindi, before there was a Billy. Now there wasn't a Billy any more. And sometimes, in the silences, he wasn't sure she was there—or was it he who was not there.

"You all right, Ed?"

"Huh?"

"I said you all right? Chrissake you got tears in your eyes. Your hand hurt that much?"

It was Ohan. Like a flipping nursemaid hovering around her charges, worrying about every nick and bruise. One of the college-educated types called him "Amah," whatever that meant. "Yeah, I'm all right. I was just getting sentimental about how nice it is to have a coupla sweet babysitters like you and Jim to look after me."

"Ed," Rawley called from the other end of the dugout, "you goin' back out there? The inning's over."

Duncan grabbed his mask and clambered up the steps.

Two innings to go. Higgins was still throwing strong and easy, but it was only a one run lead and Rawley was sure to bring in Schmidt, the closer, for the ninth. That was the new book. Used to be that you'd let the starter try to finish it then bring in the closer if he got into trouble, but nowadays that was rare, particularly with a one run lead, particularly with a rookie. There was good sense to it, but he had always enjoyed the special tension involved in going out for the last inning, wondering if he could nurse the starter through one more round, believing

144

that he could. No way he could have nursed Billy through his last inning, no sense thinking anything else. It was afterwards that was the problem for him, his real failure.

"Focus, Duncan, focus," he said fiercely to himself. That was real life, this is a game, and you can't mix them up. Play the game. This you can do. Two more innings.

He fired the last warm-up down to second, then walked to the mound. "Okay, Rick, you and me are going to play some catch. Stay loose. Sure as hell, Rawley will have Schmidt do the ninth, so don't worry about saving anything." He jogged back to the plate, pulling his mask on, the old-fashioned kind, not the hockey-style that was all the rage. He squatted.

"How's the hand, Ed?"

"It'll last two more innings, Mark. That's all I need."

On a one-two count the first batter lofted a pop-up to third. One down. The next batter, the seven hole man, dropped a flare over second base. "A pooch hit, Rick, not your fault. Pure luck. Just keep on doing what you're doing." The opposing catcher hit two fouls, took a ball, then dribbled one toward third. Higgins was off the mound like a shot.

"First base, Rick, first base," Duncan called, and the rookie threw the batter out. "Way to go, Rick."

Rawley came out of the dugout and Duncan joined him half-way to the mound. "How's he doing, Ed?"

"He's fine. As good as anyone you can bring in except Schmidt."

"They'll pinch-hit Cooper."

"Down and away, down and away, then on the fists."

"You hear that, Higgins?"

"I just do what Ed tells me."

"Can't do any better. Okay get him through it, Ed."

Cooper was a lean left-hander with a short stroke, a spray hitter with limited power, but always putting the ball in play. Higgins went up 0-1 with a fast ball on the outside corner. The next pitch was a back door slider. Cooper didn't bite and it missed the corner, then he fouled off a fast ball inside. With the count 1-2 he slapped another slider just over the shortstop's head.

145

"Damn," Duncan said and moved forward to guard the plate. The man at second, Gonzalez, had above average speed and was a smart, aggressive runner. He'd be coming all the way.

The left fielder, Willie Brown, moved quickly in and was on the ball and throwing as Gonzalez rounded third and headed home. Ball and runner converged. There was only one way to the plate and that was straight through. Duncan felt the collision in every bone in his body. His right hand clutching the ball flamed in pain.

"Was he out?"

"Yeah."

"I held onto the ball, then."

"Held on? Thought we'd have to saw yer hand off to get it away from you?"

"Did we win?"

"Yeah. Schmidt shut'em down in the ninth."

With effort Duncan raised his head to look around the room. Spare, antiseptic, like all hospital rooms. He'd seen a few over the years, but he'd never just woke up in one not knowing how he'd gotten there. Didn't make him like the place any better. Wouldn't have let them put him there if he'd had any choice. Ever since Billy died he avoided hospitals.

"So what's the damage?"

Rawley sat easily in the usual institutional chair, looking like a chaplain. Duncan suspected his manager half-wished he were, that his gruffness was a cover.

"Concussion, a few broken bones. They want to keep you in a day or so to check on internal injuries. It was a hell of a collision, haven't seen any better. Replays showed Gonzalez gave you a pretty good forearm to the head."

"Son of a bitch!"

"If it's any consolation, his arm's broken and he may have torn his acl."

"And it's only a game."

'It's your last one for the year."

"I already knew that."

146

Rawley looked at him, his brows arched, slowly shaking his head. "Your hand was already broken, wasn't it?"

"Yeah."

Rawley leaned forward, hands clasped between his knees. "You are a geezer, a throwback. You should've said something."

"Why? You saw me throw. I held on to the ball. We won the game."

Rawley stood up, a resigned smile on his face. "Well, got to be going. One more game here, then home for the wrap-up. If they let you out in time to make the team flight, fine, but don't worry about it. Don't push, no point to it. You won't be lonely. Cindi's on the way."

"Here?"

"Yeah. She was watching on TV. Called me from Lambert before I left the park. She was on stand-by for a flight. Don't know whether she'll make it before they shut up for the night, but I wouldn't be surprised."

"Me neither. Bless her heart."

"You got a good one, Ed."

"I finally learned that."

"See ya, Ed."

"Yeah. We can win this thing."

"Win it for the Geezer, huh?" They laughed together, then Rawley walked briskly from the room. Duncan waited until he was sure his manager had really gone before he pressed the call button and asked the nurse for a painkiller.

The nurse dimmed the lights when she brought the pills. In the dimness that remained he dozed fitfully. Images of the past washed over him, whether memories or dreams he did not know. So when he saw the silhouette in the doorway—a tall, lean feminine form, long hair down to the shoulders, the right hand raised to touch the door frame, hesitant—he wasn't sure whether she was dream or reality.

"Ed? Are you okay."

"Yeah, Cindi. Ready to tango."

147

She moved across the room and as she did her features emerged into reality. She sat in the chair next to the bed and placed her right hand lightly on his. "Not quite. I talked to the nurse. She told me the particulars. I saw it happen. On TV."

"Yeah, Rawley told me. I'm glad you came."

"It was awful. They kept replaying it. I couldn't bear it, but I couldn't stop watching. Finally I just ran out of the room, got some things together and went to the airport. I was scared." She looked away. "Again. But you're okay?"

"I'll be fine. Better than ever. Smarter, too. I'm coming home."

"Yes. Jim told me you were finished for the season."

"Not the season, Cindi. I'm coming home. I'm retiring."

Something like hope and something like disbelief played in her hazel eyes. Carefully, fearfully she spoke. "You're going to be fine. When you feel better. When spring...."

He turned his hand to hold hers. "I can let go of the ball now."

The Secret of Walter Johnson's Balls

I promised never to reveal her name. She's gone now, so perhaps it doesn't matter, but I made the promise and I will keep it. I need to tell the story, however, so I will invent a name. I need to tell the story because of how she died, not so that I can understand it or anyone else can understand it, but just to say it, say how it was. I will call her Maribeth.

For as long as I had known her she had been promiscuously religious. She was variously, consecutively and occasionally simultaneously a Free Will Baptist, a Nazarene, a Roman Catholic, a Methodist, a Quaker, a Christian Reformed, a Unitarian, a Presbyterian, and a Wisconsin Synod Lutheran. All that in nine years.

I know all this because, though we never discussed religion, she talked about it all the time. I listened and heard what amounted to a tourist's view of these various denominations. She did not so much join all these churches as pass through them.

She was not a seeker, but a finder. She would wander into a church and find on that day something which particularly appealed to her or suited her at the moment. It might be the singing of the choir or the fact that there was no music. It might be the preacher's well-tempered baritone voice rolling out polysyllables or the pleasantly distant sound of something being said by rote. None of the reasons had much to do with God. Not that she didn't believe in God, but since most all the churches did too that wasn't really an issue. That does explain, however, why her briefest passage was with the Unitarians since at the particular place she attended there did seem to be some question, not so much about the usefulness of having a god, but about the probability of there being one in spite of the utility. She lasted one and a half Sundays there and talked to me about it for a year.

That meant of course that the priest, pastor, minister, elder, what have you, never really had the opportunity to nurture her in the particular faith. She might plunge right into the lady's guild or the faithful singles group or the softball team, but she wasn't a candidate for inquirers' class since she wasn't so much inquiring as she was grabbing onto something that appealed to her at the moment. Which perhaps was just as well, for it spared the clergy the inevitable disappointment of losing her and thereby the pang of feeling that they had somehow failed in their vocation.

The peripatetic quality of her religious life changed when she became a full-fledged member of the New Age Temple of the Presidentially Autographed Baseballs. This had not started as a church at all, but as a special interest group within the St. Louis regional chapter of the Society for American Baseball Research. The initial purpose had been to investigate the disappearance from the Hall of Fame in Cooperstown of five baseballs bearing the autographs of William Howard Taft, Woodrow Wilson, Warren Harding, Calvin Coolidge, and Herbert Hoover respectively. They had been the prized possessions of Walter Johnson, the great pitcher and later manager of the Washington Senators. In 1968, twelve years after Johnson's death, his son had donated them to the Hall of Fame. In 1978 Hall officials had had to reveal, with some embarrassment, that in 1973 someone had stolen the balls.

Here was a puzzle and one that drew the interest of a small group of researchers for several years. But the failure to make any discoveries that threw light on the mystery frayed the spirits and tempers of the group. At that point nagging faith questions began to appear, disagreements arose, schism occurred, and the New Age Temple of the Presidentially Autographed Baseballs emerged. The problems began with a very fundamental question: what were a bunch of mostly middle-aged

150

men doing fretting about the disappearance of five old baseballs? Agreed, they were interesting and, to be sure, valuable pieces of memorabilia, but that's all they were.

"Dead artifacts that don't prove a thing," was how Morley Brown put it. He was the newest addition to the group, a high school civics and drivers ed teacher whose real interest was in identifying all the people who had been in the presidential box on every occasion when a president had attended a baseball game. In a graduate history course which he took at St. Louis U. to keep up his certification he had read something about prosopography. He had had a sudden insight that knowing about the people who surrounded a president when he threw out the first ball at a game would reveal something deep about... well about something. In the teachers' lounge at his school he had been poring over a photograph of Calvin Coolidge wearing an Indian head dress while attending a baseball game when Willard Waters had said, "Hey! You might be interested in this group I belong to. We're trying to figure out who stole Walter Johnson's balls."

Willard was the one who responded to Morley's dismissive remark about artifacts, perhaps feeling aggrieved, even betrayed, by Morley's attitude since he had introduced him to the group. "Hey! These aren't just any artifacts. The Taft ball was the one thrown out at the opener in 1910. Thinka that! That's the first ever presidential opening game throw." Willard said 'Hey!' a lot. He was a one-time bat boy for the Cardinals and a retired army sergeant who was a part-time assistant football, basketball and baseball coach at the school where Morley taught.

"So?" Morley shrugged. "We know Taft was the first president to throw out a ball. We know the date and time and place. We have pictures. We know who caught the ball. We know everybody who was in the box with Taft. The ball itself doesn't prove anything except Taft could write on a curved surface."

"Prove? What's to prove? It's probably worth a couple a hundred thou." Alvin Reese, who would know, made the rejoinder. He was the only real collector in the group, specializing in authentic hats. He ran a baseball card shop, having previously

151

run a hot tub store, before that a tanning salon, and before that a waterbed outlet. He was a hardcore entrepreneur, having ridden the waves of each successive rage and selling out just over the crest of the wave to some bright-eyed naif who would end up in the trough. Rumor was he was about to sell the card shop and those that knew him were speculating about his next move.

"It's worth nothing." Morley did have an annoying smugness about him. "It's stolen goods. It belongs to the Hall and if it ever turns up it goes back there. They'll pat you on the head and maybe give you a lifetime pass. What's that worth?"

I know all this because I was there, being one of the original members of the special interest group. Having said something about the others, I should say something about myself. I'm in my thirties, a dropout from an MA program in English Lit and now a hair-dresser by trade. That's how I met Maribeth: she said that she had never had a perfect page-boy until I did her hair when she came into the place where I was working. When I scraped together enough money to open my own shop with three employees, Cardinal Cut'N'Curl, she became a steady customer. We talked a lot in the shop and also sometimes afterwards we'd go out for dinner, though she always insisted on paying for her own meal despite my efforts to pick up the tab.

She was medium height, slender, though not everybody could tell that because she liked to wear baggy sweaters and loose-fitting jumpers. I knew from the times she let me hold her. She had dark silken hair that she always wore in a page-boy cut. It made her look girlish. I have no idea how old she was, she never told me, though I had known her for nine years and she wasn't a teenager when I met her. Her eyes were... her eyes were cerulean blue. I always wanted to say that, to write that out, because that is just what flashed through my head the first time she looked at me. And there always was about her the faint scent of lilacs.

Maribeth grew up in Alexandria, Virginia, raised by her grandparents. She was the only child of her father's disastrous second marriage to a much younger woman. The first marriage too had ended in an agony of suffering after the only child, a son, had died in the Korean War. Her mother had abandoned them when she was one, running off to California with a tennis pro, and Maribeth had never heard from her again. Her father died of a heart attack when she was two. So "Grandy" and "Gransy", her names for them, had raised her. They lived into their nineties, hale and hearty to the end, both dying within a year of one another when she was a senior in college. She once told me, "I was terribly spoiled. Grandy would do anything for me."

I shared some of Morley's skepticism about the value of artifacts, but I am a puzzle and mystery nut. Ever since I had heard about the disappearance of the five presidentially auto-graphed baseballs I had been intrigued. The link with Walter Johnson cemented my interest since he is my specialty. For years now I have been writing an epic poem on his career and have reached the twelfth canto. In any case a conversation between Willard and myself at a SABR regional meeting in St. Louis had actually led to the development of the special interest group.

But I did not bring Maribeth to the first meeting at which she appeared. Of course I knew her, knew her well. In fact I loved her, but it had not occurred to me that she would be interested in the whereabouts of Walter Johnson's balls. Despite the changes that had taken place in the nature of the group as a result of the crisis to which I have referred, the mystery of the theft was still the fundamental question for me. I had mentioned it a couple of times to her, but she always seemed to shrug it off.

And I was right. She was not interested in where the balls were; she didn't have to be. I was as surprised as everyone else when she sauntered into the meeting of the group on April 14, 1990, as puzzled as everyone else to see her tossing an old, age-darkened baseball easily from one hand to the other as she walked, and as stunned as everyone else when we discovered what ball it was.

But that happened later, after the months of struggle, of discussion, of argument. By that time Morley was long gone, even though he had precipitated the crisis by his assertion that the Taft ball, or any of the others from the Johnson collection, was worth nothing. Of course he was right, right in the sense that if you had one of them you couldn't sell it, at least openly, honestly. You had to be one of those people who have a private collection kept under lock-and-key. In the dark of night you bolt the doors, pull the shades, then open the secret treasure trove and slaver over the things that are yours, yours, yours alone.

All along we had figured that's what had happened to Johnson's balls: a collector or an unscrupulous dealer had stolen them and now they were tucked away in some darkly paneled room to satisfy the lusts of one man. The question was only whether the collector was somebody well known to other baseball memorabilia types who bought and sold and showed as avidly as they, but who kept a secret cabinet, or else was an unknown, someone whose whole collection was a mystery, a black hole into which not only the Johnson balls, but other artifacts, had disappeared.

Alvin, our expert on the mentality of the collector, favored the first thesis. "I know some guys who might do that." He had remarked that early on, before the crisis. What Morley had done, what brought on the crisis, was to bring us face to face with the existential question: What would we do, each of us individually, if by some chance one or another or all of Walter Johnson's presidentially autographed balls fell into our hands?

We were face to face with it, but we averted our eyes, tried to sidle around it, pretending we were still talking about the psychology of the presumed perpetrator of the theft. But that only got us in deeper, for it allowed us to peel off layers of our own inhibitions while telling ourselves we were analyzing someone else. After about three meetings doing this, or rather listening to the rest of us do this, Morley bailed out. "What a bunch of crap," he said in his usual delicate manner. "What difference does it make what the guy was or is thinking? What difference does it even make *who* it was?"

He got up from his chair. We had arranged them in a perfect circle right in the middle of the fellowship hall of King Charles the Martyr Episcopal Church out in Clayton where we

had taken to having our meetings. I was an occasional parish-
ioner there and the rector was an ex-major leaguer: he'd pitched
two years for the Cardinals before he blew out his shoulder and
went to seminary. He didn't come to our meetings, but he was
very supportive. So Morley got up from his chair, pushed it out
of the way and started to leave. Then he stopped and looked
back.

"If you dweebs discover that it was somebody who was
sitting in the presidential box when Nixon threw out the first ball
at the Angels' opener in 1973, or better yet if you find out it was
Nixon himself, let me know." And he left.

Nobody spoke for a while. Finally Willard got up and put
Morley's chair back in place, restoring the perfect circle. He returned to his own seat and another silence ensued.

"Hey! Do you suppose that maybe it was Nixon?"

"That's a crazy idea, Willard. Morley was just...just being
Morley." Bob Wadlow spoke without conviction. He was a
pharmacist from Alton. Short (5'2"), fat (190 lbs.), he took a lot
of ribbing because he had the same name as the tallest man who
ever lived, who also came from Alton. He took it well and everybody liked him for it.

"Why crazy?" Willard came back. "It was 1973. Nixon
was having a bad year remember. He mighta done anything."

"Might have and could have are two different things,"
Bob replied precisely. "How could the President of the United
States get himself to Cooperstown, into the museum, steal Wal-
ter Johnson's balls, and get back to Washington without anybody
knowing? Especially Nixon. Jimmy Carter maybe could of, but
Nixon never."

"Hey! I didn't say he done it himself, personally. He
coulda had someone else heist them. One of them plumbers. Or
the CIA."

"Aren't we getting off the point, evading the issue?" John
Pagonas was a tall, lanky quiet guy. He didn't talk much in our
meetings and when he did it was in spurts. We all listened because he made sense, cut through the thickets of our arguments
and set us back on track. We didn't notice his silences until he

155

spoke, because that was the way he was. Also we never got the feeling he wasn't listening to the rest of us and so we appreciated his silences almost as much as we did his conversation.

Easily the most educated and intellectual of the group, John taught history in a community college. An ABD from Minnesota he always said he hadn't finished his degree because he couldn't find a dissertation adviser who would let him write on what he wanted to, the cultural and social history of the old Three I League. "I am sorry, as we all are," (we weren't), "that Morley has left, but we need to focus on his real question. Forget his exit lines, they were mere rhetoric. His real question posed several meetings ago, though not so bluntly as I am about to pose it, is simply this: what would we do, each of us individually, if through some happenstance one or more of Walter Johnson's presidentially autographed balls came into our possession? Would we return it to the Hall of Fame? Or would we keep it in secret? Would we become like this anonymous soul about whom we have been so freely speculating?"

We all gasped and then fell again into an even deeper silence than had followed Morley's departure, marred only by the whir of the refrigerator in the parish hall kitchen. No one was looking at anyone else. Our heads were all bowed as if in prayer. It was eerie, eerie as can be, because we even seemed to be breathing in unison. Then we heard the faint sound of the organ playing in the church, maybe the organist practicing for Sunday, but whoever it was he or she was playing "I sing a song of the saints of God," an old children's hymn that almost got thrown out of the new hymnal because it's theologically incorrect. It was a favorite of mine when I was growing up. In Sunday School whenever the teacher asked what hymns we wanted to sing to fill up time at the end of lessons I always called out, ahead of everybody else, "Number 243". Just like in school music class I always asked for "Red River Valley."

Well, that's not important. What's important is that the organ was playing in the distance and I looked up to see if the others heard and they did and though I was the only quasi-Episcopalian among them they all seemed to know the hymn and we started to sing, almost whispery at first, then finally full voice:

> I sing a song of the saints of God
> > Patient and brave and true,
> Who toiled and fought and lived and died
> > For the Lord they loved and knew.
> And one was a doctor, and one was a queen,
> > And one was a shepherdess on the green:
> They were all of them saints of God and I mean,
> > God helping to be one too.

We sang it through, all three verses, and when we finished we were all standing in our perfect circle and holding hands. There was something powerful and scary happening there. Awkwardly we let go of our neighbors' hands, but stood still in the circle, still in our hearts, and still in our voices.

Finally, Jimmy Longo spoke. He was the youngest of us, a junior at SIU-Edwardsville. He had played ball for Willard in high school and first came with him and kept coming on his own after he had gone to college. He had this thing about the Zen of baseball. "I wanted to say this before, but I couldn't. Morley would have laughed so I couldn't say it. If I got one of those balls I'd keep it, but not just for myself. I would want to show it to you. I would want you to be able to touch it, to hold it, to read the name. I love you guys."

He turned, picked up his chair, and put it back against the wall. Without looking back he left. One by one they all did, putting their chairs away and departing wordlessly, till only John and I were left. He repeated softly the refrain, "..and I mean, God helping to be one too." Then he too left. I stood in the quiet of the fellowship hall thinking about what Jimmy had said. I heard the outside door close behind John. The organ had stopped. At last I picked up my chair, placed it against the wall, turned out the light and went home through the lilac-scented night. Morley's chair stood alone in the middle of the room.

Our meeting times were irregular. Usually we decided at the end of each meeting when we would get together next and I would check with the rector to see if the hall was available. If it wasn't I'd set another date and call around and tell everybody. Obviously we hadn't talked about another meeting. The spooky thing is that two weeks to the day later we all showed up (except Morley) at St. Charles without any of us having talked to one another since that night.

Even spookier, Ted Green, the only regular who hadn't been there, also showed up. Ted had played briefly in the old Negro League just before it folded. When it did he went back to school and got an accounting degree and now did the books for a half dozen area motels. We called him "Stats" because that was his thing.

I asked him the question we were all dying to ask each other: "How did you know there was a meeting?"

He looked a little funny, his eyes narrowed a little bit, and then I realized that he figured we had set the time and hadn't called him. He could be touchy sometimes. So I quick added, "The fact is we forgot to set a time, yet we all just sort of showed up."

Then he really looked funny and stared at each of us in turn. "I just figured it was about time and decided to stop by. I was out getting a six-pack."

"Yeah, but Stats, you live in the city, this is Clayton."

"Well, I was right, wasn't I?"

We had all been right though nobody knew why. I could explain to myself why I had come: I had had a bad day and was looking for something to take my mind off the only thing I was thinking about at the moment. I had been alone in the shop when Maribeth had come for her appointment. I hadn't arranged it that way; it just happened and because it seemed serendipitous, it also seemed so auspicious. When I finished with her hair she stayed in the chair like she didn't want to leave. I was sitting on the floor, cross-legged, leaning against the cabinet where I kept the towels. We were talking, about nothing much, but I was watching her every minute. Couldn't not look at her she was so lovely.

She was saying something about the revolutions of the earth when I interrupted her in mid-sentence: "Maribeth, will you marry me?"

That wasn't the first time I had asked her. As a matter of fact it was the fifth. She'd always said no. Not "I'll think about it" or "Not now," just "No." Yet not just no, no softly, tenderly, even a little sorrowfully. She always stayed away for a few months afterwards, then one day I would come into the shop and find her name down for a 3:30 appointment and she would tell me everything she had done since I saw her last.

But this time she stood up, took me by the hand. I scrambled to my feet expectant. She brushed her lips across the back of my hand. She looked at me and smiled. I could feel a mighty yes well within me, but before it broke I saw her shake her head, heard her whisper "No," and felt her hand withdraw from mine. Then she was gone. I pressed my hands to my face and smelled the sting of lilacs.

So there I was, but I couldn't explain that to all of them and they could give no words to their reasons. We were uncomfortable with that and uncomfortable, not with Stats being there, but with the problem of how to explain what had happened last time and where we were. That problem was more difficult since none of us were entirely sure what had happened.

John was the one who got us off the mark. "Well, Stats, since you couldn't be here last time maybe we should recap things a bit, for your sake. Really for all our sakes, since the meeting was a bit unusual." As John continued to talk we all got chairs from along the wall and placed them in a perfect circle in the middle of the hall. Jimmy put in an extra one.

"As you know we were all a little frustrated by the lack of progress on the problem of the disappearance of the Johnson collection. We were simply going over the same ground again and again, rehashing the same theories with no new evidence. That frustration peaked two weeks ago. Morley, everybody really, got a little upset and he left."

Everybody looked at the empty chair and Stats asked, "Where's Morley?"

"I don't know. Perhaps he didn't *feel* the way you did, the way we all did. Let me be direct. When we broke up last time we had not set another date. I had no idea when, or even if, we would meet again. Tonight I was driving back to school for a concert and without even thinking about it I came here instead." As John was recounting this everybody else was nodding. Without speaking we each acknowledged the force that had drawn us.

"When Morley left I suggested that we all needed to face up to a question which he had really posed some while ago, albeit elliptically, but which we had managed to avoid. Let me repeat what I said: what would we do, each of us individually, if through some happenstance one or all of Walter Johnson's presidentially autographed balls came into our possession? Would we return it to the Hall of Fame? Or would we keep it in secret? Would we become like this anonymous soul about whom we have been so freely speculating?"

John's flawless repetition of the question was like an incantation, a versicle in a great litany. It hung there in the air, anticipating, requiring a response.

"That's easy," Stats said invading the quiet, "I'd keep it. But not just for myself. I'd want you guys to see it, to share it with me."

"I agree," Bob and Willard said almost in unison.

"Me too," Alvin said.

"And me," I added.

"And I," said John.

"Amen," Jimmy concluded.

There was once more a stillness, but a stillness filled with light and silent rhythms.

Willard coughed nervously, then spoke. "Hey! I guess we all made a promise."

"A commitment, I'd say," Bob replied.

"A sacred promise and commitment," Stats added in his rich baritone voice.

"Perhaps that is all we need say tonight," John spoke in his most measured professorial tones. "Shall we meet here again in two weeks?"

"I'll check it with Father Hughes." Then I added, "What about Morley?"

Morley was the first question two weeks later. We set up a chair and he didn't show, but after some debate we decided to keep the chair in the circle. Jimmy clinched it when he said, "I got a feeling, I just got a feeling. I don't know whether he's coming back or it's someone else."

So we kept the empty chair. That was the first of the decisions we made. Not all the others were so easy. We knew without saying it that we were something different from a special interest group of SABR, but we didn't know quite what to call ourselves. It took us three or four meetings to work our way through the questions which hovered in our minds though we avoided talking even thinking about a name until the last.

We agreed we would meet Wednesday evening every two weeks. We agreed that we should have some general order of procedure though with latitude for spontaneity. Stats, John and I formed a committee to develop an outline and we spent one whole meeting hashing over the proposal. What we settled on was for John to open every meeting restating his question. Then we would all say together Jimmy's answer. Then somebody would read from a document, maybe about the theft, maybe some article about one of the five opening games, maybe about the particular president's interest in baseball, and we would all discuss it. There would also be a time for talking about something one guy in particular might have on his mind. We'd always close by singing the hymn.

"Hey! We're startin' to look lika church."

Everybody laughed at that except me. That thought had already occurred to me and I was a little nervous about it. Father Hughes had been very nice about letting us use the hall, hadn't even charged us, but he assumed he was helping out a bunch of baseball mavens, not breeding a cult in his own basement. What would happen if he decided he wanted to drop in on us some

161

night and we were in the middle of our...well our...it was a ritual of sorts. Obviously at some point we were going to have to talk about another place.

Alvin said "If it walks like a duck and quacks like a duck, it must be a duck."

"If it's a church it has to have a name," Stats interjected.

"Hey, how about Seven Guys Looking for Five Balls?"

"No good, Willard," Bob replied, "what if we got new members? We can't be changing the name all the time."

"Well then, what about A Bunch of Guys Looking for Five Balls?"

"You got anything against girls, Willard?" Alvin asked.

"Not at the moment."

That made us all laugh, but it also killed the conversation for a bit. Somehow it seemed to mix the sacred and the profane though we probably wouldn't have put it that way then. It must have been a whole minute we sat there. At first it was a kind of awkward silence, but then it became a stillness, a stillness like after we had first sung the hymn. Again Jimmy resolved the stillness. Looking around the circle at each of us, as if he were reading something in our eyes, he said quietly, but firmly, "The New Age Temple of the Presidentially Autographed Baseballs."

So that's how we got the name.

The day before the next meeting, which would be the first at which we used our new ceremony, Alvin called me all excited. "What time do they unlock the church basement for us?"

"Usually around a half-hour before we start. Why?"

"I got a surprise for everybody, but I want to get it there before anybody else comes. You the first one there most of the time?"

"Yeah. I try to get there ten minutes early just to be sure the place is unlocked and the lights are on. Say, what's this all about?"

"You'll see tomorrow. You'll love it."

I did and so did everybody else. When I got to the hall, Alvin was already there. He had set the eight chairs up in their perfect circle along the edge of a round white rug that was marked like a baseball. It wasn't a new rug so it had yellowed some, there were spots on it and it had a faintly musty smell, but right across the middle of it was a replica of the signature of William Howard Taft!

"Where'd you get this?" I asked in wonder.

"Cincinnati," Alvin answered with his biggest grin. "Had to go over to look at some hats: a 1931 Reds road hat, you know, gray with a red bill, and a Cleveland Spiders hat, but that one's a fake and I told the guy. But he had this hanging on the wall. Told him I'd buy the fake to get it out of circulation if he'd throw in the rug."

So we began the meeting in great style, that momentous meeting in the all too short, sweet, and finally sad history of the New Age Temple of the Presidentially Autographed Baseballs.

Bob had just finished reading aloud the newspaper account of the Washington Senators' opening game on April 14, 1910. William Howard Taft had thrown out the first ball, the first ever presidential opening day first pitch, he had autographed the ball for Walter Johnson, and Johnson had shut out the Philadelphia Athletics 3-0 on one hit. An auspicious beginning.

We heard the door to the hall open and turned to see who it was, all of us assuming it was Morley. It was Maribeth. She sauntered into the room as if she knew she was in the right place. My first thought was that she had completed her passage through Wisconsin Synod Lutheranism and was now coming through the Episcopal Church, though it was odd she hadn't mentioned that to me. But then, I hadn't seen her since that day in the shop when, for the fifth, and as it turned out the last, time I asked her to marry me. Anyway, I thought she must be expecting a meeting of the St. Charles' the Martyr quilters guild or something.

Then I saw she was tossing an old baseball from hand to hand. She hardly watched the ball as she walked, but she never missed it as it arced from left to right and right to left with hypnotic regularity. Wordlessly, she sat down in the empty chair, smiled individually at each of us, then handed the ball to the person on her right, me. I could feel the age of it, almost smell the history of it. Without looking I knew, but I had to look, and looking I saw through the dark patina of age, eighty years to the day, the signature of William Howard Taft.

The others stared at me. When I nodded they all drew in their breath as if to inhale something emanating from the orb I held in my hand as gently as a chalice. I turned it carefully, now touching it only with the tips of my fingers. Then I passed it to "Stats" who was seated to my right. Slowly we passed it around the circle, each person holding it, touching it, sniffing it, reading the name. There was no hurry and while there was anticipation there was no anxiety. Each held it, touched it, sniffed it, read the name as long as he needed. Finally the ball returned to Maribeth and she placed it gently in her lap.

"Where," John, the cool rational one among us, asked, "did you get this?"

"The same place I got the other four," Maribeth replied in a low, casual voice.

At which I thought Alvin was having a stroke. He gurgled, he strangled, his face reddened before he finally croaked, "A million dollars, easy, a million...Jeez, at least a million."

"A pat on the head and a free pass to Cooperstown, nothing more." I spoke, but they were Morley's words.

"Hey! Not even that. It's our secret. We made a promise, a sacred promise and commitment, remember."

"Right, Willard, right." Stats spoke with evangelical fervor and everybody, myself and Alvin included, nodded vigorously.

"And where..."

Maribeth stopped John before he could finish. She didn't interrupt him, just raised her hand and he stopped. She let the nervous wave of seat-shifting, rustling and heavy breathing fade before she spoke. "I have been waiting. It took you a long time to get here, to this moment, but now you are here. And so am I. Now we can begin."

She reached over and took my hand, but spoke to the others. "Silly boy. You know that he has asked me to marry him

164

five times..." I coughed, got red in the face. This was not something I had exactly talked about to these guys. "He really didn't want me, he wanted the balls." Don't bet on it, Maribeth, I thought. "But he didn't know that, he didn't understand. Of course he didn't know I had them and I couldn't tell him. Not yet. Not until he began to understand, until he had made the promise, until you all had made the promise."

"But Maribeth, how..." she squeezed my hand and I fell silent. I was either in the midst of the most passionate or of the craziest moment of my life or, perhaps, of both.

"I want to teach you all a song," she said, "a song you all know, but have never heard." Softly, in a clear soprano voice she began to sing "Take Me out to the Ball Game." Yet it was different: the same words but a different tune. The unfamiliar notes enveloped the words and changed them utterly, giving them a meaning we had never heard before. It was not a rollicking seventh inning stretch rendition, nor a jolly piece of nostalgia. It was an anthem, a litany, a sacred canticle.

"Stats" was the first one to catch on and he began to sing in his elegant baritone. Her voice was one of those that choir directors pray for: clear, light, able to blend with other voices, becoming one with them, enriching them, making them better. It submerged in "Stats" voice, but transformed it. Then I joined in and the others followed and the sound we made was beautiful, making even our hymn-singing of the last few meetings seem trite. Once "Stats" had started we never heard her voice, but she was with us all the way, and carried us. We sang it three times, all the verses. The third time around we were standing, still in our circle, and were tossing the ball back and forth, randomly but unerringly. As we reached a crescendo on the last chorus I caught the ball and handed it to her.

And Father Hughes' voice came crashing in: "Damn it, Joe, what the hell do you have here, a fucking cult?"

I don't know how long he had been watching us, but I knew we would have to move. Next time we met at my place, but that didn't work too well. It was too small and my landlady raised her eyebrows about seven guys and a girl getting together on her second floor.

We ended up renting a space from the Human Potential Movement of Greater St. Louis which itself seemed to have a few quirky trappings. They even let us store the rug there, which saved Alvin a lot of trouble. The executive director was a large shapeless woman who always wore purple muumuus and seemed thrilled to open her arms (figuratively) to an interracial, intergenerational, intergender league. That was John's idea of how we ought to describe ourselves to the curious.

Whatever, the place worked for us and in it over the next year and a half there were numerous magical moments which I will not describe. Suffice it to say that to every meeting Maribeth brought one of Walter Johnson's balls. Indeed in the depth of one of the worst snows to hit St. Louis in decades she brought all of them and every one of us made the meeting.

She never said how she happened to have them. After the first meeting we never asked directly although during the open discussions we laid some pretty heavy hints around about how nice it would be to have a little history. Smilingly she evaded them all. She did occasionally make an elliptical reference, but nothing that a bloodhound could take a sniff of and go racing off after.

At first I did spend some sleepless nights trying to sort it all out, but I didn't have much to go on and after a while it didn't seem as important. She always sat next to me and she seemed to like to hold my hand, but she made it clear, not in words, but looks, that I should not broach "the previous topic" ever again. Which was hard I will admit, because all the contact and all the mystery made me ache a bit. But mostly in the meetings my attention did stay fixed on the fragile beauty of sharing this secret with those seven other people. And I did get to see more of her than before: often I would pick her up and take her to the meetings and afterwards we sometimes would go somewhere and talk. Once we even went back to her place and she showed me where she kept the balls.

It wasn't all peaches and cream. All of us had some baggage of one kind or another we carried around and sometimes we unloaded it. But the center held. We all drew strength and some joy from the New Age Temple of the Presidentially Autographed Baseballs and from the serenity which, from one meeting to another, seemed to emanate more and more from Maribeth. We did not grow in numbers. We had decided that we would not evangelize, assuming that if there was someone out there they would be drawn to us. Sometimes we talked about Morley coming back, but the consensus was he wouldn't.

I hadn't seen or talked to Morley in almost a year when he called. "Joe?"

"Yeah?"

"This is Morley."

"I know." And I did know right off, but I wasn't sure I was glad to hear from him, so I didn't know what to say. My response was maybe a little cool, but he didn't notice, or at least he pretended he didn't.

"How things been? You and the others still trying to figure out who stole Walter Johnson's balls?"

I paused. Was he angling to come back? Did I, we, want him back? If he was tuned in, wouldn't he just come? If he wasn't tuned in, what would happen if I brought him along?

"Joe, you there?"

"Yeah."

"Thought you'd died on me or something. This connection all right?"

""It's fine. As good as it's going to get. Yeah, I'm still working on it." Intentionally I used the first person singular, diverting him a bit. "It... it figures in my epic, you know the Walter Johnson thing I've been working on."

"Well then, I got something to show you. Something that might interest you. You free tonight?"

"Sure."

"I'll be over. Seven-thirty okay."

"Yeah." Click. I wasn't certain it would be all right. I had a feeling, a feeling that I didn't want to see Morley, a stronger feeling that I didn't want to see what he had to show me, a feeling blunted, however, by an edge of desire. I thought of calling Maribeth, but I didn't.

Morley showed up on the dot. He seemed really excited. He had a briefcase with him. After a few strained preliminaries, including my opening a beer for him, Bud Light, he put the briefcase down on my kitchen table and took out of it two manila envelopes. He placed one of them on top of the briefcase, then opened the other and carefully extracted five 8x10 photographs which he arranged in a row on the table.

I looked. Right off I saw that they were pictures of presidents throwing out the first ball at a game and I quickly recognized William Howard Taft, Woodrow Wilson, Warren G. Harding, Calvin Coolidge and Herbert Hoover. Each had a date marked in the corner in Morley's script: April 14, 1910; April 14, 1915; April 12, 1922; April 15, 1924; April 17, 1929.

"You seen these."

"Yeah, I guess so. You may have shown them to me." I remembered Morley's own preoccupation, his prosopographic analysis of the presidential box.

"Well you know what I've been working on. And I've really been making some great progress. There's really something in this, Joe. But that's not my point here. One day I got a little bored. You know how it is, Joe; you don't spend every day spinning lines about Walter Johnson. For all I know you write limericks about Ossie Bluege for relief. Anyway, I got bored, so I started looking at the other people in the picture, the ones who aren't part of the presidential party. That's when I saw it. Take a look. You see anything."

At first I didn't; my mind was diverted too much by wondering what Morley's game was. He stood back watching me, occasionally glancing at the pictures as if willing me to see what he saw. And finally I did. A man and a boy in the upper left hand corner of every picture. I saw the man first because, though the pictures spanned nineteen years, it was obvious it was the same guy. In the first one he was probably in his mid-twenties, in the last his mid-forties. A little stouter, hair thinning on April 17, 1929, but the same guy. In the first picture he was holding a boy in his arms, maybe two or three years old. In the second a boy, seven or eight, was beside him, standing on his tiptoes or maybe hoisting himself on a railing, the man steadying him. The third picture was the fuzziest, focused too sharply on the foreground, but the father was still obvious and there was a youth beside him, about fourteen if I had to guess. And it was the same one two years later hovering there just beyond the ball in Calvin Coolidge's upraised right hand. And there he was again in 1929 now twenty-one, now a young man, looking not unlike his father in 1910, looking not unlike...no I couldn't say that.

Without speaking I pointed out the man and boy, father and son, in each of the pictures. Morley clapped me on the shoulder, "Right, I knew you'd see it. What do you think?"

"A father and his son attending the Senators' home openers over two decades. We can perhaps interpolate and assume that they were at the others too. You have pictures from the others?"

"Yeah, all of them. But the angle's different in some, so assuming they were sitting in the same place I couldn't pick them out. But that's not important. These five, these five, my friend, are the ones from which Walter Johnson got the autographed balls!"

"So?" Morley was almost over-wrought and I was beginning to feel strangely queasy. I still didn't know what he was driving at, where he was going with this thing, but I had a feeling I didn't want to know.

He moved the five photographs out of the way, though leaving each still visible. With both a certain relish and a kind of ritual solemnity he opened the second envelope. "Act two," he said. "The saga continues."

He placed three photographs side by side, each of a president throwing out a first ball, again carefully dated: John F. Kennedy, April 8, 1963; Lyndon B. Johnson, April 10, 1967; Richard Nixon, April 7, 1969. This time I needed no hints. In all of them in the upper left corner there was a man and a child, only this time the child was a girl. The man was elderly, mid-seventies at least, but in the Kennedy picture he was holding the girl who was about three. In the Johnson picture the girl was seven or eight and seemingly was leaning against him as she stood on her seat. In the third picture only the top half of her head was visible as she peered over the people in front of her. The man, a distinguished octogenarian, with white, thinning hair stood protectively beside her. I had no doubt that this was the "father" of the earlier pictures. I also knew that if these weren't black and white pictures, if they were living color precise to the detail, the girl's eyes would be cerulean blue.

"So what are you trying to say, Morley?" I strained to sound natural.

"You see it doncha? You see the connections doncha?"

I replied as coolly and non-committally as I could, "I see a father who likes baseball and manages to get to a lot of opening games with his son, then keeping up the tradition by taking his granddaughter," I paused then quickly added, "or maybe even great-granddaughter to games."

"That's a real fan though isn't it? A fanatic even, maybe the kind of guy that begins to think wouldn't it be great to *own* some of those baseballs."

"Morley, I thought you were the rational one, the cautious logician. That's wild speculation." Maribeth had told me that her grandfather had attended every Washington Senators' opening game from 1908 until 1971, the final year of the second incarnation of the Senators. "I may have been with him from the time I was a babe in arms. My first memory of one, a dim one, is 1963." Her grandfather regarded Calvin Griffith as a traitor to family and class, Bob Short as the worst sort of carpet-bagger. His greatest hero was Walter Johnson. In his gloomiest moments he would mutter about the great betrayal of Walter Johnson by those midgets, Cal and Bobby.

Morley smiled, that cocky little smile he would get on his face at times, the cat with the mouse smile. He reached into his briefcase and produced a third manila envelope from which he drew a single 8x10 photograph which he placed on the table. As I looked at it he read what he had written on the envelope. "Hall of Fame week, Cooperstown, 1972. Some of the many thousands of fans who toured the exhibits. Here a group in the 'President's Room' examine the five baseballs once owned by Walter Johnson and autographed by William Howard Taft, Woodrow Wilson, Warren Harding, Calvin Coolidge and Herbert Hoover."

The picture showed a cluster of people staring intently at the exhibit. Behind, slightly separated from them, looking intensely, almost angrily at them, was Maribeth's grandfather.

"Who is that guy?" Morley asked almost fiercely. "You find that out, you solve your mystery."

I don't really know how I got Morley out of my place. I expressed some fascination with his theory, enough that he left the pictures. "I got copies, don't worry. If I can be of any help call." And he left. I slumped down into a chair at the table and stared at the pictures without seeing a thing. It wasn't the theory that upset me: in a way it didn't surprise me at all and if I really had worked hard at it I could have developed such a hypothesis using what I had come to know about Maribeth.

But after the first couple of weeks of wondering where she had gotten the balls, I hadn't worked hard at it, hadn't worked at it at all. Things were too good. I was too happy. We were all too happy. The meetings of the New Age Temple of the Presidentially Autographed Baseballs filled a need for each of us and the sense of unity, the satisfaction of commitment to and for others, was so great that it hadn't mattered. What mattered is that we had them, we shared them, we touched and held them, we read the names and could incant them like a mantra: "William Howard Taft, Woodrow Wilson, Warren Harding, Calvin Coolidge, Herbert Hoover."

Now with Morley's pictures in front of me, with Morley's insidious suggestion "You find that out, you solve your mystery" echoing the room, I could feel this deep ache in my brain, this craving to know. I had started this whole thing because I had wanted to solve the secret, and the solution was surrounding me in its glittering power. The worm of certitude was alive in my gut.

I couldn't not make sure-- could I?

We had a meeting the next night. I was in a fret, but I don't think it was that which produced the electricity in the air. Maribeth was radiant, like she was bursting with something she wanted to say, yet she was strangely quiet. I had planned to ask her out for a beer or something afterwards, and then I'd tell her about the theory and see what she said.

During the meeting, however, Morley's name came up in the discussion period and I found myself talking about his call. Then I couldn't stop myself and I started to describe his whole visit, the pictures, the way he had presented them. I never looked at Maribeth, but I could feel her tense up. Partway through she took my hand and squeezed it and though she said nothing I could hear her voice silently screaming, "Don't, don't." And the worm cried back, "I got to, I got to." I rushed on, spilling it out till I reached Morley's challenge and as I said it I turned and looked at her.

I never saw such a look. It wasn't hate, it wasn't fear, it was something powerful and beautiful and fragile, breaking breaking breaking....She suddenly stood up shouting, "It doesn't matter, it doesn't matter. Don't you understand that? Can't you understand that?""

Then she started to run for the door. I followed her, but she turned. She had the Calvin Coolidge ball in her right hand. She wound up and threw it. She didn't throw like any girl. She hit me, hit me hard right...well in a very vulnerable spot. I went down like a gut-shot cougar and she was on top of me in an instant pummelling, pounding, crying "Go back. Go back." Suddenly she screamed, staggered away from me, bent over in pain, and fell on the baseball rug in the middle of the circle, the mystical circle of the New Age Temple of the Presidentially Autographed Baseballs, a circle that would now break forever.

As she lay dying I was with her. I was with her a lot those last few days. I went to her place and got the rest of the balls and took all five of them to the hospital, figuring I would try to bluff my way in saying I was her husband. Funny thing was that it worked so easily, then I found out that when they admitted her she gave them my name as her husband, but said not to call me because we were estranged. Estranged, a funny way to put it.

The head nurse was not too happy about having those five grubby looking baseballs in the hands of someone in critical condition. "Infections, we must guard against infections in these cases," she said in a high Arkansas twang. But I guess the doctor figured it didn't matter.

We talked some, but not much, she was too weak. At first I did a lot of blubbering about "Forgive me, forgive me." When she squeezed my hand and smiled and looked at me gently with those eyes, I knew I didn't have to worry about that anymore. And finally I didn't worry about any of the rest either, even the hardest part, the fact she died from complications after childbirth.

She was seven months pregnant when it happened. I don't know who it was. I asked, but she just smiled and said "It doesn't matter. Don't you understand that? Can't you understand that?" Finally I did understand that I was just there to love her to death. And I did. The last thing she said, the very last word she spoke, she put the tips of her fingers on my lips and whispered, "Yes." The balls are buried with her because I slipped them into the casket just before they sealed it.

All the others figured it was me of course and they hated me for it. They all came to the funeral, but they didn't speak to me and I haven't seen them since. Once, months later, on an impulse, I stopped by the Human Potential Movement building, but the executive director told me the group hadn't been meeting. She did say that "Mr. Waters, Mr. Green, and Mr. Wadlow are now regular attendees at the Movement's Friday evening seminars which I conduct." She said it like a cat licking cream. I read in a collectors' paper that Alvin Reese had opened a shop in Cincinnati. In a SABR newsletter I saw a note about John Pagonas working on a history of the Three I league with the help of his research assistant James Longo, a grad student at St. Louis U. Morley calls every couple of months, but I'm always out.

It keeps me busy earning a living and raising our son. I've promised myself I will never search his features for some tell-tale sign. At the moment he mostly looks like that kid in the photograph of the 1910 opener. I named him Walter Johnson.

[Author's Note: Subsequent to the appearance of this story in *Spitball. The Literary Baseball Magazine* the Hall of Fame announced they had recovered the baseballs and created a new display for them. Believe who you want to believe.]

Silent Sig Sprecher's Last Hit, But One

His milky eyes stared at me intently from beneath abundant brows, a look of surprise. Not surprise at my question, for it was the question toward which we had danced through our long and convoluted conversation, but surprise again at the answer with which he had lived, in which he had reveled, for fifty-plus years. A low, gnarled laugh rumbled within him, delaying his response, allowing him to savor it alone one last time. Then he said, "The sumabitch couldn't count."

After five years of searching I had found him at the Dunkard Brethren Home at the end of Mt. Hope Road, a long twisty country lane in rural Central Pennsylvania. There, on a wooded ridge overlooking the neglected farmlands of the once faithful few, in an unadorned brick and cement block building that housed two dozen elderly Dunkards and a few strays, I finally met Sigmund ("Silent Sig") Sprecher, the last survivor of the Granite City Gray Sox.

I first encountered the Gray Sox while doing research for my doctoral dissertation, a comparative socio-economic study of a group of southern Illinois towns during the depression. I devoted one chapter of that study to the role played by local semi-pro baseball teams that had sprung up in most of those towns, providing a focus for community spirit in a time of distress. In the towns I was studying, the teams had formed the Cis-Mississippi League. The founder and president of the league was Elijah Lovejoy Borden, a classics professor at Shurtleff College, a now defunct Baptist institution in Alton. Borden once had a tryout with the St. Louis Browns, an experience that had left

175

him with the enduring belief that, apart from the full immersion of adult baptism and the poetry of Virgil, both of which he understood to have limited appeal, the only thing capable of sustaining hope in times of despair was baseball. He said as much in a public statement made on April 14, 1930, the founding date of the Cis-Mississippi League.

The league, I learned, lasted for eihjy and one-half seasons to July 4, 1938; it originally consisted of seven teams-- the Alton Bluffers, the Wood River Oilcats, the Collinsville Toms, the Lebanon Freeswingers, the Principia Polymaths, the Grafton Gazelles, and the East St. Louis Ironmen. In the second season a new team appeared, the Granite City Gray Sox, and the Gray Sox were the champions every year thereafter until the final year when the season, for reasons I did not know, was abruptly interrupted. The Gray Sox won about eighty per cent of their games. Their star player, "Silent Sig" Sprecher, seemed to be a hitting machine.

That sort of detail was not very important to my dissertation, but it piqued my curiosity. After finishing my degree I continued to dabble in the history of the league and of the Granite City Gray Sox. Increasingly my interest centered on Sprecher himself. All the other Gray Sox had been local boys or had settled in Granite City after the league had folded, but Sprecher seems to have appeared almost simultaneously with the organization of the team and to have as abruptly disappeared after it disbanded.

When I began my search fifty years had passed since the last Gray Sox game: a 4-3 loss to the Alton Bluffers. Not surprisingly, most of the players were dead and for a time my main occupation was establishing a necrology. I did find some interesting memorabilia— pictures, a few old gloves and uniforms, programs from victory banquets— now owned by children or grandchildren. And I had one memorable interview with Billy Maginnis, the second baseman, who I thought was the last survivor.

The daughter of Clyde Veale, the first baseman, led me to Billy. Clyde had died in 1987. According to the daughter he

176

and Billy had been best friends and right up to the time of Clyde's death they had gone to ball games together. Any ball games, little league, American Legion, high school, college, even a couple of times over to Busch Stadium in St. Louis, but they didn't like that very much. Billy, she told me, now eighty, lived in a mobile home near the new high school, the easier to get to their games, and that is where I found him.

"It's been tough since Clyde died, nobody to talk to. Ya'see Clyde and me had two things to talk about: what we wuz seein' and what we seen. The first we could talk to anybody about, though most couldn't really see what we saw. But there wasn't nobody but Clyde and me anymore that seen what we seen. Oh you could always tell stories and some folks would listen, but after a while they'd stop and there was always stories ya couldn't really tell. Except to somebody who wuz there and finally that was just Clyde and me ya know."

From that beginning he rambled on, apparently feeling good that he had a listener. He talked about the games and the players, the victories and the infrequent defeats. Now and then he would stop and cackle as if at a memory that suddenly had emerged. Sometimes he would reach over and touch my arm and say "I jus' remembered" and tell me what had come to mind. Other times, however, he would chew his lower lip a bit, scowl, then shake his head, and revert to talking about Clyde.

He went on like that for two hours, but, for all he said, what struck me most was what he didn't say. Never once did he mention Sig Sprecher. It was as if he had never existed. Several times I was on the verge of raising the subject, but Maginnis always rolled on before I could get my question out. Finally, however, in a rare lull I interjected, "Mr. Maginnis, you've been talking for almost two hours about the Granite City Gray Sox and never once in that whole time have you mentioned 'Silent Sig' Sprecher."

"SSShhhiiit." It was a hissing, sibilant sound and I was not sure whether it was an exclamation or a name.

He stared at me with squinty eyes. Then abruptly rose from his naugahide chair, hobbled over to the kitchen area, and took a glass out of the sink. He opened a cabinet and removed an unopened bottle of Jack Daniels. Cracking the seal, he poured out a tumbler of the dark amber liquid and in one motion tossed it down. Wiping his mouth with the back of his hand he repeated "SSShhhiiit."

"Mr. Maginnis, I..."

"Ten years I been dry. Kept that bottle there jus' to re-mind myself. It was a kinda bargain I made. And I ALWAYS KEEP MY BARGAINS!" The last was an anguished shout and as he said it he slammed his hand on the counter jiggling the bottle and glass. He picked them both up and hobbled back to his chair clutching them. Sitting down he poured another tumblerful and tossed it off as quickly.

The air seemed heavy and threatening. For a moment I thought of leaving, but decided to press on. "Mr. Maginnis, you would obviously prefer not to talk about Sprecher so I won't ask you all I would like to, but I do want to ask one thing."

"Might not answer," he growled.

"But I hope you will. Mr. Maginnis, from what I can tell reading the old newspapers, the last game that the Granite City Gray Sox played was against the Alton Bluffers on July 4, 1938."

"Yep."

"The Bluffers won that game 4-3."

"Yep."

"Sig Sprecher had three hits including two homeruns, but in the last of the ninth inning with the bases loaded and two outs he took three strikes without taking the bat off his shoulder."

He only nodded, but in a way that suggested he felt physical pain in making even that slight motion.

"And that was it. The team never played another game, the league itself folded, and Sprecher seems to have disappeared. Why? What happened?"

He glared at me defiantly, poured himself another drink and downed it as swiftly as he had the first two.

"The papers don't say anything. There's a vague state-ment from the Elijah Borden saying that due to circumstances

178

beyond his control the Cis-Mississippi League was suspending operations for the year, but hoped to resume play in 1939. And that's it. No other explanations. No other stories. The league never started up again. That's strange, Mr. Maginnis."

"The truth is stranger still, boy."

"What was it? Was there a fix? Did Sprecher throw the game?"

"You're sniffin' at the wrong hydrant, boy."

"Then what's the answer? You obviously know it. What is it?" I was getting a little shrill. I knew I was onto something. I knew I was close to the truth. I knew Maginnis could tell me.

"Ask Sprecher hisself," was all he said and in a voice that raged bitterness. Those were the last words I got from Billy Maginnis. He began to cackle, tears rolled down his cheeks. He poured himself another drink and laughed. Drank and laughed, laughed and drank, until he was unconscious in his chair.

I left him there. I called Clyde Veale's daughter and told her what had happened. She said she would take care of him and I suppose she did. I checked back later and learned he had gone to a nursing home, but maybe a year after that I read in the *Alton Evening Telegraph* that he must have returned to his trailer because there had been a fire and he had been burned to ashes. "Fire in one of those trailers gets pretty hot," the fire chief said, "with all that plastic. Hot as hell. As good as a crematorium."

That saddened me. By then, however, I had another lead and had figured I could manage without whatever it was that Billy Maginnis knew and would not tell about Sigmund Sprecher. At the Alton Historical Society I had discovered the papers of Elijah Lovejoy Borden. The papers contained several items of note: a ledger book with the statistics from every season of the Cis-Mississippi League, a series of letters from Billy Maginnis and one from Sig Sprecher.

The ledger book had the annual totals for each player, but for one player and one player only, Sig Sprecher, there was at the end of the volume on a separate page a career summary:

G	AB	R	H	2B	3B	HR	RBI	SO	BB	SB	AVG
425	1742	634	<u>999</u>	127	83	101	874	1	212	95	.573

A spectacular career by anyone's measure. Two things struck me about the entry: that the number of hits had been neatly underlined though in a different color ink from the statistics themselves and that he had struck out only once, an amazing, indeed almost unbelievable stat— and, of course, that one time was the last time he batted. What had happened?

The letters from Maginnis all concerned Sprecher's statistics and may have prompted the neat underlining of his hit total.

```
                                    14 July 1939
Dear Mr. Borden,
To settle a friendly wager between pals I
am wondering if you could provide me with
the official stastics [sic] of my team-
mate Sig Sprecher during his career in
the Cis-Mississippi League.
                    Respectfully yours,
                    William B. Maginnis
```

```
                                1 September 1939
Dear Mr. Borden,
Thanks for your prompt reply to my let-
ter.  I am wondering if you would please
check your figures particularly in refer-
ence to the number of hits Sig Sprecher
got.  I kep [sic] a record myself and
come up with 1000 hits.  The matter is of
some concern.
                    Respectfully yours,
                    William B. Maginnis
```

```
                                30 September 1939
Dear Mr. Borden,
This is very important.  You got to have
made some mistake somewheres.  I know for
sure Sprecher had 997 hits going into the
```

game of July 4. He went 3 for 4. That's 1000 hits. Please confirm.
                        Respectfully yours,
                        William B. Maginnis

                                    11 November 1939
Dear Mr. Borden,
I got no answer to my last letter. Have you made some deal with Sprecher. He is a liar and thief. He has made off with what is mine. You have got to hold me up on this one.
                        Maginnis

The letter from Sprecher himself was brief, but it put me on the trail:

Dear Mr. Borden,
I enclose a stamped and addressed envelope. Will you put in it a copy of my stats for the years I spent in the League. I would like them for my scrap book now that I am through playing. As you can see I have moved to Lebanon.
Sincerely yours,
Sig Sprecher

Obviously I had here some hint of a quarrel between Sprecher and Maginnis which might explain the latter's attitude, but I also had a lead as to where he had gone. I spent three days in Lebanon, Illinois, trying to locate any trace of him. I got the idea that he might have ended up coaching at Greenville College, a small Free Methodist school nearby, but I could find no reference to him. One afternoon I was chronicling my difficulties to the college librarian there, a dear lady in her forties who wore her hair in a bun and had granny glasses. When I had finished my plaint she looked at me sweetly and said, "Did you know, Mr. McBride, that there are twenty-two Lebanons in the United States?"

Ah yes. Among them Lebanon, Missouri; Lebanon, Indiana; Lebanon, Arkansas; Lebanon, Iowa. All of which I came to know over the next several years as I pursued my one faint lead and none of which yielded a thing. None that is until one hot summer day I pulled into Lebanon, Pennsylvania. It is not what you would call an attractive town. It's an old town that once had a Bethlehem Steel Plant in its center. That's gone and all there remains is a long scar that cuts across its center. The main street is either dying or trying to struggle back to life. It's hard to tell, but on a steamy afternoon in July dying seemed more probable. It is, I learned, close to the heartland of Pennsylvania Dutch country.

The light dawned: Sprecher, German. I had figured he was from St. Louis. Maybe he wasn't. Maybe this rolling land below the Blue Ridge had been his home and maybe he had come back to it.

Assuming that if he had come back to this area he might have hooked on with a local baseball team I checked the archives of the local paper, the *Lebanon Daily News*. No sign of him in the late summer of 1939, but I noted a pretty good semi-pro team that played in Jonestown nearby, so I decided to follow it in particular. And there he was: in April, 1940, in a write-up about the upcoming season the manager talked about having added a pretty good-looking pitcher, Sig Sprecher, who had recently moved to the area from the Middle West. Sprecher was, the manager Hal Wengert said, a bit on the peculiar side since he had made clear he wouldn't ever himself swing at a pitch, but that was no problem if he pitched as good as it looked like he could.

Apparently he could. He won five games in a row, giving up no more than one run in any game. Then he was gone, not a reference to him in any other games. Finally in an end-of-the season wrap-up Wengert remarked, "It was a pretty good year. Woulda been even better if Sprecher had hung around, but he had some odd-ball religious ideas. Said he couldn't stand the

182

temptation of standing up at the plate and not swinging so he wasn't going to play anymore forever. Though what's so immoral about swinging at a fat pitch over the heart of the plate I don't know. Think he got sweet on a Dunkard girl though I don't even know what that's got to do with not swinging at a good pitch. He was a funny one."

Knowing nothing about the Dunkards I was as much at a loss as Sprecher's ex-manager. I went to the local college library to learn what I could about them. The main thing I learned was that there were not very many of them and that this area was one of the few where Dunkard congregations existed. I concluded that what I needed to do was to find me a Dunkard, preferably an elderly one, and see if he or she could tell me anything about Sigmund Sprecher. I mentioned my dilemma to the reference librarian to whom I returned the volume of *The Mennonite Encyclopaedia* from which I had garnered my information. She, a sprightly young woman who looked more like a long distance runner than a book-lady, said, "Why there's a Dunkard Brethren retirement home not all that far from where I live. I've ridden by it on my bicycle." Ah, the wisdom of asking questions of librarians and what better place to find an elderly Dunkard than a retirement home.

I presented myself to Benjamin Elias Kesler Diefenbacher, an austere gentleman of indeterminate though not advanced years who was the administrator of the Mount Hope Dunkard Brethren Home. He, in the plain tieless garb of the faithful, eyed my peach polo shirt with some suspicion, but was otherwise friendly enough. I stated my purpose, clearly but generally: that I was doing some research and thought it might be helpful to me in tracing a man in whom I had a particular interest to talk to an elderly Dunkard with a good memory who might remember the person since I had reason to believe he might have joined the denomination after moving to this area from Illinois..

"Well,"" Benjamin Elias Kesler Diefenbacher replied in measured, deliberate tones, "our oldest resident might be of some help to you. He can sometimes be difficult, a common failing of the very old, but he is a good man and does have a quite remarkable memory for detail. His name is Sigmund Sprecher. He..."

"Sigmund Sprecher?"

"Why, yes." I hardly needed to say that this was the very man for whom I was looking since it was written all over my face and filled my voice. With only a mild look of surprise Diefenbacher led me down the hall to the end of my quest.

Sprecher was seated in a chair facing away from the door of his room and looking out the window. The room was spare: a plain wooden bed, two wooden chairs beside the cushioned rocker in which he sat, a table with a few objects on it including an age-darkened baseball, nothing on the white walls except a single frame which appeared to contain, not a picture, but something in script. He seemed to be working at something in his lap and when we came around beside him I saw that it was an old baseball glove. On one of the wooden chairs beside him was a small can of neat's foot oil.

"Brother Sprecher, I have a visitor to see you. This is Robert McBride. He says he has been looking for you."

Sprecher did not rise or offer his hand, but continued to work on the glove while looking at me quizzically, grey eyes that had a peculiar brightness to them. Finally he nodded toward the other chair, "Set down. State your business."

Diefenbacher shrugged knowingly to me and excused himself. I sat down, watched Sprecher for a moment at his task, then carefully spoke. "Are you the Sig Sprecher who played for the Granite City Gray Sox?'"

"I was."

His reply puzzled me, I registered it, but moved on. "I'm an historian." I began to recite my pedigree and to outline how I had become interested in the Cis-Mississippi League, a recitation which evidently he found painfully uninteresting. When I got to the point of mentioning Billy Maginnis, however, he flared.

"So youra friend of Maginnis eh, that why you come. Nothing's changed. Tell'im that."

No, I'm not a friend of Maginnis. I have talked to him, but only once and that was several years ago, not long before he died."

"Died. Not likely. Jes' went back where he come from more likely."

I decided that it served no purpose to talk further about Maginnis because the enmity on Sprecher's side seemed as strong as it had been on Maginnis'. Since my interest was in Sprecher, not Maginnis, that was easy enough. "As I told you I became interested in the Cis-Mississippi League as a result of some broader research I was doing about that area in the 1930's. And, well having that interest, I became particularly interested in your career since you appeared to be, well one of the premier players in the league."

"Was that."

"So I wanted to learn a little more about your career. About how you got started. And about why you stopped."

He looked away from me, out the window, out across the fields and rolling hills, to some distant point I could not see. He had started to rub the glove again as if in the leather there was a remembrance. "Tell you how I got started. As for the other, I don' know. See where the telling gits me. So what's yer question?"

"I gather from what I know that you weren't from Granite City?"

"Nope. Come from Poplar Bluff, Missouri. Farm boy, but mostly wanted to play ball. I'd go anywhere, do anything, to play ball. Even went to a college for a while, but just to play ball. Not sure I ever made it to a class. Least nothin' rubbed off on me. Left Poplar Bluff in '28, played ball here and there. Ended up in Granite City."

"Is that why you left? To wander around playing baseball?"

At first Sprecher did not answer. Again he was looking to some far horizon and the habitual kneading of the glove became more labored like he was trying to squeeze something out —or keep it in. Finally he spoke. "Marguerite was the prettiest little girl ya ever saw. I was real taken with her. More than taken; knew I wanted ta marry her. Her people were Church of the Brethren like mine. But in '26 they went with the Dunkards when they split off. Mine didn't and I couldn't. I mean I was twenty years old, a bit of a sport. Liked to dress a bit stylish, smoked now and then, and liked my beer. The no necktie thing didn't bother me, but they wuz drab dressers. I coulda forgotten the tobacco too. But after a hot afternoon playing ball in the sun I couldn't see not having a beer or two to slake the thirst. Course they wuzn't much for ball-playing either.

"Anyways she wuz pretty sweet on me and I figured there warn't no need for me to change all that much. Figured she would kick over the traces for me. Well her father warned me off. Said I wasn't sanctified. Hell, I knew that. Then they sicked ole Kesler hisself on me."

"Who was Kesler?"

"Benjamin Elias Kesler, the head dunker hisself." Sprecher turned his eyes toward the door, then whispered "The chief jailer here likes to pretend he's a direct descendant. Don't believe it."

I admitted my ignorance about the Dunkard Brethren and we spent some time reviewing the particulars which had prompted Kesler to lead a small group of Brethren out of the church in 1926. The critical difference appeared to be the main body increasingly believed that the purpose of the Church was service to the world while Kesler and his followers believed it was to hold up a standard to the world. That conviction found expression in various dress and behavior codes which were the obvious obstacles in the course of Sprecher's courtship.

"Anyways I will confess my response to ole Kesler was not what ya might call polite which didn't help me any. Was just about that time that...." Sprecher paused. He was thinking something out, thinking how to say it, or whether to say it at all. He rose, slowly and stiffly, from his chair. He shuffled over to the table. I watched closely. Until that moment I had not even been sure that he could walk, but there was an odd sureness in his movement. It was not the teetering shuffle of age, but of a tired-

186

ness after a hard-played game. He placed the glove carefully on the table next to the ball, then went to the frame and looked silently at whatever was therein inscribed.

Then he turned slowly toward me. "What did...what did he tell you?"

"About you? Nothing." I described my conversation with Maginnis, noting that I had thought it odd that his ex-teammate avoided any reference to him until I forced the issue. And I described Maginnis' reaction when I did. "Then when I asked him what had happened in that last game the only thing he would say was 'Ask Sprecher hisself.'"

Sprecher found that funny. He laughed and snuffled, slapped his leg several times, then with his arms spread he made a slow and strikingly graceful turn which belied his years. He ended his turn in a batting stance looking out the window and swung with a fierce youthful joy at a ball which only he could see but he saw all the way and watched as it rose high and far over the fields and rolling hills.

"That was the longest home run I ever hit."

"But you took a called third strike."

He looked at me smiling, shuffled back to his rocking chair. Once he had settled in, he resumed. "Was just about that time that he showed up. He wuz a slick one he wuz. Sorta short and skinny, but a natty dresser and a real talker. Said he wuz puttin' a team together for a friend. One that would do some travelin', make some real money. Said he'd seen me play and figured I could be a star with the right, instruction he called it.

"Well acourse, he caught me at a real vulnerable time, what with her father ordering Marguerite not to see me and she buyin' into the program about bein' more sanctified, more righteous, more holy and more perfect through faith and obedience. That was Kesler's talk with special emphasis on the obedience part. So I wuz going nowhere with her.

"So our mutual acquaintance," he made the reference in a sing-song voice, "our mutual acquaintance tells me not to waste my time, that if I play on his friend's team I'll make some money, meet some fetching women, generally have a good time.

He also hinted about that if I played the game right he had a strategy in mind that I could eventually have my way in regards to Marguerite.

"That all sounded pretty good to me and I said so. So he produces what he called a personal services contract which I wuz to sign."

Sprecher paused, set the rocker in motion with a hard push of his feet, and waited unspeaking while the results of the effort were expended and the rocker creaked to a halt. ""Ya gettin' my drift, sonny. Ya Startin' yo understand what I'm tellin' ya."

"Sure, sure. Maginnis was an agent for a touring team. That was a common phenomenon in those days. Major league players did some touring in the off season, but there were others. A couple of black touring teams, the House of David."

"Well, ya might say that. Yeah, he was some kind of agent all right. But ya don't really get my drift. He wuzn't no Billy Maginnis. More like Billy Z. Bubb. And his friend wuz more like the midwestern sales rep for the archfiend hisself."

"Are you saying...wait a minute." I was getting his drift though I'm not sure I was understanding him. Faust as barnstorming ballplayer is what it was sounding like and that seemed too fantastic to believe. I let my rational, social scientific mind absorb that premise a bit, tried to identify it as a primitive metaphor of some sort, and finally decided I would have to suspend disbelief until I had more information. With effort I framed my question. "You were being asked to sign a contract with...with the forces of evil?"

"You can call it that, but it was more like the devil from what I could tell."

"And what were the terms?"

"Well they wuz pretty attractive to me at that point. Remember I wuz a ball-playin' fool, plus badly smitten with Marguerite and awful frustrated with the turn that had taken. The deal was that I could play ball year round on what looked like it was goin' to be a pretty fair team and there wuz some indication that I would git a little extra help now and then, ya know, an in-

188

fielder not quite gittin' to a ball and that sort of thing, not that I thought I needed much help bein' pretty full of myself.

"Course I coulda played ball for lots of people. The big hook was the contract stipulated that when I got my one thousandth hit three things wuz to happen: I wuz to get a major league contract with the St. Louis Cardinals — Billy hinted they had some special connections there; he wuz to put in effect the strategy for me to git Marguerite; and my soul would become the permanent possession of the devil hisself to be collected whenever…

"Lookin' back that don't seem like such a bad deal for a twenty year old who'd already been told by no less authority than Benjamin Elias Kesler that he wasn't sanctified and stood about a snowball's chance of bein' so."

"But when you were almost there you didn't finish the deal. Why?"

"Fetch me that ball and glove, sonny."

I did as he asked. The glove was small, hardly much bigger than my own hand, an artifact from the distant past, yet the leather seemed still supple and new. Sprecher I thought must work on it with oil every day. In contrast the ball was dry and hard. I could almost feel it draw the moisture from my fingers when I picked it up. It was prickly with ancient scuff marks. Eagerly he took both from me, slipped the glove on his left hand. The ball he held in his right hand, gripping it with his thumb and first two fingers across the stitches, contemplating some long ago pitch.

"Ya ever play ball, sonny?"

"Up through my freshman year in college."

"Whadya play?'"

"I was a pitcher."

"Then ya know what a hangin' curve is."

"I threw a few. Well maybe more than a few. That's why I stopped."

"That last pitch was a hangin' curve, big as a balloon. Bases loaded, two outs, and we're down by a run. Took two fast balls for strikes and then here came that big melon. Coulda hit it

189

a mile. But like I said it went even further cuz I didn't swing. It still hasn't come down."

""So by not swinging, you..." I paused uncomfortable with the language, but knowing no other way to say it I blurted out "You, you saved your soul?" surprising even myself.
"Yep."

"But why? What made you change your mind?"

He tossed the ball in the air and deftly caught it in the glove. As earlier I was struck by the flashes of youthful vigor that he occasionally showed. Like the glove he was old and used, but amazingly supple. "Here I bin talkin' and talkin'. Never know they useta call me 'Silent Sig.' You know that, sonny."

"Yes I did."

"Never did talk much. Always liked to act, rather than talk. But I wuzn't dumb. Had a good mind for numbers. And I thought a lot. Loved to play ball. Couldn't imagine doin' anything else. Heard some people say playing ball was like life. Hell, then I woulda said it wuz life. But couldn't help seein' the world around me. Couldn't help seein' the depression. Couldn't help seein' the hurt in the eyes of the men, the sorrow in the women's eyes. And I knew that baseball wuzn't life; it wuzn't even like life. It wuz a game, a good game, but a game.

"Saw a family one time. father, mother, little boy about seven, come to see us play. They wuz a sorry lookin' trio in a way. Shabby, lookin' tired and poor. Father caught a foul ball and gave it to the boy. Ya woulda thought he'd given'im the world, that boy was so happy. Now we wuzn't into lettin' the fans keep balls like that cuz we wanted to save money. Maginnis went over ta take it back, but the father stood there between Maginnis and the boy, his arms spread out, and the mother hugged the boy to her. Maginnis was shoutin' and carryin' on, but they just stood there. Like some statue. There wuz somethin' beautiful about it. I went over and pulled Maginnis away. Told him to bag it. I'd pay for the ball, but to let the kid alone.

"I did. And I never forgot that picture. The family standing there strong and lovin' in some way that seemed beyond me. Began to think of that picture with me as the father, Marguerite

190

as the mother. And I knew there was nothin' like that that could ever come to be because of some strategy devised by runty little second baseman like Billy Z. Bubb. That's when I knew I wasn't goin' to get that last hit. But I wanted ta squeeze every last bit of juice out of it if I could. I went back and figured out where I wuz and I kept careful count from then on. So I let that hangin' curve float by."

"What happened then?"

"Jus' walked back to the dugout. The fellas was all upset acourse cuz we hadn't won the game and wonderin' too why I hadn't at least swung. I wuz what you'd call a contact hitter. But it waren't any sort of critical game. Anyway I got my stuff together and said in general to everybody 'I quit. I'm goin' home.'"

"What did Maginnis do? He knew what you were doing? It wasn't the game that mattered to him, but that last hit?"

"No, he didn't. He was jus' sittin' on the bench sort of smirking. Sez to me, 'Might as well keep on playin', Sprecher, you got your thousand an' I got what's comin' to me.' Well, I sauntered up to him real slow, laid my bat down across his knees, and said, 'Sorry to disappoint you, Billy, but by my count that's nine hundred and ninety nine. There ain't goin' to be another.'"

Sprecher chuckled in remembrance. "'Billy went about crazy at that. He jumped to his feet shoutin', my bat fell off his lap and hit 'im in the foot. He yowled something dreadful. Called me a liar, among other things which is a kind a language the keeper here don't like. Pulled a note book outa his pocket and waved it under my nose. So I pulled out my book and waved it at him. Other fellas couldn't figure out what was goin' on, so they left, all except Clyde who was always hangin' around Billy. Always figured Clyde was tryin' to sell his soul to Billy for a coupla base hits, but Billy wasn't buyin'.

"Anyway, wouldn't do but we had to sit down and go over the books. When we did that old Clyde finally looks at Billy with these big wonderin' eyes and sez 'Sorry, Billy, he's right. Only adds up to 999'"

"How, how did that happen," I asked.

191

He laughed again, this time a long, low sound like the bumpy, winding road at the end of which I had found him. "The sumabitch couldn't count."

We sat quietly for a time, Sprecher savoring again the story in its retelling, me trying to absorb all the details of what I had heard. The slap-slap of ball against mitt broke the silence and brought me back from the intricacies of my reflections. "Pardon me, Mr. Sprecher, but you referred to that strikeout as the longest home run you ever hit. Did you mean because you beat...beat the devil with it?"

"That, yeah, and more. I went home. Went home to Poplar Bluff. Went home to see how things were with Marguerite. She was there, lookin' after her mother, cuz her father had died. She'd never married. Said she had loved me too much. I said I wuz through with my sportin' days and wuz thinkin' the Dunkard ways made more sense to me than they had when I wuz twenty. Ole Kesler said somethin' about findin' lost sheep. We got married, but decided to move out here to Pennsylvania.

"Tried playin' some ball, jus' pitchin', not hittin'. Told the manager it was against my religious principles to hit anything, but throwin' was fine. But ole Billy Z. Bubb had followed us, first back to Poplar Bluff, then out here. He kep' hangin' around, watchin', hopin' I'd take a swing. So I chucked it. Took to farmin' full time. Lived forty fine years with Marguerite, till she died.

"And here I am."

"Did you ever talk to Maginnis?"

"Nope. But he talked to me plenty. Every time he got within hearin' distance he would talk. Said he was checkin' the records cuz there had to be some mistake, said he was keepin' his eye on me, whined about didn't I know what I'd done to him, to his career, even started beggin' me. When I stopped playin' he hung around another year or so, then disappeared.

"So that's the story sonny. Funny, eh. Never told it to anyone, though it mighta made a good article in the *Bible Monitor*, a good witness ya know. Feels good to have told it though."

It was now late afternoon. The sun was shining brightly into the sparely furnished room, giving it a brilliance that made me blink. But Sprecher looked out the window, toward the source of the light, smiling, kneading his glove. Silent. Again. At last.

Homer Happy

I had a plan. Some of it was pretty obvious and easy, but it took real foresight. Of course, as early as spring training there was a lot of talk about this being the year someone would break Roger Maris' home run record and it didn't take a genius to figure Mark McGwire was the prime candidate. By then, however, I had already set my plan in motion.

First, I had two season tickets for section 282 (loge reserved) at Busch Stadium. That's in left field, off the line and about half way up, roughly 425 feet from home plate. I'd graphed McGwire's home runs since he came to St. Louis, and fixed that area as the most likely landfall for his four-baggers. Also the seats were on the end of a row near a cross aisle. Having studied crowd behavior I knew most people stand there watching the flight of the ball with their mouths open, hoping it'll come to them. As a one-time outfielder (I played decently at the semi-pro level till just a couple of years ago) I've got a pretty good sense for tracking a ball and I'm off at the crack of the bat as they say.

Sure there're some holes here. If he went upper deck or into the centerfield terrace there'd be no way I could get the ball, but you got to go with tendencies. Those upper deck shots are something, but he doesn't do that every day, ditto for centerfield. And I had a theory: when he got close to the record his adrenaline would really be pumping and his bat would be faster, increasing the likelihood he'd pull the ball. That made me give some thought to the upper deck or moving closer to the left field line, but I concluded he'd drive the ball so hard it wouldn't have as much lift. Also I decided to stand pat on location banking on my range to get me closer to the foul line if it came to that.

After he hit sixty-one I was watching Sports Center and one of their pundits was waxing eloquent about studying McGwire's swing and noting his bat speed seemed to have picked up and how he was almost pulling too much. I was on my feet, punching my fist in the air, shouting "Right buddy boy, but I had that figured last January. Where were you then?" Annie was a little startled by that outburst and looked into the den, but when she saw I hadn't busted anything she went back to fixing supper.

She was also a good sport about the traveling. Obviously my strategy involved covering some road games. I got two tickets to every road game in September (Florida, Cincinnati, Houston, Milwaukee) and one ticket to Cards' games in the immediately preceding series in those same cities, all in what I'd calculated was the best location in those parks. The earlier trips were to get the lie of the land and practice a little. All the parks were a little different and each presented particular problems. Florida was the worst because of the big section of seats covered with a tarp. I'm pretty agile, but I didn't fancy scampering across that mine field. And as much as I love Wrigley I was glad it wasn't on the list since the most likely spot there was Waveland Avenue and the crowd out there is too testosterone-driven to suit me.

One reason Annie was such a sport about the traveling is the thinking I'd put into the finances. We're not flush and she's pretty careful minding what we've got so early on I sat her down and went through things. The extra tickets were not for entertaining friends and family, and she had to understand that since she has a brother who's a bit of a pest. (Actually so are his wife and two kids.). I figured I could always sell the extra home game ticket at face value because Card tickets are generally a good commodity, especially on weekends. Actually early in the season I sold both of them and so was making good progress at recovering costs. Once McGwire had the record in sight I knew I could ask a premium for the second ticket both at home and on the road and end up a little ahead even with expenses.

Something I hadn't figured on that worked in my favor was the mania that developed long before he was close to sixty-one. I discovered I could get more than face value for my home tickets earlier than I had anticipated and the same goes for my road tickets. Those early road series I ended up going to only one game each and selling the single for the others. Even devised a way of renting my ticket for batting practice at the games I went to. Annie was pretty pleased when I reviewed the income and expense flow after getting back from the Florida series. This wasn't like a lottery ticket, all outgo unless you won. From the beginning I promised it wasn't going to cost us and here we were already in the black and climbing. And I was having a ball.

That's the basic framework of my plan: coverage and finance. I felt pretty good about the general conception, but it's the particulars of technique and purpose I was proudest of. My basic technique is simple and I've used it ever since snagging my first home run ball, a Ted Simmons in 1978. I never try to catch the ball: I wait for the rebound. Nine times out of ten the guy who touches the ball first muffs it. It'd be easy if you were standing there with a glove and nobody within ten feet, but there are people ducking, people spilling beer in your shoes, and at least ten other guys pushing, jumping, reaching. So you make your move after the first guy has muffed it. In certain special situations you can even guarantee that he does, but that's a trade secret. If you're lucky you get the rebound, but more often than not there'll be a bit of scrum.

The important thing is that you have to know beforehand just how far you're willing to go for a particular ball. If you're a regular, you'll see a lot of the same people and you don't want to get a reputation because they'll start ganging up on you. I've been pretty successful just playing it straight and half the time when I do get a ball I'll give it away to some kid. That's worked in my favor in a few scrambles, people knowing me and figuring I'm a good guy so they let up a little. I didn't expect that to be a factor in this campaign. Even so I was amazed at what some people would do for just a McGwire batting practice ball. When he was closing in on the record I got more particular about who I sold my extra ticket to, preferring codgers, scrawny kids and women in that order. No use introducing another muscle-boy.

Most importantly, I was focused. I had two goals: the ball McGwire hit to break the record and the ball he hit for his last home run of the season. Every now and then I'd make a practice run, particularly for balls a few sections away, just to see how my timing was, what the best route would be, stuff like that. McGwire talks about visualizing where the ball's going to be. Well, that's just as important if you're chasing as if you're hitting. And McGwire has things easy: it's him and the pitcher. I had at least seven thousand maniacs to worry about. I made good runs at sixty and sixty-one, not because I wanted them, but because if I had just stood around people'd think I was queer or something. I got close to both without mixing it up too much. On the night of September 8, 1998 I was as ready as I could be

McGwire said afterwards that when he came to the ballpark that night he knew he was going to do it. That sounds good, but it's easy to say after the fact. If you don't do it you just keep quiet. Well, I'll be a man and tell you I was dead certain that ball was going to be mine. Until he hit it.

Upper deck? Centerfield terrace? Forget it. It's a laser beam that goes 341 feet, his shortest home run of the season, hits the wall above the yellow line and drops into the slot behind the inner fence where some kid on the grounds crew, for heaven sakes, pounces on it! I got no more than five feet away from my seat. Bam, boom, over that quick. I never had a chance.

Of course the whole place went bonkers: cheering, clapping, flash bulbs popping, generalized happy times chaos on the field, delirium. I cried. The only guy there who felt worse than I did was Steve Trachsel. No, I was the only guy in Busch who felt worse than Steve Trachsel. The lady next to me, a bleached blonde grandmother of ten to whom I had sold my extra ticket for two c's and who had so much red on she looked like a chili pepper, gave me a big hug and blubbered, "I know just how you feel; I'm so happy I could cry too." Sure lady, sure. You got no idea how I feel. I up and left before they resumed the game.

Annie was great. She did know how I felt. And it wasn't just the money though that was something to cry over too. That's right, money. No way was I giving that ball away. Six people in a row—the ones who got the homers that tied Hack Wilson, that beat Hack Wilson, that tied Babe Ruth, that tied Roger Maris (and the piddling ones in between which don't count for much) —gave the balls back to McGwire. Back? He never had them in the first place! His bat touched them for a milli-second and redirected them. And I hear this groundskeeper kid did the same thing. In the post-game ceremony he hands it to him and says, "Mr. McGwire, I have something of yours to return to you" or some such thing. I didn't watch, it would've made me sick. And Annie didn't tell me. She knew better. She knew how I felt. It was her sniveling brother who just had to tell me, mouthing some flim-flam about how it was a sacramental act, representing the pure heart of America. I hadn't heard garbage like that since bailing out of catechism class. His wife was worse, blathering on about how proud the kid's parents were and how wouldn't any of us like to have a child like that, which wasn't a good subject to bring up around Annie and me.

So, yeah, I would've sold that ball to the highest bidder, paid my taxes and invested the rest to make things easier for Annie and me. That's the pure heart of America. That's what I would have done, but....

Of course the campaign wasn't over though I figured the last one was going to be harder to come by. I'd have to go hard for every one. Well not really every one. The Cards were going on the road to Cincinnati and Houston, then would be home to close the season except for three games in Milwaukee. I decided to bag Cincy and Houston, figuring there was no way he was going eleven days without a dinger and to be honest I really wasn't up to that trip anyway after what had happened. So I gave the tickets to Annie's brother. You would have thought I'd given him the crown jewels. What I got out of it was five days without him and his wife and their chattering about their kids. I already had those days off from work, so I just hung out with Annie, didn't even watch the games. That was good, and I got back a little of my fire.

I was pretty sure the last one would come at Busch and so I gave some thought to bagging the Milwaukee trip too, but decided not to risk it. I'd read an article in the *Chicago Tribune* right after the Cards' last trip to Wrigley in which the writer plotted McGwire's course to sixty-two. He projected it would come in Milwaukee between September 18th and 20th. Well, as he was smart enough to say, "We're the ones who gave you Dewey over Truman." Now, there was a chance Milwaukee would see the last one, though I didn't want Bud Selig to have the pleasure. So I decided to go to Milwaukee and offered to take Annie along, another chance to avoid her brother and family.

September 13th wasn't a Friday, but it might as well have been. That day really blew a hole in my plans. McGwire hadn't done much on the road, but in the first two days of the Cubs-Brewers series in Chicago Sosa got a couple. I saw the clips on ESPN and figured he was heating up again—and I knew the wind was blowing out at Wrigley. The notion that he might actually end up setting the new record did not escape me. Now I've got a thing about McGwire, him being a Cardinal and all, but I wasn't in this thing for sentiment. Looked like there might be another chance to get a number sixty-two. So I decided on an unplanned trip to Chicago.

When I mentioned the idea to Annie she said she'd take a quickie trip to Chicago over three days in Milwaukee any time. I was more than happy to have a second driver. Also I figured a second pair of arms and legs might be useful dealing with the mob beyond the left field wall. Turned out they were, but not like I thought. I've already made clear my feelings about the Waveland Avenue crowd and in retrospect I should've maintained my principles. Unfortunately I let the lust of the chase overcome my usual good sense. Anybody watching the TV coverage of the event will remember what happened in the street when Sosa connected on his number sixty-two. It was like the running of the bulls in that Spanish town. I got close, I got oh so close. I could almost feel that ball in my hands. Almost. But I tripped and fell and nine-tenths of that mob ran right over the top of me.

The first person who showed any interest in my plight was Annie who was jogging along at the back of the pack. A Chicago cop did come over and offer to call an ambulance, but I begged off. I was bruised, battered, a little bloody around the edges, but I figured nothing was broken inside or out and I didn't fancy being imprisoned in any hospital overnight. Annie read my mind and fibbed to the cop that we lived just around the corner. She got me to the car a few blocks away and headed out of town. As soon as we cleared the city she checked us into a motel, put me to bed and hustled out to get bandages, Advil, Ben-Gay.

I was feeling achy, a little stupid, but cared for, in other words bad but not awful, until I caught the late Sports Center and heard McGwire had left his game against the Astros with back spasms. Then I felt more than awful. When McGwire was ahead of Sosa my plans were still in good shape. With them tied I had to make a choice since I couldn't be in two places at once, but given what had just happened to me in the streets of Chicago I'd stick to my original strategy, having learned where improvisation got me. But if it was down to a one-horse and it was the other horse? Even as I was lying there in agony the Cubs were headed to San Diego for four games. They had only three games left at home, against Cincy the next weekend, then wound up with road series at Milwaukee and Houston. In my condition physically San Diego was out—and that trip would have put a real dent in the finances. I couldn't face the Waveland cement mixer again, so I would have to bank everything on the last two road series. I groaned.

"Does it hurt that much?"

"Worse than that, Annie, worse than that."

She hugged me and I screamed.

Fortunately McGwire's back spasm didn't amount to much so it was going to be a two-horse race after all. Sosa did catch up and actually passed McGwire for forty-two minutes, so they were tied at 66 going into the last weekend.. If they'd stayed neck-and-neck I had to figure on making an emergency trip to wherever the Cubs might be in a play-off for the wild-card. To me the wild card is a crock and this year with a three-way scramble right up to the final day, I thought it even crockier. Of course, all them over-paid TV journalists were cooing about how such a race proved what a great idea it was and how nobody now would complain about it. Think again, buddy boys, I complained plenty about it, mostly to Annie who was very sympathetic. The idea that I might grab McGwire's last home run and then have it turn out to be second best if Sosa got an extra game made me sick.

When McGwire took two deep on Saturday my blood was up. Didn't get either one ,wasn't even close on sixty-seven having gotten blocked in the aisle by some over-weight, over-wrought female. But that didn't matter: I knew McGwire was hot and he'd be sure to hit at least one on Sunday, the location of all the shots Friday and Saturday fed right into my calculations, so instead of diminishing, my confidence was growing. On Sunday, September 27, I left our apartment for Busch as cocky as a jaybird. But then like they say though, the best laid plans....

Number sixty-nine should've been mine. I was in perfect position for the rebound. The guy with the glove who caught it even closed his eyes for god's sake and the ball stuck in his mitt! I was half-a-second off applying my sure fire technique to cause a muff. The near miss rattled me some, but I still believed this was going to be my day, that all my hoping and planning and hard work was going to bear fruit. So I got back to my seat and waited for the next one.

I've already expressed some indignation that it was a groundskeeper who got number sixty-two, but that feeling was nothing like what I felt about number seventy. It was the same kind of ball as the other, not one of the typical high arching moon shots, but more on the line and right into one of those party boxes! A bunch of research scientist types from one of the local universities, probably yakking about the uncertainty principle or something. I never had a chance. All those months of planning, all those weeks of preparing and hustling and making choices and I never had a chance.

I didn't leave like I did the other time. Told myself he might get up again. The Cards would have to have a big inning in the eighth or the Expos would have to rally, but neither was out of the question. So I sat there and hoped——but I knew it was hopeless. I thought back over all my planning and maneuvering trying to figure if there wasn't something I could've done differently. Maybe if I'd gotten one of the others or kept the early season one I did get, it would have been worth a little cash, not what I'd wanted, not enough to really ease Annie's disappointments, but something anyway.

I sat through the rest of the game and the post-game ceremony too, doing automatically all the things one's supposed to do, but I sure didn't feel like there was much to celebrate. Even sat for a while after the crowd started to leave. I guess I didn't want to admit the chase was over. Started to consider the possibility of Sosa hitting four dingers in a play-off game, but dismissed that with a sad chuckle. I began to understand that while I'd never said it was a sure thing, this plan of mine, something inside me thought it was and was banking on it, dreaming on it. Now that something was broken. Didn't even want to go home.

Thinking that made me sadder because I knew if I did Annie would do everything she could to make me feel better. Even if she'd been as certain as me this was going to work, even if she'd been depending on it, even if she'd been having dreams about how things were going to be when I came home with that golden ball, she'd put aside all her disappointment and try to move the world to make me happy. I didn't think there was anything she could do that would. And I didn't want her to make the effort-- I wasn't worth it.

I ended up down near the arch: the Gateway to the West celebrating all those pioneer types who had ventured westward in search of land and wealth and adventure and happiness. Only I was looking eastwards and framed in that great silvery span all I saw were riverboat casinos and East St. Louis. Not an inspira-

202

tional sight.   What if, I thought, all that time and energy I'd spent chasing home runs I'd used going in the other direction?

It was dark by the time I got back and I was still trying to think up an excuse for being so late, not wanting to say I was afraid to come home. But before I could put the key in the lock, Annie had opened the door and put her arms around me and hugged me. As she drew me into the apartment she was talking a blue streak. She pulled me over to the couch, sat me down beside her, and held both my hands. When I got the courage to look at her I thought, sometimes, sometimes you make a great catch and you don't hardly know it.

Stealing Home

When the Zanesville Grays folded, Skeeter Thomas had a decision to make. He could have tried other places, other teams, adding to the sixteen years he had played professional baseball. Age had slowed him, but that wasn't the reason for stopping. Zanesville just seemed a natural end point, completing the circle since he was only a few miles from Cambridge where he had grown up. In his two years with the Grays, he had never traveled those few miles. Now, with the future uncertain, he pondered the famous Zanesville Y-bridge. Had he known about such things he would have considered it a metaphor. As it was he simply thought it defined the decision facing him.

. He could take one of the branches west and end up who knows where, maybe in the too cold Northern League again or in some forlorn Louisiana ballpark. Or he could follow the old road east, back to where he had come from. "Well," he remarked to the four faded walls of his boarding house room, "if I'm not going to play, I might as well go take a look. Last time I left there I knew where I was goin'. Maybe it'll have the same effect now." He packed his duffel bag, paid his landlady and started walking east on US-40.

Skeeter Thomas ran like a deer. Thin and wiry, he stood only five foot eight, but had the legs of a six-footer. He ran with passion, with ecstasy, rising laughingly from a slide at second or third or home. He fielded like a starving chicken in a barnyard, picking up everything within reach or snagging looping fly balls over the infield. He savored the look of sullen wonder on the faces of batters who had thought they had a sure hit. If he had ever made it to the majors he would have been on ESPN's top plays every night.

But he never did. All his other skills paled beside the fact that he never could hit. That fact explained the arc of his career from the Elizabethton Twins in the rookie Appalachian League, as high as the Denver Zephyrs in the triple-A American Association and then downward to the independent Frontier League. The record was a litany: Elizabethton, Wisconsin Rapids, Kenosha, Visalia, Orlando, Knoxville, Denver, Tabasco for God's sake! Harrisburg, Birmingham, Duluth, Zanesville. For most of that ride he was a utility player, a late-inning defensive replacement or pinch-runner.

That's not how he started, of course. Coming out of junior college he had the "good field, no hit" tag on him, but hitting was a work and he was willing to make the effort. "Skeeter," Fred Waters, the Elizabethton manager, told him, "you run aggressively, you field aggressively, but you bat like you were afraid to hurt the ball."

They taught him to bunt because the art of bunting is catching the ball on the bat and dropping it where you want and Skeeter got to be pretty good. You can't bunt all the time though. At Kenosha Charlie Manual taught him the fine art of "accidentally" getting hit by a pitch. But you can't do that all the time either. Between bunting and getting hit by pitches he made himself a pest to the opposition, but never a real threat.

"Hit down on the ball, Skeeter," Manual kept saying. "Hit grounders. With your speed you can beat some of them out." He tried with marginal success. If you can't hit a ball on the level, how are you going to hit it swinging down? The only injuries he ever had were bone bruises on his feet from hitting himself with foul balls. There were just some things he never learned, like how to forget what he'd given up to take this ride along the byways of baseball.

By the time he reached Visalia he was already playing only part time. He hung on because what else was he going to do. He could have gone back to college, but higher learning was as much a mystery as hitting. Or he could have returned to Cambridge, but what was the sense. His folks had retired to Florida. His high school sweetheart had waited a while for him, but she'd finally married somebody else. And when it became clear that maybe he ought to find another line of work all the jobs back home were drying up.

He had regrets though he knew there was no point to them. He'd made his choices. Like stealing home, once you commit to it there's no sense thinking too much about alternatives.

"Marvin, look out for that man walking along the shoulder. You're going to come too close to him."

"Oh, shut up Nance, I'm drivin'."

To show her who was in charge, Marvin Bellows gunned the engine of his Durango and stayed on course. Skeeter, trudging eastward on US-40, his duffel bag over his right shoulder, heard the approaching vehicle and turned to thumb a ride. He had barely turned and raised his arm when he saw how close the pick-up was to the edge of the road. Instinctively he dove to his left, like diving back to first on a pick-off move, but as the truck sped by the front fender hit the bottom of his duffel and spun him crazily into the dust and gravel of the roadside.

Nancy screamed. For one awful moment she had been almost face-to-face with Skeeter and the sudden fear in his eyes seemed frozen in her mind. When her own first fright had passed, she shouted at her husband, "Marvin, stop. You might have killed him."

Marvin glanced in the rear-view mirror, then laughed. "Naw, he's already gettin' up. Just gave 'im a fright is all. Maybe it'll teach 'im to keep on movin'. We don't need no tramps in Guernsey County."

Disbelieving because she had to, she held back the knife edge of understanding. Knowingly she held her tongue. She looked in the side mirror and in the receding distance saw Skeeter struggling to his feet. Then another thought dawned and she whispered, "I know him."

"What's that you say, babe."

She looked at her husband, at the once sharp features of his face now turning flaccid, the puffiness that made the once deep-set eyes seem squinty. "Nothing, nothing."

He laughed. "Damn, that made my day."

When they got home, a small, wood-frame house on the west side of Cambridge that, aside from the carefully tended window boxes and front garden, betrayed neglect, Marvin went directly to the refrigerator and took out a beer. He opened it and was taking a long draught when Nancy appeared in the doorway.

"Marvin, I completely forgot. I meant to ask you to go by the grocery store so I could pick up a few things. I'll just run out and get them if you don't need the truck."

"Naw, take it. I'm just goin' to enjoy my beer, watch a little NASCAR." He belched. "Oh, and pick me up some more beer."

"All right." She paused. "And I may stop by Mother's to see how she's doing, so I might be a while."

Her words trailed unheard after him as he slouched into the front room.

Skeeter walked slowly, his legs stiff from the fall. "Real Guernsey County redneck greeting, that was," he muttered to himself. He wondered if he could have done anything differently. If he had dropped the duffel bag he might have reached the grass safely, but then, of course, the pick-up would have run tight over the bag, ruined everything he owned. Not much of a loss that, he thought. He walked on nursing a grudge, but then let it go. "He's still a son of a bitch, but I don't wish hurt to any man," he announced to the wildflowers, the kildeer and the roadside detritus. And he wondered again if he could have done anything differently, but now it was a bigger question.

He had just passed Peters Creek Road not far from town when he saw the Durango driving slowly westward. "Come back for more, I suppose," he said aloud. He didn't watch it, but was aware that the driver had made a U-turn. He edged more off the road, but kept walking, even when the pick up drove onto the shoulder behind him and stopped. He heard the cab door open and close.

"Skeeter?"

He halted, straightened, unsure if he had heard right. He turned slowly. She stood beside the truck, the sun almost directly behind her, so he couldn't make out her features, but deep memory prompted by the sound of her voice made them clear to him even after all those years.

"I'm sorry, Skeeter."

"So am I, Nancy. So am I."

Release Point

When I signed my first pro contract right out of high school, the question was whether I'd turn out to be another Sandy Koufax or another Steve Dalkowski. That wasn't my question acourse. I had no doubt what with the way I could throw the ball, clocked at close to a hundred on those jugs guns scouts carry around, that I was a sure bet to make the majors. Just a question of when. Besides I only knew Koufax's name as an old-timer, same way I knew Bob Feller's name. I mean Koufax was retired before I was born. And I'd never even heard of Steve Dalkowski. You got to be one of those trivia nuts to know that kind of thing. Anyway, turned out I was just Bubba Floyd.

The book on me back then was that I was the hardest thrower in the state, maybe the country, but I was missing something when it came to control. Well, pitching high school ball in rural Illinois control didn't much matter. At least it didn't much matter to me. Coach Doolittle cared a lot more about it. He'd played a coupla years of minor league baseball back in the early fifties and he had a whole lot of "lessons he'd learned" from this guy or that guy. He always mentioned 'em by name, but nobody else in Farley ever heard of 'em so far as I could tell. Farley, Illinois, population 737 on a full day: that's where I grew up. In the middle of nowhere in the back of beyond though now an interstate just west of us has changed things a bit. "Bubba," Coach would say to me, "you're not so dumb as you're acting. You know those kids couldn't hit you if you were throwing a lot easier, so back off and learn how to place your pitches. If you want to go places in this game you've got to pitch smart as well as hard. Fact is smart will get you farther than fast dumb. Bobby Shantz taught me that."

I'd nod my head and say "Yeah, coach. Yeah, coach." But when Jimmy Swartz, my catcher, would put down the old number one, I'd forget all that and just throw. I was having too much fun rearing back and firing the ball as hard as I could as long as I could and watching the hitters' knees go wobbly and their eyes near pop out of their heads when that sucker came at them. Even got called the "Farley Flame Thrower" by the Peoria paper when we played a tournament game up there. Acourse that only encouraged me. Anytime a scout was around--and that wasn't hard to tell since whenever a stranger was in the stands like as not it was a scout, I mean why else would somebody you didn't know show up at a high school game in Farley or Plain City or wherever—I'd crank it up as far as I could. I think I was trying to see if I could break one of those jugs guns.

Oh, occasionally one of them would say to me, "Son, you got a great arm, but all that speed isn't going to get you any-where until you learn to use it right." But they lost my attention as soon as they called me "Son." I wasn't anybody's son except my Mom's. By then Pops was long gone. He'd been a no account farmer, then a no account gas jockey at the only station in town—a job he got only because my Uncle Fern, Mom's older brother, owned it. He'd always been a no account father as far as I was concerned, and probably a no account husband, too, though Mom never complained. Then he was just no account and took off for places unknown. "I got to find myself," I heard him saying to Mom. I was ten then and had a habit of listening in on their conversations which only added to my less than favor-able opinion of him.

He was always whining and complaining about how somebody else was to blame if things didn't work out for him. He'd say the extension service gave him bad advice, or the seed Harry Hunt at the feed store sold him was moldy or Uncle Fern got the accounts mixed up somehow. He even blamed Mom. "Essie," I heard him say more'n once, "I'd be fine if you'd jus' have a little faith in me." Well that was getting to be a harder and harder sell I can tell you. I suspect he even hit Mom a few times though I never saw him do it and she never said. I know he could be a mean drunk cause I got in his way a coupla times when he'd been up to Whitaker where the nearest tavern was. That didn't happen much the last year or two he was around cause Mom finally kept him on a short leash as far as pocket money goes. Whatever he earned at the gas station, Uncle Fern gave to her, figuring otherwise it wouldn't make it home. And by then Pops didn't exactly have the best credit around town—or even up in Whitaker. Despite all, Mom cried when he left. Why, I couldn't understand.

Mom sold the house and what was left of the farm, some of it he'd already had to sell off. It had mostly been her family's in the first place. She moved us in with Uncle Fern, who was a bachelor, and took work as a waitress at the Farley Café. He said "You don't have to do that Essie. I can support us fine. You jus' stay home and mind the boy." It was true: he had some land he let out, the gas station was the only one for miles, and he was a whiz at small engine repair, so he made out fine.

"No, Fern," she'd stand up her full five foot five to his six foot three—it's from her family I get my height, Pops wasn't much taller than her, "I mean for Bubba to go to college so I got to put something aside." Like as not if I'd gone to college it wouldn't have put her out much since coaches from some of the big state schools were looking at me too. But Mom had her heart set on me going to Eureka because that's where Ronald Reagan went and I suppose if I'd gone anywhere it'd been there. I'da got lost in one of those big places. Anyway, when I got drafted pretty high by the Orioles and they offered me a contract with what looked like a nice bonus, I convinced her it made no sense to spend money on education given what I wanted to be was a major league pitcher.

That wasn't long after the end of the state tournament where I'd pitched a helluva game in the finals, but lost, 1-0. I gave up only one hit, struck out twenty, and walked ten. Three of those walks came in the bottom of the ninth. After the second one—we had two out by then—Coach Doolittle came out and said to me: "Bubba, do me a favor. I been waiting for this moment for twenty years, so will you listen to me this once. Just put it in there easy and let your fielders take care of it."

Well, I did, and the next batter hit a hard two-hopper to Billy Baldwin, our second baseman, who muffed it. Bases loaded. So I had listened once and that was enough for me. Next guy I hummed it in there, ran the count to three-two, then walked him to force in the winning run. It wasn't the first time and I figured it wouldn't be the last. I shrugged my shoulders and walked off the mound. Our guys were standing around, looking stupid, tears running down their cheeks. Billy was sobbing up a storm, begging people's forgiveness right and left. Coach Doolittle stared at me for a bit, not saying a word, then walked over to Billy and hugged him.

Meanwhile four or five scouts came up to me, shook my hand, and said "Too bad, but nice game, kid." Of course, the other team was whooping and hollering and slapping and hugging each other like they had won the Universal World Series. .All except their pitcher, guy by the name of Andy Avalon. I'd been on a coupla all-star teams with him. His guys were whirling around him, happier than pigs in slop, but he stood like a statue, glaring at me talking to the scouts. None of them bothered with him. He'd pitched a good game—six hits, no walks, coupla strike-outs. Tough kid, tough pitcher, a gamer, but mostly junk ball stuff. I finally went over to congratulate him.

"Nice game, Andy," I said. "If anybody beat me I'm glad it was you."

"Screw you, Bubba. If I had half the stuff you did, I'd never lose. But you, you just don't have a clue." He turned and walked away. I just laughed.

Betty lit into me a little bit for that, saying I wasn't sensitive enough to other people's feelings, and even then I supposed she was right, but heck what could I do about it. That was the way I was. Betty was not only my girl, she was my best friend. We'd been going together since sophomore year, but it went back further than that. Not long after Pops took off, her mother died of some wasting sickness, and we sort of hung together in our sorrows. Her dad was a good farmer, the kind of farmer and man I wished Pops had been. Anyway she could say about anything she wanted to me and I'd listen—though I got to admit it didn't always have effect. She'd just shake her head and say, "I don't know why I bother with you sometimes. You're just Bubba" But she'd smile a little and squeeze my arm.

Well, like I said, my Mom gave in. Took some convincing, but I was helped in that by Vince Poteat, who was my agent. He'd come swooping into my life right before the draft and assured Mom he could negotiate a deal that would not only include a nice bonus up front, but also some money for educational expenses. That way, he said, we could both have what we wanted and it wouldn't require any stretching the dollar on her part. So I signed with the Orioles and off I went to Bluefield, West Virginia.

Coming like I did from Farley, Bluefield seemed big, but I could handle that, I mean I had been to Peoria. I even enjoyed the town itself, but the hills really got me. Couldn't figure out how they even found enough flat ground to put a ball field. For the first month or so, I felt all closed in, though I sort of got used to it. That was the Appalachian League, what they call a rookie league, which basically meant everybody was like me, fresh out of high school. We were all either full of ourselves or scared to death. Some guys were one, some the other, and a few were both, going from one to the other one day to the next. I was mostly full of myself. There wasn't anybody I saw who could throw as hard as I could and I figured it was just like high school only you were playing against high school all-stars. I just kept on doing what I had always done.

The Appalachian League is a kind of sorting machine. You take a bunch of seventeen, eighteen years olds and let them play themselves up or out. It's not a place you spend morena coupla years developing. And whether you move up to A ball or out of your boyhood dream before you get a real taste isn't simply a matter of stats. The organization types are evaluating you all the time, but a lot of that is guesswork. Take me, for instance: they knew already how fast I could throw the ball cause they had all those scouting reports and it didn't take long to see they was right. I mean why did they sign me in the first place? What they didn't really know was whether I'd ever get the ball over the plate often enough to suit 'em. But acourse, at that level, every-body is scared to give up on somebody who could throw like me. So there wasn't much chance I wouldn't move up, unless I got hurt or busted by the cops, either one of which was always a possibility. I don't mean I was a hell raiser once I got away from home. Mom brought me up right and I had the opposite example of Pops' shortcomings as reminder. But take a kid out of Farley and plunk him down a long way from home and he's likely to be a little frisky.

First game I started was against Elizabethton, a Twins farm team. They had a hotshot lead-off man, Cleotis James, cen-ter fielder, who could run and throw and was hitting about .500 after four or five games. During warm ups I was cutting loose and the ball was going all over the place, into the dirt, over the catcher's head to the backstop The catcher, Bobby Welliver, was working up a good sweat before the game even started. James just stood there, watching, looking cool as could be. Well my first pitch went over his head, my second behind him. Got to admit that didn't scare him. I knew by looking at 'im that he al-ready had himself down to first base with a walk and stealing second. He got there a little early because my third pitch whacked him on the knee. He jogged on down to first, pretend-ing it was a flea bite, but I could tell if he was alone on a country road he'd be limping some. First pitch to the next hitter James tried to steal second to prove his point, but Bobby, who had a helluvan arm himself, though he never did hit what they were hopin' he would and so only got as far as high A-ball as a back-up, gunned him down. Trotting off the field James gave me one of those looks that's supposed to scare you, but I just told him "See ya in the fourth innin', gimp." Walked two guys, struck out the rest that inning and went to the bench pretty pleased with myself.

"Not bad for starters, Bubba," the pitching coach, Ed Sweet, told me, "but keep your mouth shut out there. Swagger in a seventeen year old isn't very appealing."

"I'm eighteen."

"Same difference. If you get to the bigs, it'll be with your arm, not your mouth."

Sweet was what gets called grizzled by sportswriters. He had two years with the Orioles at the tail end of the bullpen after about eight in the minors, all of which provided him with what amounted to wisdom and lots of patience. Patience is probably what it took to deal with the likes of us. Most managers and coaches in the league moved on as quick as the players. After all, they were looking for a ticket to the majors, too. Sweet, I guess, enjoyed working with seventeen and eighteen year olds and was good at it, there being no other way to explain why he stayed in Bluefield. And I'd have to say he did help me, though I didn't think that way at the time. Patient handling maybe wasn't what I needed—though even he had a tough time providing it in my case.

As it turned out I saw James again in the second not the third, the result of a coupla more walks. He came up with two outs and two on. Again he played cool, though I had seen a little hitch in his walk. Anyway this time my first pitch was up and in. He threw his left hand up to protect himself and the ball hit him on the back of the wrist, pretty well shattering it I heard later. Apparently he never did really recover from it. I know he didn't play again that summer.

My hitting James a second time did produce one of those general bench clearing, milling around, marginal pushing and shoving things you see in baseball, but nothing like a fight. Lots of posing and yammering, but not a lot of action. Still, our manager, Jim Pamlayne, decided to quiet things by taking me out of the game which didn't make me very happy cause I thought I was really grooving, but hey he was the manager. Later somebody suggested I should go and apologize to James, though why I should was never clear to me. I didn't throw at him on purpose. Never but once threw at anybody on purpose. I mean I hit enough guys without even trying. And James was the one who threw his hand up. If he hadn't done that the ball woulda just skimmed his helmet at worst. Anyway I didn't apologize. That's baseball.

I didn't pitch again for a week. Sweet worked with me in the bullpen, "to refine my mechanics" was what he said. "Right now, Bubba," he'd say, "you're not a pitcher. You're just a thrower. And you're a good ways from being ready to even try to be pitcher. So we're not going to do anything too fancy with you. We're going to concentrate on one thing, the release point. Even if you're just flinging your fastball you got to give some thought to when you let go of it. Right now you're so excited by just how hard you can throw, that's all you're thinking of. Doesn't seem to matter to you whether you hit the backstop or the catcher's mitt." He scratched his chin a bit, a habit with 'im, then squinted at me "You know the difference between what happens when you let go too soon as opposed to too late?"

Well he was right. I hadn't given it much thought. I mean when you let go, you let go. So I said, "Can't really say."

"Thought not. Throw one to Bobby there."

I did and it sailed over his left shoulder so that he almost had to jump to catch it.

"Wild high, Bubba. So can you tell me where your arm was when you let the ball go?"

That's what it was like. For a while he had me throw real easy, "Like you're playing catch with your mother," he said. And he kept after me to tell him where the 'release point' was. "Now I'm not saying you have to think about this all the time, Bubba. You do that and you'll have another kind of problem. But you got to train yourself so it's natural, it's instinctive." I felt like I was playing soft toss, but I went along only busting one if he wandered off to talk to somebody else. Some days he even had me throwing a softball over hand. Said I'd have to let go of it right or it'd go straight up in the air or into the ground. He was right about that.

Finally they started me against Johnson City. They had a good club and were off to a fast start so Pamlayne thought I might try to be a little careful. Well, of course it only juiced me up a bit. First inning I struck out the first batter, then walked the next two, which brought up a sharp looking kid by the name of Ray Lankford, whose done all right for himself since then. Anyway, I went two and one on him. On the fourth pitch I threw one that probably woulda gone through a brick wall. It happened to come into the strike zone, middle of the plate knee high. Didn't stay there long. They say lefthanders like the low ball and he loved that one to death. Damn, did that sucker go. That was the first home run I ever did give up in my life starting from Little League and it was a beaut.

Well, I settled into my groove after that. Pitched about four more innings, walked six or seven, gave up a piddling hit that might have been caught by a faster left fielder, and struck out eight, including Lankford on another low fast ball. Left the game losing three-zip and we never did catch up so I was 0-1. After I came out Sweet sat me down and asked me, "What did you learn tonight, Bubba?"

Didn't take me long to figure that one out. "That anybody can get lucky every now and again."

We were sitting at the end of the bench. Sweet was leaning back, arms folded, giving the appearance of watching what was left of the game. I had picked up a bat and was moving an empty paper cup around with the business end of it. Well, when I answered him, he unfolded his arms, turned and stared at me without saying a word for a bit. When he did he spoke real slow.

"How long have I been working with you?"

"Not much above a month, coach."

"That all. Seems longer than that." He leaned back again, folded his arms, concentrated for a bit on Teddy Lee, our reliever, big lanky fellow with less speed than he imagined, but a loosey-goosey, side arm delivery that took a while to get used to. "See what he's doing, Bubba?"

"Lookin' like a turkey buzzard, throwin' the ball."

Sweet took a long breath. "You try me, boy. I gotta lot of patience, but you try me. Listen to me a minute. Yeah, he looks funny, but what he's doing is pitching. Not throwing, pitching. I

217

don't know how far he'll get in this game, probably not above double-A, but that's a lot farther than you'll get unless you learn a little something down here. Teddy doesn't have the stuff you have, but he knows what pitching is about. What you shoulda learned from what Lankford did to you is that no matter how fast you throw, if you put the ball in the wrong place there's hitters that will crush it. Maybe you didn't happen to notice that the pitch you got him on the second time wasn't quite so dead center on the plate as the one he belted. Down here you won't see many that can catch up with you the way he did, so you can get by doing just what you're doing. But my job is to get you ready to move up the ladder. When you do—if you do—you'll see more and more guys who can take a pitch, even your best pitch, deep on you. So you better start learning now what you need to know to do it right."

"Yeah coach, I understand," I said, though probably I didn't.

He rubbed his chin, maybe wondering whether I was really listening, or maybe knowing I wasn't and considering whether to call me on it. Then he said real slow and quiet, "I've been talking to you for a month about control, but I been doing it by baby steps, hoping you'd begin to think about it. Not actually being able to do it yet, 'cause you got a long way to go, but at least thinking about it. Let me tell you just how far it is you got to go. When I talk about control I don't mean just putting the ball over the plate. I mean location, putting the ball in a particular zone, if you got good enough, in a particular spot. That's what pitching is. I got high hopes, but low expectations for you, Bubba. This season I just want you to begin to understand that."

Then he got up without looking at me and went over and patted Teddy on the back as he came in from the mound.

"Old fart," I said to myself. "What's he know?"

What he knew was he could keep me from pitching in a game for better than a week. Sweet "worked with me" in the bullpen, more of that mechanics stuff, though mostly he just watched. I said something to Pamlayne, but he just shrugged. "Sweet thinks you need to take it easy. Don't want to throw your arm out. And we got the organization's roving pitching coach coming through pretty soon. We want to make sure he's here when you see game action."

Not long after that Poteat showed up, "to see if they were handling me correctly," he said. I didn't complain, but he was upset I hadn't pitched more. He was all for a meeting with Pamlayne or calling the Orioles farm director, but I told him, "Don't fret, it's gonna happen. They know I can throw better'n anybody else they got."

Well he may have said something on his own, I don't know, but the roving coach arrived a little sooner than expected and I was back out there. We were playing Bristol at home. I went five innings, walked nine and struck out everybody else, except one guy who got on by an error which cost me a run. I wasn't happy when they took me out. I mean I had a no-hitter going. Palmayne muttered something about pitch count when he told me I wasn't going out for the sixth. I think it was just Sweet tweaking me, hoping I'd throw a fit and embarrass myself. Anyway the roving coach—I forget his name now, but he was a slightly younger and tidier version of Sweet—took me out to the bullpen and talked to me while he had me throwing some more to Mickey Perez, our back-up catcher. Good catcher, but couldn't hit diddley as it turned out.

"Son," the guy said, "I've heard a lot about you and seeing you makes me a believer in what I heard. You've got a major league fastball right now, no doubt about it, but you got a high school approach to the game--and maybe pony league control. Ever hear of Steve Dalkowski?"

"Nope," I answered letting go of a hummer that went over Perez's head and temporarily halted the game as it bounced across the infield.

"He's sort of a legend in the organization. Hardest thrower ever, the story is. Threw bb's. In high school he'd throw no-hitters and give up a stack of runs because he walked so many. Same thing in the pros. Everybody oohed and aahed about his stuff, but he never got his stuff together. Bounced around and out. Never made the bigs. Not even close. Ended up…well with some social problems, I hear. Whole lot of talent, but not much control—of his pitches or himself. Sad story."

I fired another flamer that bounced in the dirt and caught Perez in the crotch. He went down like a gut-shot cougar.

"Damn you, Floyd," he moaned from his curled up position on the ground.

"What the hell, Mickey, that's what cups are for."

"That's enough, Floyd," the rover said. "Go take a shower. And remember what I said."

"About Dalkowski?"

"Yeah. That too." He walked back to the dugout. I saw him talking to Sweet. I took my shower.

That's like my season went. Didn't pitch anywhere near enough to hit my stride, but I thought I was looking pretty good though I ended up just 3-4. Sweet kept preaching to me and sometimes he'd introduce an anecdote or two about Dalkowski, like maybe he'd been told to keep reminding me. They were interesting, some of them, but I didn't see the point. I mean from what I could tell his problems weren't just pitching mechanics, but, like the roving coach had said, "social." And while I sorta got from the look he had given me that he wondered whether maybe I was into that kind of thing, I shrugged it off. I mean I was no angel, but, like I said, Mom had brought me up right--no thanks to Pops.

My last game of the season was against Wytheville. I was battling against Frank Castillo, their best pitcher who did make it to the majors and stayed there though he bounced around some. I was doing my usual conveniently wild bit and had 'em 2-0 after six innings. I'd walked eight or nine, but they only had a coupla bleeders for hits, and mostly were fanning the breeze.

I hit the first two batters in the seventh, one of them not even trying to get out of the way which wasn't too smart of him as it turned out because he got a cracked rib for it, but the ump didn't call 'im on it. Probably felt sorry for 'im because he was obviously hurting. Anyway Pamlayne took me out and brought in Lee who had started warming up even before I hit the first guy. Maybe he thought it was too hot and I was tiring, but hell, I

220

had pitched double headers in the prairie heat. Lee gave up a double and both runners scored. We went on to win the game, but I came out with a no decision when I coulda been 4-4.

"I coulda finished 'em," I told Sweet afterwards.

"Maybe yes, maybe no, Bubba. But remember this game isn't just about you. We need to see what everybody can do. Teddy hadn't pitched in a while and it's getting to be time when we have to make some recommendations for next year."

"Well, he sure didn't help himself," I said.

"And you think you did?"

I looked at him a little surprised. I mean the answer was obvious to me. He had to be kidding right? He musta noticed my reaction because he got this sly smile on his face.

"Attitude, Bubba, attitude. The thing we don't know about you hot shots when we draft you is whether you got the attitude to learn what you need to make the right use of your ability. Like I told you before, Teddy doesn't have anywhere near what you got in that arm of yours. But, so far, he sure beats you between the ears."

After the season I got the last laugh though. The Orioles released Teddy Lee and assigned me to Erie in the New York-Pennsylvania League. Nobody was dumb enough to let a guy with my stuff go.

Betty was the same way. She'd been writing all summer wanting some assurances I'd been true to her and all that kind of thing. Now I was never one of those fellows who played around a lot though acourse in a town like Bluefield there were always some baseball Annies hoping to hitch their wagons to a rising star or at least get some summer diversion from the local boys. And what with my obvious talent I certainly had some opportunities. I won't say I didn't dabble a bit, but by my standards I was able to assure Betty, the few times I managed to send a letter back, that she was my one true love and I couldn't wait to see her again and such like.

Partly for that reason and partly to make Mom happy I went right home after the season. Got to admit, too, I missed the nice flat country around Farley. All the going up and down in

221

West Virginia got a little trying to me. Anyway I went home. Did a little work around the Farley Cafe. Bessie Mae Buck, the owner, liked having me there mornings so the coffee crowd could talk baseball with me if they wanted. And I helped my uncle around the gas station.

Which is what I was doing in late January when a black Lincoln pulled in and a guy in a dark coat and black hat got out. I was sitting inside reading the *Sporting News* and decided just to wait there since he looked to be coming in. No sense going outside on a cold January day when you don't need to. When he did come in, I thought he must've come right out of an old grade-B gangster movie like they show on TV late nights.

"Can I help ya?"

"I'm looking for Clarence Floyd."

"You're lookin' right at 'im."

That seemed to take him back a bit and he gave me a pretty careful gander before he said anything else. "You aren't the one I'm looking for."

"Well, I'm the only one there is hereabouts."

"Fellow said he was from Farley, Illinois."

I didn't particularly like the looks of the guy and pretty quick decided he must be somebody that Pops had got himself in hock to one way or another. No particular business of mine though so I said, "Maybe he was *from* here, but he ain't here now."

"You sure about that?"

"Sure as I can be."

"You some kind of relative of his. Must be in a dump like this. Everybody must be everybody's cousin or in-law." Guy never looked at me. His eyes kept darting this way and that.

"Some kind, yeah. He was my father."

That caught his attention and he turned and glared at me. "Was? What the hell does that mean? He can't be dead. I just saw him two weeks ago."

That sort of slowed me a bit, but I didn't let it show. "Didn't say he was. I only said he *was* my father. Don't count him that way anymore. I haven't seen him in more'n ten years. Don't care to. Nobody else hereabouts has seen him neither."

The guy laughed. Wasn't one of those laughs that suggest he was much amused. Sort of dry and hard. "Damn. Looks like I got taken. Must have took you too."

"Yeah."

"We had a little…a little business arrangement over in Ohio. He was supposed to meet me to settle accounts, never showed. Son of a bitch."

"Yeah."

"He got any other family around here?" He sorta looked me up and down, then added, "Any property?"

No way was I going to let him near Mom so I said, "Just me and he took with 'im whatever was his." Fella went and looked out the window. I had a thought he was going to pull a gun out from underneath his overcoat and try to rob me. Settle Pops' account that way. But when he turned back, he just pulled his wallet out, tossed a dollar on the counter, and grabbed a coupla packages of gum. "Keep the change. And on the long chance he ever does show up here tell him J. J.'s looking for him."

He walked out to his car, glanced up and down the street, then got in and peeled away in the direction he'd come from. When my uncle came back he asked if I'd had any customers. I figured there was no sense giving him many details about the conversation since like as not he'd tell Mom all about it and it'd only stir her up. ""Just some slicker who got lost. Bought some gum."" Then I went over to see if Betty was home yet.

Didn't see as much of Betty as I'd expected given the tone of her letters. She'd started taking classes at the community college twenty miles away. Said she was bent on eventually getting herself a degree in teaching.

"My Aunt Mabel taught for years up near Peoria," she told me, "and I've always admired her. Besides," and here she gave me a sideways look,"it will give me something to do if…if things don't happen the way they're suppose to."

223

Well, I knew where she was headed with that one and I shied off. I mean, I liked her an awful lot and guess I assumed we'd get married down the road, but in my mind that road was longer than it appeared to be to her. "Yeah, that's probably a good idea. Maybe I ought to take some courses in business or something. With what I'll be makin' in a coupla years I ought to get some background."

She got a little cool on me for a while after that which made being in Farley less interesting than it had been. But that didn't last too long. Like always she said "I don't know why I bother with you. You're just Bubba." And she put her head on my chest. I always did like the smell of her hair. She warmed back up some more the last few weeks before I left for spring training, maybe figuring I'd needed some reminding about why I ought to come back to Farley the next winter.

Actually, it was in my head that I wouldn't, which didn't have anything to do with Betty. Just seemed that what with my ability and what I intended to accomplish my second season the Orioles would probably send me to one of those instructional leagues. Didn't say anything about it to anybody since I didn't want to cause unnecessary grief. Probably thought, too, that it was about time since once I made the bigs, not more'n a year or two from then, I'd only be coming back for visits anyway.

Maybe Mom and Betty figured out what I was thinking without my saying. Mom started acting real sentimental at times. One evening, right before I left for training camp, she said, "Ever since...ever since..." and here she got a bit weepy, "we got left to ourselves, I've known there'd be a time when you'd grow up and go away. You got your dream about baseball and Farley, well Farley's a wonderful place for regular folks, but a major league ballplayer.... All right to be from here, but not to be here. It's just...." And then the tears really started.

"Now, Mom, I ain't goin' nowhere," I said, though to myself I added 'yet.'

"Pish and tush, Bubba, don't pretend."

Betty, she didn't exactly get sentimental, but like I said warmed up real nice the last coupla weeks and I wasn't likely to

224

forget her. Fact is I was already thinking it'd be good for her, for us, if maybe she came and visited me for a while wherever it was I got sent to over the next winter.

Bessie Mae was watching all this. Day before I left she took me aside. "Clarence," she declared, "there's something different about things and what it is finally come to me. I think you're thinking you won't be coming back to Farley. At least not regular. Well that's all right, doing what you want to do is going to take you places you might want to stay awhile. But don't you ever forget who's raised you and who loves you. I won't name names, but don't you ever be like him and hurt your own people." Bessie Mae had a way of getting to the nub of things it was hard to forget.

So off I went to Florida to get ready for the season. Since I'd still be in one of those short season leagues, we had what they call extended spring training which meant a good spell in Florida. For me that meant a lot of time with the "pitching gurus" as my manager-to-be Bobby Tolan called 'em. They kept calling me a "work in progress," complimenting me on the physical shape I was in, but saying I needed to work harder at pitching fundamentals than I seemed willing to do. Same stuff Sweet had harped on.

It was good to see some of the guys again though it struck me that none of 'em were what you might call friends. I hadn't paid much attention to making friends in Bluefield. That made me think some more about Betty though I didn't get moony about it. Coupla of the guys from Bluefield were going to Hagerstown, a step up from Erie and that torqued me a bit since none of 'em were any better than me, but I figured that would all come to rights soon enough. There were some new faces around and some, like Teddy Lee's, that had disappeared. Heard that he'd tried to hook on with another organization, but had no luck and decided to give college a try. Well, good for him I thought.

Sweet was around and now and then he'd come by and watch me throw, but he didn't say much. He might say something in a near whisper to whatever other coach was working with me, but that was it. I got bored enough just throwing to a

225

catcher that I'd try some of the stuff they were telling me and you could see their heads bob in approval. But when it came to the games we played, sort of inter-squad things with players from the various teams, occasionally even a big leaguer who was on the disabled list and was working his way into shape, I just did my thing. There was nobody else could bust a pitch like me. I still got my biggest kicks from the sound a fast one hitting a catcher's mitt or seeing a batter look a little uneasy in the box when he saw how hard I threw and how my control was questionable. Wildness was part of my game and I hadn't seen a good reason yet for focusing on accuracy.

Just before we broke camp Sweet came by while I was limbering up for a one-inning go in a game. "Well, Bubba, up a notch this year. I wish you well."

"Thanks."

"I've been watching you a bit and I've seen some things that encourage me a little about you. I got to thinking I'd like to send you off with one more story."

About Dalkowski, again," I said a little lippy.

"Naw, it's a different story. Little sad too, but that's not why I'm telling it."

"Go ahead," I answered backing off a bit. I mean I thought I wasn't exactly a favorite of his since I was pretty strong-minded about the way I oughta do things. But here he didn't have any responsibility for me and coulda just ignored me; the tone of his voice though suggested he was serious about offering advice. I didn't need to take it, but I could listen.

"Dalkowski was a guy who never learned to control his stuff, but there're pitchers who have good control, have success for a few years, and then suddenly something happens. They lose it and can't get it back. I'm thinking of Steve Blass, for example, a Pirate pitcher. Y'ever hear of him?"

"Don't remember," I grunted as I let go with fast one, getting close to being ready for my stint.

"Well you were only a toddler I guess when he was finished. Anyway a good solid pitcher for five, six years. One year, 1972 I recollect, he won nineteen games, came close to getting the Pirates into the World Series. Never had great control, but good enough. Then the next year he came to camp and just couldn't throw strikes. That season he walked about the same number of batters in less than a hundred innings as he had in two hundred and fifty or so in '72. Never got it back. Out of baseball a year or two later. Nobody could figure out exactly what went wrong. No physical problems and he was all right on the sidelines, but put 'im on the pitching mound and he lost it. Sad story."

I stopped throwing. Couldn't figure out where the old man was going with this one. He'd been talking all last season about focus and mechanics and working hard. Now he tells me this story which says you can bust your butt on those things and it finally don't matter. "That's real encouragin', coach."

"Well, my point is that sometimes finding control comes just about as suddenly and you can't exactly put your finger on the why of it. We like to say hard work and attention to fundamentals like the release point is what did it. There's a lotta truth to that, but what makes it all come together who knows? Like I say I've been watching you and there's just something that tells me one of these days you're going to have it and you'll start putting the ball right about where you want it. What's going to make that happen I don't know, any more than I know why I got this feeling that it will. Just enjoy it Bubba and use it right."

Then he just turned and walked away. Don't even know if he heard me say, "Thanks, coach."

Finally it came time to start the season so off to Erie Pa. we went. In camp guys kept referring to Erie as "the mistake on the lake," and laughing about it. Well, it wasn't paradise, but after Bluefield it seemed more interesting and the lake was nice. Sometimes I'd go down to the shore and skip stones, never had a real chance to do that growing' up in Farley. They'd skip three, four, five times, a few times more than that, sending ripples out that'd run into each other, then one last plop and they'd disappear. Once I got one to skip twelve times, but as hard as I tried I never managed that again. Thought some about what Sweet said, but more often I thought about Mom—and Betty. Don't know

227

that I would have enjoyed Erie and the lake much in the winter, but so what. Come winter, I wasn't planning to be there—or in Farley. Somehow that idea wasn't as exciting to me then as it had been when I first had it. Tried skipping another stone. Best I could do was ten.

I was slated to start the second game of the year, against Batavia if I remember right. Had a good outing too. Pitched seven innings, gave up a coupla hits, only one of them solid, walked six, and hit three batters, two of 'em starting the seventh. A wild pitch in the third cost me a run, but we were cruising 6-1. When the seventh started the way it did, it looked like Bluefield all over again. Glanced down at the bullpen, but nobody stirred. That boosted me up some and I got out of the inning. When I got to the dugout Tolan slapped me on the shoulder, "Good going, Floyd. You can take your shower now. You've thrown enough pitches for the day, but you showed me you can get out of a tight squeeze. I left you in to see what you could do."

I wished Sweet had been there. Seemed like Tolan was willing to give me regular work so I was looking forward to a good season.

And things did go well for the first few weeks. My record was only 2-2 which was a drag because overall the team was playing pretty good, but Tolan was putting me out there every fifth day. I was averaging almost two strikeouts an inning and was pretty stingy with hits. Oh I was still averaging close to a walk an inning and hit somebody every now and then, but that went with my style. And I was getting some press too, both in Erie and on the road. Like when we got to Utica the local sports section had a headline "Wild Bubba Floyd to Face Blue Sox." and the story talked about "The Farley Flame Thrower coming to town." I thought it was a hoot, but as it turned out the publicity led to my big troubles.

I was scheduled to pitch the first game so at the usual time I strolled down toward the bullpen to warm up. My catcher Luis Paulino — good player, made the all star team that year, but I guess never made the bigs — was walking with me. Outa the corner of my eye I saw some guy leaning over the railing.

228

About the time we drew even with him he called, "Bubba, Bubba Floyd."

I stopped and looked at him and right off I knew it was Pops. Fatter than he had been, flabby I would've said, and pasty-looking, not weathered like when he had farmed, but it was Pops.

"Can I have a word with ya, Bubba?"

For a moment I thought of just going on to the bullpen, doing my warm-ups, pretending he hadn't called me, I hadn't heard him, nothing had happened. Took a deep breath to settle myself, then, reluctantly, I walked over to him.

"Yeah.

"Ya know me? Ya know me?"

"Yeah, I know ya."

"Thought ya would. Hoped ya would. When I seen the story in the paper I knew it was you, had to be. Like I said to the mis...." He paused, flustered, licked his lips. "...To my friend," he made a vague gesture with his left hand.

I looked through him, beyond him. About three rows up, sitting on the second seat in from the aisle, watching us like a hawk, was a bleached blonde who I can only describe as a floozie. Overweight, too much make-up on a pudgy face, dressed not well, but all wrong for a minor league baseball game.

"Like I said to my friend, I know him. I mean there can't be too many Bubba Floyds from Farley, can there now." He forced a laugh that was more like a chicken cackling then a man in honest humor. "So acourse I had to come see ya. See how yer doin'."

"I'm doin' fine."

"Paper made it sound like yer a real phe-nom. Maybe on a fast track to the big leagues."

"Don't know how fast the track is, but I'm goin' to be there. Aren't many pitchers throw harder than I do."

"Good, good. Makes me feel real proud."

He patted me on the shoulder like he used to when I was a kid and had done something he liked which wasn't too often as I remembered. But he took his hand away pretty quick. Maybe from surprise at the feel of a man's muscles instead of a skinny kid's bones, maybe from an instinct that told him I didn't much welcome the gesture. He coughed.

"Say, Bubba. Paper said you got drafted pretty high."

"Yeah."

"Musta…musta gotten a pretty nice bonus to sign."

Right then, it came to me. I was ticked enough at seeing 'im and at the fact he hadn't even bothered asking about Mom, though I had been willing to consider that he might actually have some shred of interest in his family left. But nothing had changed with him. "So that's why you're here. You walk out on Mom and me ten years ago. All that time, not a word. Then you think I might have some money you can bum so all of a sudden you come buzzin' around. You don't even bother to ask about Mom, but you beg me for money."

"Now Bubba, it's not like that. I woulda come anyway. Wanted to see ya. But ya see, my friend, she…"

"That your woman?"

He paused, looking a little sheepish, licking his lips nervously. "Bubba, I…I mean a man's gotta….It ain't much fun livin' alone."

Somehow he shrank in my eyes into a trembling old man, almost pitiful, but I didn't feel anything like pity. I didn't raise my voice, but spoke so fiercely that he acted like I was shouting. "So she told you to come beg your son for money."

"Bubba, keep it down will ya." He glanced nervously over his shoulder. "I…I didn't exactly say you was my son. She, she doesn't know about…. That would raise…some questions. I tole her you wuz my nephew."

"Bubba," Paulino called from the bullpen. "Time to warm up man. You got to be loose."

I turned away. "Bubba," Pops' voice had a desperate sound to it. "just a little. We…I'm sorta short of ready cash."

"Maybe your friend J. J. can do something for ya."

I didn't even look back to see what effect that remark had on him but walked to the bullpen and started loosening up to pitch the game. Short tosses to Paulino, easy like playing catch in the side yard, moving backwards a step or so at a time until I was behind the mound, then a few easy throws from the mound itself. At one point I looked beyond Paulino and saw Pops still standing where I had left him. The floozie had joined him and they were having a lively discussion. He had obviously told her I hadn't exactly offered to put him on easy street. I was still steaming. I fired a coupla hard ones to Paulino. They were scorchers and right down the heart of the plate.

"Easy, Bubba, easy. I no want you to break my hand before the game starts."

I snap caught his throw back to me, kicked the dirt a coupla times, walked around a bit, rubbing up the ball. My head was in a tangle, but I had a sudden burning thought. I had just thrown two pitches that went pretty much where I wanted them to.

"Hey Bubba, this is warm-ups, not the bottom of the ninth."

I saw Pops staring at me, his face looking like a whimper. "Luis," I called out, "don't even try to catch this one." I wound up and threw as hard as I could. The ball flew high and wide of his mitt as he waved hopelessly at it. Wild high and right on target it caught Pops flush on the jaw with a crack that sounded like the best Louisville Slugger giving a ride to a hanging curve. He fell backwards and over the railing onto the field. People started screaming and players, coaches, fans, you name it, were running toward him. I ambled slowly that way. Luis was just standing there with a strange look on his face. As I passed him, he said "Jeez-us, Bubba. Sweet Jeez-us."

When I got to the crowd, people gave way to let me get near to where Pops was lying. The floozie was whipping up a storm, crying and moaning. She saw me and screamed, "You kilt him. You kilt your own uncle."

I stared down at Pops lying twisted on the ground, his jaw outa whack, blood all over. He was moaning, and every moan hurt. "He ain't dead, just feelin' the pain. If I'd wanted to kill him I woulda aimed for his ear." I glared at her hard, then slow and clear so she could hear every word, I said, "And he ain't my uncle. He's my father."

All that was more than ten years ago now. I was right: I didn't kill the old man, only shattered his jaw and made sure every bite he ever took after he'd remember me and Mom. Acourse, there was quite an uproar about the whole thing. The Orioles' organization tried to make out it was an accident and pointed out my record showed I wasn't exactly a control artist, but I told them to forget it. That throw went exactly where it was supposed to and I made sure everybody knew it. I got suspended by the league and there were some legal shenanigans, too, charges of reckless endangerment or some such thing. But Pops lammed out of town as soon as he could — whether the floozie followed him I don't know — and they gave me some kind of probation, probably the result of a smooth-talking Baltimore lawyer. It didn't much matter to me.

I had to stay in Utica while all that was going on which wasn't the most exciting place to sit and twiddle your thumbs. And I was pretty depressed. I mean I didn't regret doing what I had done, but I got no special satisfaction from it and I had no particular idea about what to do next, about how long I'd be suspended, about whether I even cared. Poteat called a coupla times and said he was working on an appeal of the suspension and that he had prepared a statement for me to sign. He sent it Federal Express, but after I read it I just put it aside. Mostly wasn't true and it certainly wasn't me. Then, all of a sudden, there was Betty and Bessie Mae come all the way from Farley.

"We come to take you home, Bubba," Bessie Mae said and I didn't object. That was where I wanted to go. On the way Betty told me she'd read about my trouble in *Baseball America*. "I've been reading that regularly," she said with a little smile, "since someone I know isn't exactly the best correspondent in the world. When I read about what happened I would have come myself, but it didn't seem proper so Bessie Mae said she'd come along."

They didn't know all the particulars, like who it was I had hit, so I took a deep breath and told them the whole story. Bessie Mae turned and looked at me — she was in the front and Betty was driving. "Well Bubba, the idea was a bad one in a lot of ways, and I can't say I approve of it. But what moved ya to it I find no fault with. Bless you for that. Still in all, let's agree we won't tell your mother what she don't need to know."

I live in Farley. Have ever since. I own the gas station now though I closed the one in town and moved over to the interstate access. Built a nice little restaurant next to it that Mom and Bessie Mae run. I call my business operation the Release Point Gas and Diner. It's a good conversation starter with folks passing through though I never tell them the whole story.

Play some first base in a slow pitch softball league, but haven't picked up, let alone thrown a hard ball since. And Betty, me and her got married after she got her degree. She teaches at the new consolidated high school here. So things worked out all right.

Orioles finally put me on the voluntarily retired list. For a while I used to hear from them occasionally. The regional scout might drop by for a chat when he was in the area, to see what I was thinking, but they finally gave that up. Scouts from a few other organizations nosed around too, and I had some nice conversations with them though I had no interest in talking business which they finally figured out. And every now and again Poteat would wheel into town in his BMW "to talk turkey" with me is what he said. Last time I saw him, and that was quite a while ago now, he got a bit irritated and declared, "I don't get it. You got the makings of a major league pitcher in that arm of yours. But you let a little bump in the road turn you off. For what," and he sort of gestured like he was taking in Farley, "living in a corn field?"

"I dunno," I answered 'im, "there's probably no explainin' it unless you've lived it. Just seems to me that once you've thrown the perfect pitch what else is there to do, except come home to them that love you."

William J. McGill is a graduate of Trinity College (CT) and Harvard University. A retired college administrator and history professor, he is author of numerous articles, essays, book reviews, short stories and poems. He has published a short story collection, *The Rock Springs Chronicles* and a study of two major poets, *Poets Meeting: George Herbert, R. S. Thomas and the Argument with God* and a biography of Maria Theresa. An ordained Episcopal priest he has also served as managing editor and poetry editor of *Spitball: The Literary Baseball Magazine.*